IT'S IN THE RHYTHM
NOW AVAILABLE

Coming Soon

Can A Sistah Get Some Love? An Anthology with stories by Tinisha Nicole Johnson, Nathasha Brooks-Harris, Zana Kane, and Gail McFarland

Death At The Double Inkwell- Shonell Bacon

LADY LEO PUBLISHING

She felt a heat wave wash over her. Of course he made her nervous. Very nervous. She was more attracted to him than she cared to admit. She was nervous about what was happening between them now.

Kayla shrugged. "No. I'm not nervous," she lied. Not sure what to do with her hands, she hugged herself.

Paul closed the small gap between them.

Determined to prove that he wasn't having an effect on her, she boldly looked up into his eyes as his tall frame towered over her. He reached out, embracing her in his arms. "There's no need to be nervous," he whispered, gently pulling her to him.

Despite Kayla's effort to put up a brave resistance, her body automatically leaned against him. Her heart rate sped up. She watched as his lips slowly descended to meet hers.

LACE & HONOR

SAMMIE WARD

LOVE STORM ROMANCE
An imprint of Lady Leo Publishing

Lady Leo Publishing
P.O. Box 14283
Silver Spring, MD 20911

This is a work of fiction. All characters, places and events are from the author's imagination and should not be confused with fact. Any resemblance to person's living or dead, events or places is purely coincidental.

Copyright © 2008 by Sammie Ward

ISBN-13: 978-09841076-2-9
ISBN-10: 0-9841076-2-2
Manufactured in the United States of America

Second Edition
Visit us at www.ladyleopublishing.org

To my mother Georgia Tims, thank you for all of the love and spiritual support. To my sisters, Betty Fowler, Lisa Jenkins, Shirley Fowler-Tillman, and Barbara Ezenekwe. DeMarcus, Dominick, and Eugina, you are the best. I love you.

To all my brothers and sisters in uniform, I salute you.

Chapter One

$\mathscr{S}$ergeant Kayla Perry was running late for army formation. It was the second time this week. She could just hear the supervisor, Staff Sergeant Maurice Cage's mouth, scolding her on her responsibilities as a new non-commissioned officer in Delta Company, 32nd CSH Combat Support Hospital, Fort Bradley, Maryland. The mission of the unit was to provide medical care to patients.

She took a quick glance at herself in the hallway mirror. Her hair styled in a French bun, she adjusted the army beret on her head. After tucking in strands of hair that had come loose from her French bun, she adjusted the army beret on her head. Looking closer, she noticed circles under her eyes. She had been up late after returning from a date, but no excuse was valid enough for being late for formation. She grabbed her car keys and hurried to her car.

Kayla turned the key in the ignition and pulled out onto the highway. After she made a left turn at the light, her black Mustang quickly ate up highway. Luckily, not many vehicles were traveling at 0530. She should make it to the unit in no time.

It was Cage who persuaded her to re-enlist for another four years after her first enlistment ended six months ago. He believed in her capabilities as a leader, helping her prepare for the sergeant's board and recommending her for the army's Green to Gold Nursing Officer's Program.

Trained as an army medic, Kayla planned to continue her nursing degree by enrolling in University of Maryland at College Park. She submitted her package and was now waiting to see if she had been selected. Upon graduation, she would pin on officer's bars. Fort Meade was a good duty station, but after nursing school, she was looking forward to another duty station—preferably overseas in Germany, Hawaii, or Japan. At this point, she'd even take Korea. She'd heard so many wonderful, exciting stories from soldiers coming from abroad that she couldn't wait to receive orders.

Besides education, traveling was another reason for enlisting. A southern girl from Mobile, Alabama, Kayla wanted to get as far away from home as possible. After two years at Tuskegee University, her father was laid off from work. Her parents could no longer afford to pay for her education. After speaking with a campus recruiter, she discussed the educational opportunities with her parents. They displayed mixed emotions. Divorced since she was thirteen years old, her mother, Olivia, was surprised at Kayla's decision to enlist, but she was supportive. Her father, Douglas Perry, was the opposite. He had never served in the military and didn't believe it was the proper career choice for his only daughter. Not only was Kayla no longer under their watchful eye, but there was also a lot of political unrest going on in the Middle East. He was worried about the possibility of a war.

Kayla stepped on the gas and zoomed across the intersection. She knew the role of the army. It didn't bother her to put her life on the line for her country.

Before she knew it, she was parked in front of the

company. She got out of the vehicle and scurried along the sidewalk. Formation had already begun.

Kayla stood quietly in the back row. Cage nodded at her and gave her a frustrated look.

After the group was dismissed, Cage sauntered over, looking at her intensely. He stopped in front of her, inhaled deeply, and slapped the rolled up paper in his hand.

"You're supposed to be here before formation, not during."

"I'm sorry, Sergeant Cage," she tried to interject. "I—"

He waved her off with a hand. "Save it."

"It won't happen again," she managed to get in.

"That's what you said the other day. Don't make me regret that I recommended you for advancement. A big part of your job is to set an example for the troops under you."

Kayla dropped her head. She knew Cage was right. She admired him for his honesty, dedication, and leadership to her and the other enlisted personnel in the unit. He was her mentor. She wanted him to be proud of her. She desired to follow in his footsteps. All of the soldiers spoke highly of him. She wanted the same type of respect.

He pointed the paper at her. "We lead by example. Understand?"

Kayla gave him her undivided attention. "I understand."

"Outstanding. Now that we have that out of the way, I need you to select two soldiers to support B 2/4 Infantry Division on a field training exercise."

"How long is the exercise?" Kayla asked.

"Two weeks."

Whomever she chose wouldn't be happy. Fourteen days on a field training exercise was never easy, especially for women. A woman's personal hygiene was a major problem.

There weren't hot showers, decent food, or the proper sleeping facilities. Your residence was a large tent with other members of your unit. You had no privacy, worked long hours, and had very little sleep. Not to mention not being able to get your hair, nails, and toes done. After several weeks of living in the woods, women were a sight to see.

"Each platoon is sending two bodies," Sergeant Cage continued. "If you can get volunteers, great; if you can't, then choose them. Report to me this morning with the names."

"Consider it done," Kayla answered, as she watched him turn and walk through the large set of brown double doors. His powerful, well-muscled body moved with easy grace.

Standing under six feet tall, with a smooth, nut-brown complexion, he was average looking, but his personality and intelligence made up for what he lacked in appearance. Divorced and a father of two, Cage didn't fit under Kayla's dating guideline of no men with children or ex-wives, but he could make a woman break her rules.

Kayla pushed the thought aside. What was she thinking? They couldn't date. Sergeant Cage was in her immediate chain-of-command; according to army regulation, they could not date.

"Forget it, girl," she said. It would never happen, but it didn't hurt to think what could be if the situation was different.

"Sergeant Perry."

Kayla jumped at the voice calling from behind her. She turned around. "How was your date with Jamaal?" Liz asked. "I waited up for you to call me last night and give me the scoop."

"Good morning to you, too, Liz," Kayla teased.

Not put off by Kayla's sarcasm, Liz continued. "Good

morning—now fill me in." There was genuine pleasure in her voice.

Kayla hugged Liz's short, medium-built frame. Sometimes it was hard to make friends in this line of work, especially for women, but when Kayla first met Liz, an Administrative Assistant with the unit, the two hit it off immediately. Kayla wasn't sure if it was the infectious smile Liz always wore on her light-complected face, her humor, or a combination of these things that made her like Liz so much.

Kayla inhaled, then slowly let out her breath. The interrogation was about to begin. "It was all right. He took me to a movie, to dinner, and then took me home."

"That's it?" Liz prompted, as she shook her head and fell in step with Kayla.

Kayla shrugged. "That's it. There's nothing else to tell."

Liz frowned, then asked in her southern drawl, "Are you going out with him again?"

Kayla had met Sergeant Jamaal Trip one day while driving on post. A member of the Military Police, he presented her with a speeding ticket and at the same time asked for her phone number. After avoiding Jamaal's phone calls, she'd finally given in and gone out with him. It wasn't a bad date. Sergeant Tripp made it clear that he was looking to settle down. She made it clear she wasn't—which marked the end of the conversation and the date.

"No," Kayla answered smoothly. "We have nothing in common."

"So it didn't work out with Jamaal. We will find you someone else."

Liz was happily married to an army sergeant and felt it was her job to find Kayla a man.

"I know the perfect guy for you."

Kayla playfully placed her hands over her ears. "I'm not listening."

Liz giggled. "His name is—" she began, removing Kayla's hands from her ears.

"I don't care what his name is."

"Anyway," Liz continued, "he's never been married and no children, so you don't have to worry about baby mama drama. He's a friend of my Timothy, a sergeant, a country boy from Durham, North Carolina, and he is *fine*."

Kayla had to admit his resume sounded interesting, but she'd have to pass. She frowned and said, "As good as he sounds, I'll pass. I'm not interested in meeting anyone right now. My focus is on nursing school. That's it."

"Look, all I'm saying is just meet him. You never know what can happen. There are other men in the sea besides Sergeant Cage."

Kayla's eyes stretched. Liz was always insisting that she had a crush on Cage, no matter how often she denied it. She playfully punched her in the arm. "Don't even go there. He's my boss. That's how rumors get started."

"All right. All right," Liz raised her hands in surrender. "I'll change the subject. Have you had breakfast yet?"

"No. I'm on my way to the dining hall. You know I never get up in time to prepare breakfast. I have to be here too early."

"Hmm. That's why you're so bony. I don't know why you ever bother going to breakfast. You eat like a bird, anyway. I'm the one who needs to miss a meal or two."

"Oh, please, you're a perfect eight." Kayla enclosed her arm around Liz's waist. "Your husband isn't complaining."

Kayla glanced from Liz to see Specialist Marissa Poe coming toward them. Trained as a Pharmacy Technician, she worked at the main hospital in the pharmacy department.

A tall, statuesque white girl with blonde hair and blue eyes, Marissa only dated African-American men, a habit she admitted picking up after joining the army. Not many women cared for Marissa—whenever she entered a room, she commanded attention from both men *and* women—but Kayla and Marissa got along well. Besides being a little naïve, Marissa proved to be a good friend.

"Good morning, Sergeant Perry and Liz."

"Morning, Specialist Poe," Liz grumbled.

Kayla was aware that the two women didn't get along well. Every chance she got, Liz made it a point to let Marissa know she didn't approve of her dating black men. As far as Kayla was concerned, it didn't matter about a man's color; love was blind.

"Good morning, Specialist," Kayla said, returning the greeting. "How are you?"

"I'm fine." Marissa adjusted the black backpack on her right shoulder. "I had a hard time getting up this morning." A huge grin spread across her face. "I'm so anxious; two weeks and I will be out of this man's army and onto Penn State in the fall." She clasped her hands together in excitement. "I can't wait."

"You don't have to rub it in," Kayla said, feigning sadness. She was happy for Marissa. She had been accepted to college, majoring in pharmacy. She was also a little envious that she hadn't heard anything on her own admission package. "I'm happy for you. I hope to hear something soon."

"Still no word yet?" Marissa asked.

"No," Kayla answered.

"Don't worry. The packet will be approved," Marissa said. "I have my fingers and toes crossed."

"I have my fingers and toes crossed also," Kayla added.

"Me too," Liz chimed in.

"I had a hard time getting in here this morning, too," stated Kayla, changing the subject. "I was late again. That didn't set well with Sergeant Cage."

"Oh, no," Marissa gasped. "Did he chew you out?"

"No more than usual. Nothing to worry about. How are things going in the pharmacy?"

"Busy. I met my replacement the other day." Marissa smiled. "A male. He came in from Korea. He seems to be very nice. Can you believe it? He pulled strings to come here to Fort Bradley."

"Soldiers like it here, and why not? You're living around DC, the most powerful city in the world. Not to mention being close to Maryland and Virginia." Kayla had come across a large population of soldiers who'd decided to remain in the area after retiring. They enjoyed the power, glitz, and economy. "Are you sure you don't want to re-enlist?"

"I'm not a lifer, Sergeant Perry," Marissa said. "I will leave that up to you. Where are you guys headed?"

"We're on our way to grab some breakfast," Kayla answered.

Liz positioned herself between Marissa and Kayla, letting Marissa know her presence wasn't welcome.

"I'm headed in that direction," Marissa said, sounding irritated. She fell in step with Kayla. Liz frowned.

Once inside the dining hall, Kayla followed Liz. She carefully selected a light breakfast of orange juice, two slices of toast, jam, and a boiled egg.

Liz loaded her plate with grits, scrambled eggs, sausage,

and a biscuit. Marissa grabbed a box of Frosted Flakes, a slice of toast, and orange juice. They found a seat in the center of the dining facility.

Marissa frowned. She pointed to the southern grits on Liz's plate. "What is that?"

"I bet your latest boyfriend knows what it is," Liz quipped, shoving a spoonful of grits into her mouth.

Marissa rolled her neck with attitude. "What does that mean?"

"It means," Liz snapped, "you need to get those brothers to teach you more than the mattress mambo."

Marissa leaned across the table. "You better watch your mouth."

"Or what?" Liz threw back. "What are you going to do?"

Kayla could see the situation getting out of hand. Whenever the two were in the same room, it was a sparring match. "Come on you two, knock it off."

Liz rolled her eyes. "She gets on my nerves."

"You get on mine," Marissa answered right back.

"And you *both* are getting on mine." Kayla pointed at both women. "Why don't you kiss and make up?"

Liz made a face. "I don't even get down like that."

Marissa puckered up her lips and blew Liz a kiss. "You know you want to kiss me. I see how you be looking at me."

Liz dropped the spoon on her plate in disgust. She was doing her best to compose herself. "Keep dreaming, white girl. The only thing I want to do right now is smash your face in."

"Any time. Any place. You let me know when."

One thing Kayla could say about Marissa—she never backed down from anything. She could hold her own.

"You both are dreaming," Kayla joked, to ease the

tension. "No one wants either one of you. It's me you want."

They both laughed.

"No one wants you," Liz said, taking a bite of her biscuit.

"I received an e-mail from a friend of mine," Marissa said, her voice serious. "His name is Andrew Schwartz. We went to high school together. He joined the army a year ahead of me. Anyway, he's stationed at Fort Sill, Oklahoma. My mother told me he's being deployed to Iraq. I can't believe it. He's leaving on Friday. He just got married. Has a new baby boy." She shook her head. "Now he's on his way to Iraq."

"I feel sorry for his wife," Liz commented. "I don't know what I would do if that was me. Left behind to try to manage without my husband and raise a newborn baby. Talk about stress."

Marissa's eyes widened. "Do you think we're going to be deployed?" She focused on Kayla. "Have you heard anything?"

"I haven't heard anything," Kayla said in a calm tone. "I'm not going to worry about it."

"Always the cool one," Liz joked. "Well, I am worried about it. I don't want my husband to go. We're trying to start a family. I don't want to wind up like Mrs. Schwartz. Left behind to raise a baby alone."

"He will be back," Kayla said.

"I hope," Marissa added, in a quiet tone.

Kayla and Marissa looked at each other. She didn't want to push the issue. She knew where Liz was coming from. In times of war, a lot of men and women lose their lives. It is unfortunate.

Marissa's face twisted in disgust. "I only joined the army

to attend college. I didn't join to fight in nobody's war."

"No one wants to go to war," Kayla said. "I also joined to earn money to attend college. That's a chance you took when you enlisted."

Liz leaned back in her chair. "Is that you talking or Sergeant Cage?"

Marissa burst out laughing. "Good question."

"This has nothing to do with Sergeant Cage. When you join the army, there's a chance of going to war. That's what the army does."

"So you want to go to war?" Liz took a sip of orange juice.

"Of course not," Kayla explained. "I'm just saying that when I joined, I knew that was a possibility. So did your husband."

Liz threw her a no-you-didn't look. She sucked her teeth.

"Don't look at me like that. I'm just telling the truth," Kayla replied.

"In two weeks, I'm out of here," Marissa added.

"Then you better hope that nothing happens within that time," Kayla explained, "or you will be headed to Iraq." She spread grape jelly on a slice of toast.

Marissa's face paled. "The army can stop me from getting out?"

"Yes," Kayla said.

Marissa looked as if she were going to pass out. "Let's talk about something else," she said, shaken. "This conversation scares me. I don't want to even think about it."

"Hey, baby," came a voice from behind them. The ladies turned to find Specialist Randall Spivey standing next to Marissa. He acknowledged them with a nod before refocusing on Marissa.

Marissa's facial expression was blank. "We have nothing to talk about." She turned away from Randall, folded her arms across her chest, and looked straight ahead. "Leave me alone," she said, pouting.

Liz leaned over to Kayla and whispered, "Trouble in paradise."

Kayla hit her on the arm. "Be quiet."

From the day they began dating, six months ago, Marissa and Randall's relationship had been love and hate. For Kayla, it was difficult watching Randall take Marissa for granted. As a friend, she tried on numerous occasions to tell Marissa that Randall was no good for her. She would not listen. Kayla decided to let her find out on her own. In two weeks, Marissa would be out of the army and moving on with her life without Randall.

og so

Later that afternoon, Kayla sat in the training office, pounding away at the keyboard. She gave Sergeant Cage the names of Private First Class John Luck and Private Brian Mills to accompany B 2/4 Infantry on their training exercise. She couldn't believe they'd volunteered for the assignment. It made her job easier. With her mind free, she had time to think about the conversation she and the girls had had at breakfast about being deployed. Though she said she wasn't worried, she was. It would be foolish not to be.

Sighing in disgust, she exhaled and forced herself to focus on the document in front of her, the roster for the make-up physical fitness test. She glanced at the names of two soldiers in her platoon. They'd failed the initial test. Both were working out five days a week and should be ready on Monday morning.

Kayla looked up when she heard the knock on her office door. "It's open."

Liz breezed in. "You're invited to my house on Saturday."

Kayla frowned. "What's going on Saturday?"

"I'm having a cookout." She cleared her throat. "I expect to see you."

"Free food. I will definitely be there." Kayla noticed the sly grin on Liz's face. "What are you up to?"

"Nothing." Liz leaned across the desk. "I'm just looking forward to it."

Kayla wasn't buying it. She knew Liz and could tell when she wasn't telling the truth. "This isn't about the guy you want me to meet, is it? Why do you keep interfering in my love life?"

"I just want to see you happy," Liz explained.

"I *am* happy. I will be even happier when I'm accepted into nursing school."

Liz smiled. "Yes, but for the time being, you need a man in your life to keep your mind occupied."

"No, I do not."

"Yes, you do," Liz argued.

"If you plan on setting me up tomorrow, forget it. I'm not coming." Kayla didn't want to hear any more. "I have work to do. So do you."

Liz chuckled. She crossed her arms over her chest. "Uh, you already agreed to come."

Kayla shook her head in disbelief. Liz was a good friend, but she never understood the meaning of the word "no."

"I just disagreed."

"You can't change your mind. I will nag you all day."

Kayla rolled her eyes. She knew Liz was telling the truth.

She would have to go to Liz's cookout. "Fine, I'll go, but no set up, Liz. I mean it. If you do, I'm leaving."

Liz clasped her hands together in victory. "Okay. Great. No fix-ups."

"I'm glad I made your day. Now get out of my office."

Liz wasn't fazed by the remark. "It's going to be fun, you will see. I have to stop by the commissary," she mumbled to herself, turned, and headed back out the door. A moment later, she stuck her head around the door. "Don't think about not showing up. Remember, I know where you live."

Kayla leaned back in her chair as she stared at the door. She closed her eyes a moment, wondering what she'd agreed to.

ભ જ્ઞ

Sergeant Paul Lake entered the last supply order in the computer, closed out the window, and let out a sigh of relief. It had been a hectic day in the Orthopedic Clinic Walter Reed Army Medical Center, in Washington, DC.

It was Friday, and he was looking forward to stopping by Cadence Supper Club after work to unwind, something he had not done since transferring from Hawaii, six months ago. A majority of the patients being treated in the clinic were suffering from injuries and accidents in Afghanistan and Iraq. The workload was overwhelming, keeping him busy.

Cadence was known for its upscale African-American clientele, outstanding food, and music. Owned by his cousins, Victor and Gerald Sexton, the club had been founded by his mother's brother, William Sexton, a retired army first sergeant, who opened the club after leaving the army. Under his uncle's leadership, the club became very prominent. Many top performers had graced its stage: Eric Benet, Toni Braxton, Mary J. Blige, LL Cool J, Brian McKnight, and Garrett Martindale to name a few. Since their father's death, the brothers had run the club with the same grace and style.

Paul, the third of four sons, was born and raised in Durham, North Carolina. Victor and Gerald were army brats, moving every couple of years, but they spent their summers in North Carolina. Paul briefly lost contact with each of them when they went away to college and Victor joined the army. They reconnected when Victor invited him to speak at his retirement ceremony a year ago.

A third generation soldier and Victor's exceptional career in Special Forces persuaded him to join the army. He submitted a package to the elite unit and was waiting to see whether he had been accepted. He set goals for himself early on, and so far everything was on track, except for a wife and kids. He thought he'd found that once with his college sweetheart, Dina West, but it wasn't to be.

Out of four sons, Paul was the only bachelor. Brothers Devin and Jonah were married. Younger brother Quentin, a senior at North Carolina State, had recently become engaged. Even Victor was headed toward the altar. Maybe marriage just wasn't in the cards for him.

"Women think they have it bad," he said to himself. "What about the brothers? Why can't a good man find a good woman?"

People were always trying to set him up with women, and women found him attractive. He was muscular, just shy of six feet, with smooth brown skin and brown eyes. He didn't have to spend time alone. The young lady that worked at the Post Exchange where he'd purchased a computer the past weekend made it clear that she would like to get to know him a lot better. She went so far as to jot down her phone number on the back of the sales slip. If he told his cousins that he'd turned down her advances, he'd never live it down. It wasn't that he wasn't interested. She was pretty attractive. He just wasn't interested in having sex for sex's sake.

The woman he decided to settle down with had to be special. It was difficult being married to a member of the armed forces. He'd seen it time after time again, spouses not able to withstand the stress of long field exercises, deployments, and moving every two or three years. It would take a woman with patience and a lot of understanding to handle the direction his military career was taking.

A voice interrupted his thoughts, and Paul's head turned toward the door.

"Are you headed over to Cadence?" Sergeant Timothy Shupe asked, standing in the doorway. Assigned to B 2/4 Infantry, Paul was a combat medic, rotating through the orthopedics clinic for additional training. Timothy arrived at the hospital a year ago.

"Yes. I'm on my way out the door. I'm looking forward to relaxing with a good meal and good music." Paul leaned down, grabbing the black gym bag on the side of the desk.

"Check out the ladies," Timothy added, with a big smile. He moved further into the room.

Paul liked hanging out with Sergeant Shupe. He had an easy-going personality and was very straight up with everyone with whom he came into contact.

Paul returned his smile. "Of course."

"Mind if I tag along?"

"Not if your wife doesn't mind."

"You got jokes. I'm a grown man. I don't have to check with my wife. I have heard nothing but good things about Cadence. I want to check it out."

Paul threw the bag on his shoulder. "All right. I'm on my way to the locker room to take a shower. I'll meet you back here," he glanced at his watch, "say in about ten minutes."

"Fine with me." Timothy trailed Paul out the door and headed toward the nurses' station.

Paul frowned. "Where are you going?"

Timothy picked up the telephone at the desk and punched in a series of numbers. "I'm going to let Liz know I'm headed to the club."

Paul burst out laughing as he turned the corner and headed for the men's locker room. He couldn't help but feel a little envious.

Chapter Two

Kayla glanced up at the clock on the wall—five minutes until the end of the day formation. Clearing her desk, she put everything in its proper place, then grabbed her beret before heading out the door. She hoped First Sergeant Chambers wasn't long-winded. It had been a long, hard day. All she wanted to do was go home and soak in a hot bath.

First Sergeant Chambers must have read her mind. Before she knew it, she was in her vehicle and headed off post. A quick stop by the supermarket, followed by picking up her cleaning, and forty minutes later, she was parked in front of her apartment building.

A few minutes later, quick strides carried Kayla to her door. Carefully shifting the bags beneath her arms, she searched in the bottom of her black purse, found the keys, activated the lock, and entered the foyer. She strolled through the living room, heading into the kitchen, and placed the grocery bags on the counter. She put away the items and went into the bedroom.

Decorated in romantic off-white, the bedroom was a welcomed haven for Kayla. She hung the dry cleaning in the back of the closet, stripped off her tactical boots, and stepped into the shower. A few minutes later, she turned off the shower and toweled dry. Returning into the bedroom, she massaged lotion into every part of her body. When that was done, she went to the oak dresser, retrieving a brown army T-shirt and sweat pants. She brushed her hair into two large braids.

Deciding to just relax, she climbed into bed and pointed the remote control at the television before stretching out.

Then she heard it: "Soldiers of the 3rd Infantry Division at Fort Hood, Georgia, received orders today for deployment to Iraq," the female reporter stated.

Kayla thought about Marissa's friend, who had also received orders for deployment. While she understood that the army's main function was to defend the country, she didn't want to go to war. She didn't want anything to interfere with her chance of attending nursing school. Could the 3rd Combat Hospital be next? It was a possibility she couldn't rule out. During a conflict, soldiers got hurt, injured, and even killed. It was her unit's mission to provide medical care. It's what they trained for year-round. They were ready if called upon, and she would go with honor. Nursing school would have to wait.

Kayla didn't realize she'd dozed off until the ringing of her telephone jarred her awake. Groggy, she glanced over at the clock on the nightstand. It was only 6:30 p.m. With her eyes still half-closed, she spoke into the receiver, "Hello?"

"Sergeant Perry," Marissa's agitated voice came across the phone line. Kayla's hair stood up on the back of her neck. She could hear drama coming on. "Can you come and pick me up?"

Kayla sat up in bed. "What? Where are you?"

"I'm at Cadence Supper Club in DC," she explained. "Randall and I had a fight. He left me at the club."

Kayla sighed. Familiar story. Different day of the week. They fight. They make up. Back together the next day. It was getting old.

"Please, Sergeant Perry," Marissa pleaded, prompted by Kayla's silence.

"All right. I'm on my way."

‹∞›

Paul drove the Cherokee once around before he found a parking space—normal for Cadence.

"This place is packed," Timothy said, looking at the long line out the door. It wrapped around the corner, and cars were parked on both sides of the street.

"It's always like this, even on Sundays," Paul boasted. "Very influential African-Americans hang out here. You never know who you might see or meet."

"Hmm," was Timothy's response.

"You just remember you're a married man," Paul said, parallel parking the vehicle in an open space.

"Married, not dead." Timothy glanced out the passenger's window, just as a group of attractive women passed the vehicle. The three women glanced at the handsome men, waved, and giggled. Timothy nodded.

Paul chuckled. "Let's go." He exited the vehicle, followed by Timothy.

The pair stepped inside a set of massive mahogany doors affixed with brass fixtures and found themselves engrossed in a beautiful, spacious foyer, with soft beige furniture. The sound of Luther Vandross' *Never Too Much* filtered through the built-in speakers in the club. Customers' chatter and silverware clicking on china rounded out the club's ambience. As they moved through the club, Paul recognized most of the people who often dropped by to enjoy the laid-back atmosphere, whether they were someone special, or alone.

"What's going on, Sarge?" the bartender, Hunnicutt, asked Paul as he settled on the barstool.

An army veteran, having served in Vietnam with Victor and Gerald's father, Hunnicutt worked part-time at Cadence. He was a nice man, a people person, which made him perfect to bartend at Cadence.

"Nothing much, Hunnicutt. What about yourself?"

"You know me." Hunnicutt placed a shot glass in front of Paul. "Trying not to let them work me too hard. What will it be?"

"Give me the usual, watered-down," Paul replied, glancing over at Timothy who sat next to him. "Hunnicutt, I'd like you to meet Sergeant Timothy Shupe, a co-worker and good friend of mine. Go easy on him; it's his first time at Cadence."

"Welcome to Cadence," Hunnicutt said, placing a shot glass in front of Timothy. "I hope this won't be your last time with us. Nowhere else in DC will you find a club to wine, dine, and unwind you all in one night the way we do it here."

"Thank you. With what I've seen so far, I will definitely be back."

"Great. Bring a guest. What will it be, Sergeant?" Hunnicutt asked.

"Give me what you gave Sergeant Lake."

"One scotch, watered-down," Hunnicutt replied.

"I can't afford to drink it any other way," Paul explained. "You know how the army frowns on drunk driving. Can't take a chance." Paul lifted the glass to his lips to take a sip. The next sentence died in his throat when he noticed a woman coming into view. His gaze took in everything about her, from head to toe. The beautifully built body, shapely legs, and smooth, light skin were all things he liked in a woman. His eyes took another tour of her as he took a deep breath. He noticed her looking around as if searching for someone. Who was she meeting? Her boyfriend? Husband? He hoped neither.

"Having a cookout tomorrow," he heard Timothy saying.

Paul frowned, wondering what Timothy was talking about. He stole another look in the woman's direction. He saw a blonde-haired, attractive woman come up and hug her. He breathed a sigh of relief.

"I'm inviting you to cookout tomorrow at my house. Can you make it?" Timothy turned around on the stool, following Paul's gaze. He recognized the two women. "Which one has your attention? Kayla or Marissa?"

Paul couldn't believe his luck. "You know them?"

"Yes. Both ladies are friends with my wife."

"Who's the sistah?" Paul inquired.

"Oh, that's Kayla Perry."

Paul watched them settle in the booth; he wanted to get to know Kayla Perry, up close and personal.

È Ç

Kayla was a frequent patron of Cadence. She enjoyed the friendly atmosphere of the club. She liked Victor and Gerald; they were approachable, and she had spoken with them on numerous occasions. Both could often be seen in the club among the guests to ensure everything ran smoothly. The food, music, and clientele were also the best in the city. Despite all those wonderful things, Kayla didn't appreciate leaving her comfortable bed to be involved in another lover's spat.

"What happened?" Kayla slid into the beige-colored booth across from Marissa.

"We got into it because Randall took money out of my bank account without consulting me. I'm getting tired of his mess." Marissa placed her face in her hands. Kayla remained silent; she'd heard it all before. "I don't mind Randall having the money," she continued.

"Then what were you arguing about?" Kayla inquired.

Marissa placed her hands on the table. The candlelight flicking across her face showed she was trying to keep her composure. "Because he wouldn't tell me what he withdrew the money for."

"How much did he take?" This wasn't the first time Marissa had complained about Randall taking money from her account. Kayla didn't understand what the big deal was.

"Fifteen hundred dollars," Marissa quipped.

"Fifteen hundred dollars?" Kayla repeated.

"Can I get you anything?" Maya, the hostess, asked. She appeared so quietly, Kayla hadn't even known she was there. Not an alcohol drinker, she ordered a Sprite. Marissa ordered the same.

"What did he need fifteen hundred dollars for?" Kayla asked, when Kim was out of earshot.

"I don't know. That's what I wanted to know. He wouldn't tell me. I have a feeling he's up to no good."

Kayla tilted her head to one side. "You think?" she said with sarcasm. A farm girl, Marissa was naïve to game shooting, city guys like Randall. Though Kayla was from Mobile, she was aware of brothers like Randall. They took advantage of a young mind like Marissa. Randall was trouble with a capital "T" and had been since the day he arrived at Delta Company, eight months ago. Rumor around the unit was he was reassigned to the unit after getting in serious trouble at his previous unit in Belgium. No one knew the details. Whatever it was, the army was letting him go for it. As far as Kayla was concerned, it was not soon enough.

"It wouldn't be the first time," Kayla continued, as Kim placed their drinks in front of them.

Marissa leaned across the table. "I know you don't like him."

"That's not it." Kayla stirred the straw in the Sprite. "No one likes the way he treats you. What do you think he did with the money?"

Marissa blew out a soft breath. "I wish I knew." Almost on cue, the old school song, *Casanova* by Levert filled the air.

Kayla sat up straight. She believed the song was appropriate for the conversation they were having.

"I asked him, and he told me to mind my own business. Can you believe it?" Marissa face turned beet red, and her voice raised an octave. "It's my money. He tells me to stay out of his business."

"What did you say?"

"I said it's my money; that makes it my business. I still didn't get a straight answer."

Kayla took a sip. "I'm not going to ask if he's going to repay you."

Marissa almost choked. "Are you serious?" She answered with attitude. "I'll never see that money again. It's gone."

"If you could do anything about it, would you?" Kayla challenged.

Marissa's eyes skidded away. "I don't know what to do about Randall. I'm confused."

Kayla sighed. "I know I don't understand."

"Have you ever been in love?" Marissa asked.

"No," Kayla admitted honestly, "but I know that love doesn't hurt; it's loving, kind, gentle, caring. From what I can see, you have none of that with Randall."

"How do you know?" Marissa threw at Kayla.

Kayla leaned back in the booth. She crossed her arms over her chest in irritation.

"And who says that love doesn't hurt? It does hurt," Marissa defended. "That's when you know you're in love with someone. I love him. He loves me."

Kayla rolled her eyes.

"Look, I know Randall is no good for me."

"And how is that love?" Kayla prompted.

"I don't know. I just know how I feel about him."

It was no use talking to Marissa about Randall. Kayla could tell from her voice that Marissa was upset. She didn't want to hurt her feelings. She believed Marissa felt something for Randall. Lust? Whip appeal? Whatever it was, it wasn't "real" love.

"What about when you go to Penn Sate? What then?" Kayla asked. Marissa nervously looked away, then leaned back in the booth.

"Don't tell me, Randall is going, too?"

"Maybe. He's thinking about it," she added quickly. "We have discussed him joining me after he gets out."

Kayla didn't get a chance to protest Marissa's decision.

"Good evening, ladies," came a voice over Kayla's left shoulder. A second later, Timothy appeared, accompanied by a handsome man she didn't recognize. Kayla and Marissa both exchanged pleasantries with Timothy. All the while, Kayla was admiring the handsome man's smooth, brown face, full lips, and eyes that were compelling to look into.

She marveled at his long lashes. The brother was definitely easy on the eyes. She didn't miss that he was looking right at her. Her heartbeat went into a full gallop from his open stare.

"Kayla. Marissa. I'd like you to meet a friend of mine. This is Sergeant Paul Lake. Paul, allow me to introduce Specialist Marissa Poe and Sergeant Kayla Perry."

"Nice to meet you, ladies." He was talking to both of them, but his eyes never left Kayla's.

Kayla nervously cleared her throat. "Nice to meet you, Sergeant Lake," she said, her voice laced with sexual huskiness. She stuck out her hand.

Paul accepted her hand, his stomach in knots just at the touch of her warm flesh to his. She was even more beautiful up close. Her facial bones were delicately carved, her mouth full, just right for kissing, and her light complexion glowed. Her features were exquisite. Natural. Without a hint of makeup. He liked that.

"It's Paul," he corrected. He smiled, displaying straight, white teeth.

"As long as you call me, Kayla." He had the sweetest smile she'd ever seen.

"Okay, Kayla," he answered in a deep, low voice.

"Now that we have the introductions out of the way," Timothy said, as he extended a hand to Marissa, "why don't we go dance?"

Marissa glanced at Kayla to make sure it was safe to leave her alone with Paul. Kayla nodded. A wide grin spread across Marissa's face. She placed her hand in Timothy's

"Let's go," Marissa said, almost rushing to the dance floor.

Once Timothy and Marissa left, an awkward silence fell between Paul and Kayla. Paul was the first to break the tension. "Do you mind if I sit down?" Before she could reply, he slowly eased his long body into the booth across from her.

Kayla swallowed the lump in her throat. She could deal with him standing beside her, but sitting across from her was going to be difficult.

"Do you come here often, Kayla?"

She dipped her gaze. "Enough."

Paul placed his arm on the table, linking his fingers together. "Enough?" He wished she would look him in the face. Maybe she was shy. He had to restrain himself from reaching out, lifting her chin up, so he could look into her lovely face. "What does that mean?"

Kayla looked up into his face. "It means I'm not exactly a regular, but I come here often." She took a sip. She was grateful to do something with her hand. The way he was looking at her, it seemed as if he was undressing her with his eyes. "What about you? Are you a regular?"

"I come here a lot."

"Why?" She knew it was a stupid question. She couldn't think of anything to say. She just wanted to say something so that he would have to speak and she could listen to the sound of his voice.

He smiled. "The food and music are excellent, and I like meeting people."

"I like those things, too, but I have better things to do than come in here every night."

He leaned forward to look directly in her eyes. "Like what?"

Kayla gulped. Except for an occasional date, she didn't have much of a social life to brag about. "That's personal."

Paul chuckled. "You mentioned it. I'm just making conversation."

Paul was right; she felt terrible for being so rude. "I'm sorry. You didn't deserve that. It's just been a long day."

"Anything you want to talk about?"

Kayla's head snapped up. "What?"

"Anything you want to talk about?" Paul repeated. "I'm told I'm a good listener."

Kayla was surprised at how open he was. She found it refreshing. "Thank you. I'll work it out."

"Okay, but whenever you want to talk about anything, the invitation is open."

She chuckled. "Does that line work on the women you meet?"

His eyes found hers again. Hers skidded away. She wondered if he was aware of what he was doing to her inside. Every time their eyes met, her heart turned over. This was insane. No man had ever made her feel how she was feeling right now.

Paul's eyebrows bunched together. "What makes you ask something like that?"

"You look like a ladies' man."

Paul leaned back in the booth. No one had ever told him that. "Oh, so tell me, what does a ladies' man look like?"

She pointed at him. "You. He looks like you."

He laughed again. The couple in the booth behind him turned around.

"You still didn't answer my question. What does a ladies' man look like?" he prompted.

"Suave, debonair, and handsome. Women throwing themselves at you."

He blushed. She thought he was handsome. This could go somewhere, he thought. "Thanks for the compliment, but believe me, I'm a long way from being a ladies' man."

"Why should I believe you?" She enjoyed teasing him and realized she was beginning to relax.

He chuckled. "I wouldn't lie to you."

"Hmm," Kayla answered, as she continued to sip on her soda.

Paul changed the subject. "I can't believe you're in the army."

"Does that surprise you?"

"Well, yeah. You don't look like a soldier."

"Oh. What does a soldier look like?" She was proud of herself for getting the best of him. He was speechless.

Paul had to grin. He nodded. "All right. You got me. You're just so beautiful, I didn't expect you to be a soldier. My bad."

Her face warmed at the compliment, but she wasn't finished making him squirm. "So, what are you saying? Female soldiers are not attractive?"

Paul blinked. "No. That's not what I'm saying. There are a lot of attractive female soldiers."

"So you were just feeding me a line?"

"No, I wasn't feeding you a line."

Kayla placed the empty glass on the table. "Hmmm."

"I was just giving a beautiful woman a compliment. I didn't mean any disrespect." He chuckled nervously. "And can we please change the subject?"

"I guess I can let you off the hook."

"Thank you. Where are you assigned?" Paul inquired.

"Delta Company, 3rd Combat Support Hospital out at Fort Bradley."

"Isn't that a front line unit out of Maryland?"

"Yes, it is. How do you know Timothy?"

"We work together at Walter Reed Army Medical

Center in DC. I'm the NCOIC of the Orthopedics unit, and he's doing his rotation."

"A safe job," Kayla replied.

"Good evening, Paul." Kim, the waitress, interrupted their conversation. She flashed him an overly friendly smile. Kayla didn't know Paul from Adam, but she was a little jealous.

"Hi, Kim. How are you this evening?" Paul asked, returning Kim's greeting.

"I'm fine. What about yourself?"

"I'm good."

Kim turned to Kayla and asked, "Would you like anything else?"

Kayla declined.

"The usual?" Kim asked Paul.

"You know it," Paul answered.

Kim beamed at him. "Okay. I'll be right back with your order." She turned and disappeared in the crowd.

"What's the usual?" Kayla asked.

"You will see. Now back to my job being safe. It may be for the moment, but I'm waiting to see if I have been accepted for Special Forces."

"You like living dangerously or something?"

"We are in the army. We are all living dangerously."

"It doesn't mean you have to do something to make it even more dangerous. What made you decide to apply for Special Forces?"

"My cousin served in Special Forces. He had an intriguing military career. I want to follow in his footsteps, but enough about me. I want to know about Kayla. What made you join the army?"

"A college education."

"Really?"

"I was in college at Tuskegee, and my parents ran out of money." She spread her hands apart. "So, here I am. I applied for the Green to Gold Program. Like you, I'm just waiting to hear if I have been accepted."

"I guess we're both waiting to see if our career paths will change. What program are you interested in? What school?"

"The nursing program at the University of Maryland."

"A very good school. I graduated from North Carolina State with a degree in African-American History. I'm sure you will be accepted."

"I hope so. I only need two years to get a baccalaureate degree in nursing."

"Looks like I will be addressing you as an officer soon. And who knows, you may have to take care of me one day."

The smile vanished from Kayla's face. Though they had just met, she didn't want to think about him being injured or even worse. "Don't talk like that. It's not funny."

Paul's voice became serious. "It wasn't meant to be funny. I'm a realist. I know if I'm accepted into Special Forces, what I'm in for. I don't have a problem with it."

Kayla cleared her throat. She didn't feel comfortable having this conversation with him. "I still don't want to hear you talk like that."

"Yes, ma'am," he replied, already addressing her as an officer.

She smiled. "I'm not an officer, yet."

"You will be," Paul said. "I have a feeling you will be a good one."

"So will you, sir." Kayla returned the respect to him as a fellow officer.

Kim arrived with a plate consisting of chicken fried steak,

mashed potatoes, brown gravy, green beans, a dinner roll, and banana pudding for dessert. "Enjoy," she said and walked away.

Kayla admired the platter loaded with food. "That's your usual?"

Paul picked up the salt and pepper shakers and sprinkled a little of both onto the food. "Every time I dine here, this is my order. Are you sure you don't want to order dinner? It's on me."

She shook her head no.

"I feel guilty eating in front of you."

"Don't be." She watched him bow his head in prayer, then properly cut a small piece of the meat and stuff it in his mouth.

"You don't know what you're missing."

Kayla looked around for Timothy and Marissa. She didn't see them. They had been gone for over forty minutes, evidently to allow her and Paul a chance to get acquainted, but there was no need. They were headed in opposite directions. There wasn't a chance for a relationship. Deep down inside, she wished things were different.

"I wonder what happened to Marissa and Timothy," Kayla said, as she craned her neck, looking around.

"I'm sure they are fine. What's the matter? Not enjoying my company?"

"It's not that. I'm getting tired. I hope Marissa is ready to leave."

"You're ready to leave?"

"Yes. The only reason I came here was to give Marissa a ride home."

"I see, he said, sounding disappointed. Well, I hope I can see you again." Kayla definitely wanted to see him again. She just wished their timing wasn't so bad. "I don't think that's a good idea. Do you?"

"Actually, I think it's a great idea." He couldn't help it; he was intrigued by this beautiful woman and wanted to see her again. He didn't care how much time they had left together. Whether it was one hour, one day, or one week, he wanted to spend it with her.

"We're going in different directions. Let's not make things complicated."

"How am I making things complicated by wanting to see you again? There is no pressure for a relationship. We go out. We have a good time." He grinned. "Hopefully, I impress you and we go out again. We see where it goes—if anywhere," he quickly added.

"Look, Paul, I—"

Paul cut her off. He took a deep breath. "I hear what you're saying. I do, but it's a chance I'm willing to take, if you are." Then he thought about it. *What if she's involved with someone else?* "Wait. Are you seeing someone?"

Kayla frowned. "Isn't it a little late to ask that question?"

"Well?" he prompted, hoping Kayla would give him the answer he wanted to hear.

"That's none of your business," she said, being coy. She stood, hoisting the thin purse strap on her right shoulder. "It was nice meeting you, Paul."

Paul dabbed at his mouth with the napkin and stood. He was doing his best to mask his disappointment, but he wasn't turned off. If anything, he was more intrigued. "I will ask again."

"And I will give the same answer." With that Kayla turned, threading through the crowd. She hated turning Paul down. He would never know how much she wanted to say yes to his invitation. Why couldn't the circumstances be different?

A moment later, she found Marissa and Timothy at the bar, laughing and talking.

"Thanks for not coming back," Kayla said, placing her hands on her hips.

"You don't have to thank us," Timothy replied. "Paul is a great guy."

"For someone else," Kayla responded.

Timothy frowned. "What do you mean?"

"He seemed like a nice guy to me," Marissa threw in.

"Whatever," Kayla replied. "Are you ready to go? I'm tired. I want to turn in."

"Yeah, all right," Marissa replied, casting her friend a look.

"Are you ladies coming to the cookout tomorrow?" Timothy asked.

"What cookout?" Marissa quipped.

"The one at my house tomorrow afternoon."

Kayla didn't know if Timothy was aware of the tension between his wife and Marissa, or he would have thought twice about extending an invitation to Marissa.

"I have plans tomorrow." Marissa slid off the barstool. "Thanks for inviting me, though."

"Well, if you change your mind, the invitation is open." Timothy focused on Kayla. "What about you, Kayla?"

"Yes," she replied. "I told Liz I would stop by for a few minutes. Probably around two or three."

"Great. I will see you tomorrow then." Timothy slid off the barstool. "You ladies drive safely. Let me go and see what damage you did to my man." With a wave of the hand, he disappeared into the crowd.

Chapter Three

Kayla and Marissa walked outside of the club underneath a beautiful full moon, a moon that perhaps explained the kind of day Kayla was having so far. They walked up the street and around the corner in silence. Kayla had parked her car on a side street, the closest she could get to Cadence.

Kayla pulled out her car alarm remote and pressed the button, unlocking the doors. Marissa slid into the passenger seat. Minutes later, they were headed down the interstate, still in silence.

"Still upset about Randall?" Kayla leaned forward, turning on the radio. The rap lyrics of T.I. filled the car.

Marissa's head bounced along to the music. "Yes. We will work things out, but right now I'm thinking about the cookout."

Kayla looked over in her direction. "What about the cookout?"

Marissa turned in her seat. "Liz didn't invite me." She waved a hand in mid-air. "The girl be trippin'."

Kayla had to laugh. Marissa's knowledge of African-American Ebonics was impressive. If it wasn't for her skin color, she could have been black.

"She can get on your nerves sometimes," Kayla said. "I wouldn't take it personally." Kayla took the exit off the interstate onto the main street.

Marissa leaned back into the seat. Crossing her arms, she stuck out her bottom lip. "I try not to take it personally. The woman just doesn't like me."

"Sometimes people just don't hit it off. It doesn't mean that they don't like you. Your personalities are just different. Liz has a strong personality. But she's a good person."

"I think she's prejudice," Marissa replied in a huff.

Kayla stole a look at Marissa, then focused back on the road. "What makes you say something like that?"

"C'mon, Kayla. You heard her, all the negative remarks about Randall. She's always talking about black men, white women, and interracial couples. What else can it be?"

"I don't know," Kayla replied.

"She's your best friend. I expect that answer from you."

"You're my friend, too. I really don't know what's going on. I just want my two friends to get along. I'm tired of being in the middle."

Marissa was quiet a moment, as if in deep thought. "And I'm tired of trying to get along with her. Whatever issue she has with me, that's her problem, not mine." She gestured with her hands. "I'm through with it."

Kayla threw her a sympathetic look; she knew Marissa really had been trying to get along with Liz.

"I'm sorry that you're in the middle, Kayla." Marissa continued her tirade. "I have tried to be nice to her, you know that. I'm not going to kiss her butt to get along with her. I just hope you and I can still be friends."

"You know we're friends to the end." She glanced at Marissa again. "I know you have gone out of your way to get along with Liz for my sake. I appreciate it."

"Believe me, it was only because of you that I tried to get along with her." Marissa sighed. "I don't want to talk about Liz anymore." She managed a smile. "Tell me what happened between you and Paul after we left? He is gorgeous. And he couldn't keep his eyes off you. I know you gave up the digits."

Kayla tried to suppress the grin that threatened to cross her face. "He was fine, wasn't he? But I didn't give him my phone number."

Marissa gave her a look like she had lost her mind. "Hold up. Paul was interested in you, *very* interested, so I know he asked for your number."

"Not exactly."

"What do you mean, not exactly?"

"He asked me out."

Marissa's face beamed. "Now you're talking."

"I turned him down."

Marissa's mouth dropped. "You must have lost your mind. I know you were interested. You were checking him out." She pointed at Kayla. "You better have a good reason for turning him down."

Kayla stopped at a red light. She knew Marissa wasn't going to understand her reason for not wanting to get involved with Paul, or any other man. Her main focus was nursing school—that meant no distractions.

"I'm just not interested in getting involved with anyone at the moment. Just want to go at it single."

From the look on Marissa's face, she wasn't buying it. "What does that have to do with getting your groove on?"

Kayla's eyes blinked in disbelief at Marissa's question. She stepped down on the gas pedal when the light changed to green. "What are you saying? Sleep with him?"

"That's exactly what I'm saying. Men do it all the time. Why not women?"

"You're talking crazy," Kayla replied.

"No, I'm not. Who says you have to be in a committed relationship?"

"My main focus is school. I don't want anyone or anything to take my focus from that."

"A man like Paul could get my attention any time or any way that he wants it."

"Well, for your information, Paul has his own agenda. Just like I'm waiting to see whether I get into the Green to Gold Program, he's waiting to find out if he's accepted into Special Forces, so our lives are going into different directions."

Marissa shivered, as if a chill coursed through her body. "A man that is dangerous and sexy. That's good sex. You better reconsider that decision."

They looked at each other and burst out laughing.

Kayla shook her head. "You're so nasty."

"Yeah, but I'm right."

Kayla dropped Marissa off at her apartment. Forty minutes later, she found herself back in her familiar surroundings. She quickly undressed, showered, slipped into her nightgown, and crawled back into bed.

Just as she was preparing to turn out the light on the nightstand, she reached over and flipped the ringer off on the telephone. She slid down beneath the sheets. Too bad she couldn't turn off the thoughts of Paul.

 C3 80

Saturday morning, Paul placed the 275-pound weight back into its proper place in the army's weight room. He began his six-day workout with ten minutes of stretching, a five- to ten-mile run, followed by a thirty-minute workout. Keeping in shape in the army was a must, not to mention it was a good way to try to keep his mind off Kayla. It wasn't working. He had been awake half the night trying to get her out of his mind. Everything she'd said to him last night made sense. He understood her apprehension about not wanting to get involved, but Paul was never a man who gave up easily. Timothy told him that Kayla would be attending the cookout, and he couldn't wait to see her again.

Ten minutes later, Paul exited the gym through the side double doors and made his way to his truck, throwing the gym bag onto the passenger seat. He turned the key in the ignition and pulled out of the parking space. He waved to the Military Police standing guard at the front gate and pulled out into early morning traffic.

To keep his mind occupied, he turned on the CD and let Sean Paul and his Reggae rhythm accompany him on his ride home.

Paul parked in front of his Germantown, Maryland apartment building. He bent down to scoop up the mail as soon as he stepped inside. As he entered the foyer, then the living room, he quickly sifted through the mail, receiving nothing but the usual monthly bills.

He dropped the keys and mail on the coffee table. Tossing the gym bag on the sofa, he turned and headed to the kitchen. After turning the small TV to CNN news, he opened the refrigerator door and grabbed a bottle of water. The liquid vanished in seconds. He glanced at the kitchen clock on the wall; it was 11 a.m. Fours hours until he would see Kayla again.

As he headed into the living room, the phone rang. He

hoped it wasn't Timothy phoning to say the cookout was cancelled.

"Hello."

"What's up, little brother?" The familiar voice of his older brother, Devin, came across the line. Devin was also in the army, assigned to a Field Artillery unit at Fort Hood, Texas.

"Hey, Devin. What's going on?"

"Just checking on you."

Paul plopped down on the sofa. "Just working. Trying to be like you."

Devin chuckled. "You know my motto. Don't be like me. Be—"

"…better than me," Paul finished for him. Since he was a little boy, Devin, who was eight years older, drilled those words of wisdom into his head.

"Exactly," Devin replied. "Anything on Special Forces?"

"Nothing yet."

"Well, no news is good news. I'm sure you will be picked up."

"I'm just anxious to get going."

"At the rate soldiers are being deployed, I wouldn't be too anxious. Once you're picked up, I'm sure you're going to be deployed."

"I know," Paul answered. "That doesn't bother me."

A moment of silence fell between them. "Paul, my unit is being deployed to Iraq for eighteen months."

Paul leaned back into the sofa cushion. He didn't know what to say. He shouldn't have been surprised. Devin was assigned to a field artillery battalion, trained as a tanker, a skill that was needed in combat. But he didn't want his brother to go. Devin was married with two small children. It should have been him. He wasn't leaving a family behind or anyone special. He had nothing to lose, though he was sure his immediate family would disagree.

"Paul? Are you there?" Devin prompted.

"Yeah, I'm here. I'm just thinking."

"About what? I hope it's not about me. I'm going to be all right. I've been doing this for twelve years. The Iraqis are the ones who should be worried."

"When are you leaving?" Paul asked.

"Sometime next week. We go through mobilization this week to make sure all of our necessary records are in order. Then to Fort Irwin for several more months of training, then on to Iraq."

Paul ran a hand down his face. He could imagine how Devin's wife, Jennifer, was taking it. Their parents. Though they knew the danger of being in the military, it wasn't until a loved one marched off to battle that everything became a reality.

"How's Jennifer taking it?"

Devin sighed. "She's handling it. That's the best way I can describe it. She's upset. Scared."

"What about Mom and Dad?" Paul asked. "Have you told them yet?"

"No. I will phone them after I'm done speaking to you. I don't know how they will deal with one son in Iraq and perhaps another on the way."

"Mom and Dad will be fine. Dad served in Vietnam. He knows what war is about."

"I know he does. I'm worried about Mom."

"How are my niece and nephew?" Paul had to change the subject. Talking about the six-year-old twins, Aaron and Ashley, was what he needed at the moment.

"Aaron and Ashley are fine. They keep asking when they will see their favorite uncle again."

Paul had to chuckle. The last time he'd seen them had been during the Christmas holidays, six months ago. He spent Christmas with Devin and his family and New Year's with his parents. He was sure they had grown like weeds since then. "The only reason I'm their favorite uncle is because I always visit bringing gifts to the little rug rats," he joked affectionately.

Devin joined the laughter. "Watch your mouth. Those are *my* little rug rats."

Paul couldn't fathom Devin being away from his family for over a year.

"Wait until you have your own," Devin added. "I hope you're dating."

"Not at the moment, but I'm attending a cookout today."

"Are you going alone?"

"Yes, I'm going alone," Paul answered, as his mind zeroed in on Kayla, "but I hope I don't leave alone."

They spoke a few minutes more before hanging up. Devin promised to keep in touch as much as possible during the week. Paul tried to tell himself that he wasn't going to worry about Devin or let it overshadow his decision of wanting to go into Special Forces. He closed his eyes a moment. He loved his brother. If anything happened to him, he didn't know what he would do.

ও ৪

Kayla rolled out of bed and made a beeline for the bathroom. She turned on the shower, stripped off her nightgown, and stepped into the warm, inviting downpour of water. She reached for the sponge, lathering it with her favorite shower gel.

As she showered, she hoped Paul would be at the cookout. She was sure Timothy had told him about it. She didn't want to admit it to Marissa last night, but she was attracted to Paul, even though he could be leaving at any moment. To be honest, she hoped he wasn't accepted into Special Forces; it was far too dangerous, and if he stayed, she would have the opportunity to get to know him better. Kayla smiled and thought about Marissa's comment about a man in Special Forces being dangerous and sexy and capable of good sex.

It had been a while since she shared her bed with a man, but she couldn't allow herself to be distracted. She had to keep her feelings in check, and she knew that might be difficult to do, because ever since she'd laid eyes on Sergeant Paul Lake, she couldn't stop thinking about him.

A few minutes later, she stepped out of the shower and toweled herself dry. She padded back into the bedroom and sat at the vanity table. After rubbing lotion all over her body, she went into her closet and decided upon a pair of tan Capri pants with a matching top and sandals. With hot curling irons, she styled her hair in soft curls around her face, gently touching her shoulders. After applying a few strokes of lip-gloss and a few quick brushes of mascara, she grabbed her sunglasses off the dresser and was on her way out the door to her car.

CR ED

Thirty minutes later, Kayla strolled along the flowered walkway to Liz's brown, split-level townhouse. She practically basked in the weather—the sky was clear and blue, the sun warm, and a gentle breeze rustled the leaves and cooled the flesh.

She stood outside the door. She could hear music playing on the other side. She rang the doorbell. No answer. Thinking they could not hear because of the music, she turned the doorknob, letting herself in.

She entered the living room and found it empty, but she could smell the meat on the grill. Also, she could hear adult voices, and children running and screaming from the fenced-in backyard.

Kayla strolled through the open, glass sliding doors. She spotted Liz placing a large bowl on a large picnic table filled with pre-cooked platters of burgers, hotdogs, chicken wings, and tasty side dishes. There were several platters of basted and marinated meats waiting to go on the grill. Looking around, everyone seemed to be having a good time. Guests were dining, dancing, and relaxing on lounge chairs. Disappointment ran through her. There was no sign of Paul.

"Hey girl," Kayla said. She gave Liz a hug and waved at Timothy, who stood stationed at the grill.

Liz grinned. "I'm glad you made it."

"Did I have a choice?" Kayla joked. "Someone threatened to come to my house if I didn't show up."

"True." Liz, eyes shining, said, "I have something to tell you."

"Don't keep me in suspense. Tell me."

Liz smiled and said, "Let's go inside." She grabbed Kayla's hand and motioned to Timothy that she was headed inside. He smiled and nodded.

Liz led Kayla into the kitchen. She opened the refrigerator door, removing a large bottle of Sprite.

"Come on, Liz. What's the news?"

"Timothy told me you met Paul last night."

Kayla placed her hands on her thin hips. "Is that what you want to talk to me about? Paul?"

Liz raised a well-manicured finger. "That's one of the things."

Kayla nervously crossed her arms across her chest. "What's the other?"

"I'm pregnant," Liz announced, bubbling with excitement.

Both women squealed. Kayla hugged Liz tightly. She was ecstatic for Liz. Liz confided in her that she'd suffered a miscarriage eight months ago and that they were trying again. Kayla knew how much Liz craved having children.

"How far along are you?"

"Six weeks," Liz replied with glee. She put a hand to her face. "I can't believe it. You know, Timothy and I have been trying for a while. I was beginning to think I couldn't get pregnant again." She shrugged. "You know…after the miscarriage, but then Dr. Maundry phoned this morning and confirmed it."

"You suspected you were pregnant and you didn't tell me?" Kayla tried to act as if her feelings were hurt. "I thought we were friends."

"We are. I just didn't want to get my hopes up."

"Come and sit down." Kayla took Liz by the hand, leading her to a chair at the dining room table. They settled across from each other, Kayla holding Liz's hand for support. "I'm so happy for you, Liz. I told you not to worry. It would happen."

"Yes, you did. I just hope nothing goes wrong this time."

"We won't have you talking like that. Every pregnancy is different. Many women have gone on to have successful pregnancies after a miscarriage. You will, too."

A nervous smile crossed Liz's face. "You're right. You're right."

"What did Timothy say when you told him?"

"He was, and still is, on top of the world. A little worried about me, the pregnancy, but that's to be expected after what happened last time."

"Do you want a boy or girl?" Kayla asked, beaming.

"I don't care what it is. I just want it to be healthy."

Kayla leaned over, giving her girlfriend another tight hug. "I'm going to be a godmother."

"Yes, you are."

They giggled.

"Now about Paul." Liz arched an eyebrow.

Kayla let out an irritated sigh. Liz wasn't going to give up on the conversation. "What about him?"

"Looks like fate has intervened. Timothy told me you met him last night."

"It's just a coincidence."

A sheepish grin crossed Liz's face. "So, what do you think of him?"

"He's okay," she lied. "We only spoke a few minutes. But he seems nice."

"He's okay," Liz repeated.

Kayla threw both hands up in mid-air. "What do you want me to say?"

"Paul is a very nice guy. He's handsome, educated, and seems to have his head on straight. You saw for yourself what he's working with. From what Timothy tells me, he has a thing for you. Any woman would be lucky to have him. If you don't want him, I'm sure there are plenty of women who wouldn't mind him parking his boots underneath their bed."

Before Kayla had a chance to respond, Timothy came

into the kitchen, trailed by Paul. It took everything in Kayla's power to suppress the smile that threatened to cross her lips at the sight of him.

"Look who's here," Timothy announced.

Kayla didn't think Paul could look as good as he did last night, but she was wrong because the ambience of the nightclub did him no justice. Casually dressed in a pair of baggy jeans, a white short sleeve shirt, and a pair of black sandals, Paul made Kayla admit to herself that she loved what he was working with.

"Hi, Paul." Liz sauntered over to him and threw her arms around his neck. He kissed her on both cheeks. "Welcome, I'm glad you could make it."

"Thanks for inviting me. I never miss a chance for free food."

"No problem. I believe you already met Kayla." Liz grinned, looking from Kayla to Paul.

Paul's eyes rested on Kayla, moving over her from head to toe. "We met last night. Nice to see you again, Kayla."

Kayla hoped Paul would kiss her on both cheeks as he did Liz. He must have read her thoughts. A moment later, he stepped forward and did just that. She wondered what his lips would feel like on hers. The scent of his Black Suede cologne was mesmerizing. *He smells so good*, she thought.

Paul stepped back with a sly smile on his face. His eyes locked with Kayla's and he licked his lips.

"Hey, man," Timothy said, interrupting the moment. "I have a plate with your name on it. Let's get at it."

"I'm right behind you," Paul said, giving Kayla one last glance before trailing Timothy outside.

Liz cleared her throat, tilted her head to one side, and giggled. "*He's okay*, huh? That *is* what you said?"

Kayla finally let out her breath. "Yeah," she stammered.

"It's a good thing Timothy and I were in the room."

Kayla frowned. "What do you mean?"

"The way you and Paul were looking at each other. I have a feeling his boots would have *definitely* found a home under your bed."

Chapter Four

Paul accepted the plate of food from Timothy and found a seat at the far end of the table. He nodded, acknowledging fellow soldiers, their families, and employees from the hospital. His mind was reeling from seeing Kayla. He didn't think she could look lovelier than she did last night.

His eyes found Kayla and Liz strolling outside together. He took in everything about the woman who had kept him up half the night. The pair of tan Capri pants that ended below her knees accentuated her perfect, well-shaped calves and ankles. He smiled to himself, looking at her luscious lips. It took all the strength within him not to take possession of her mouth. He glanced up in time to see the object of his desire headed in his direction.

Kayla inhaled sharply as she watched Paul attack a drumstick. "Good food?"

Paul wiped his mouth with a napkin. "Very good. Are you eating?" he asked, noticing she was empty-handed.

"Maybe later. I just came over to see how things are going," she lied. As good as he looked, Kayla wanted to be close to him. If he were aware of her motives, he didn't show it.

"Things are going well. I'm surprised to see you here," Paul lied.

Kayla gave him a look. "Are you really?" she joked. "I would have guessed Timothy told you I would be here."

Paul wagged his head from side-to-side. "All right. You got me. Shupe did tell me you would be here."

She felt her face heat up. "Was that so hard to admit?" She enjoyed making him squirm.

"That depends. Did you think about what we discussed last night?"

Kayla placed her hands on her hips, then tilted her chin up. "What was that?"

Though they had just met, Paul believed Kayla was a woman running over with self-confidence, something he loved in a woman. He rolled his head to one side.

"Ouch," he mumbled under his breath. "I must have lost my touch. Women usually hang on my every word."

A smile touched the corner of her lips. "I'm not most women."

"You're right about that. Why are you giving me such a hard time?" Paul asked. "People usually like me."

"How am I giving you a hard time? We only met last night." Kayla tapped him on the arm, signaling for him to scoot over. She sat down next to him. "I don't know anything about you."

Paul's heart dropped just from her close presence. It was a struggle to compose himself. He leaned over and said, "Once you get to know me, you will like me, too."

"I never said I didn't like you."

Paul faced her. "Just not as your man."

Kayla was amazed at how forward he was. It left her speechless. She looked away to find Liz and Timothy at the cooking island staring at them. Liz smiled and waved.

"You're putting words in my mouth."

He chuckled. "You're right. I apologize. I didn't mean to put you on the spot."

"Are you always so forward?"

"Yes," he answered without hesitation.

"Ever heard of subtlety?"

"Heard of it. Don't believe in it. And you still didn't answer my question."

"What question?" she teased.

Paul burst out laughing. He wasn't going to get a straight answer from her. "You are off the hook, Kayla," he said, as he gently touched her bare shoulder. "For now."

The warm feel of his skin on hers set her aflame. She couldn't help but wonder what it would feel like if they were together, naked, flesh on flesh, body-to-body. She looked at his large hands. She imagined him caressing and stroking her, bringing her to sheer ecstasy. Looking up at him, she smiled and wondered if he knew what she was thinking.

A moment later, Kayla spotted Cage shaking hands with Timothy, followed by a woman she didn't recognize. She waited until Cage looked in her direction before she waved at him. Cage waved back, wound his arm inside his date, and walked toward Kayla. He stopped in front of her. "Hello, Sergeant Perry."

"Hi, Sergeant Cage," Kayla said, wondering who the woman was. Whomever she was, with her Hispanic heritage, long flowing dark hair, dark eyes, and medium height and build, she was very beautiful.

"Sergeant Perry, I'd like to introduce you to a friend of mine. This is Maria Rios."

Kayla smiled at Cage and his friend. "Hello, Maria, it's a pleasure to meet you."

"Same here," Maria said in a Spanish accent. "I have heard so much about you."

"All of it good, I hope."

"Of course."

Kayla forced a grin, wondering what Cage had said about her. Paul stood, letting Kayla know he was still present.

"Sergeant Cage, Maria, I'd like you to meet Sergeant Paul Lake. Paul, this is Staff Sergeant Maurice Cage and his friend, Maria Rios."

Paul extended his hand to Cage, followed by Maria. "Nice to meet you both."

"Same here," Cage and Maria said in unison. "It was nice to meet you, Sergeant Lake. I'm going to introduce Maria to the other guests. I'll see you on Monday morning, Sergeant Perry," he said, pointing at Kayla. "And don't be late."

"I won't," Kayla replied.

"You guys enjoy the rest of your weekend." He steered Maria by the elbow to the other guests.

"He seems like a nice guy," Paul said.

"He is very nice." Kayla watched the couple head over to the cooking island.

Cage grabbed a paper plate, loaded it with food, and handed it to Maria and then leaned over and whispered in her ear. She giggled, running her hand up and down his back. Gone was the serious scowl he wore around the unit. He was grinning from ear-to-ear. He appeared happy. She couldn't help but feel a jab of jealousy.

"What's wrong?" Paul asked.

Kayla turned to face Paul, who was staring intently at her. "Nothing. Just thinking about something."

"You want to take a stroll down by the lake?"

"Sure. Why not?"

Paul stole a glance in Sergeant Cage's direction, wondering if there was history between the two, and if Cage was his competition. He fell in step with Kayla. She led him from the spacious backyard, through a wooden fence, and out toward the lake. Walking down the trail, they were nearly run over by a group of teenagers on skateboards. A large group of people were out enjoying the sun. They passed couples holding hands, family members involved in various activities, roller-bladers, swimmers, runners, and bikers. They took a seat on the bench across from the large, man-made lake.

"This is nice," Paul said, as he placed the sunglasses on his face, taking in the sun rays bouncing off the waves. He loved the smell of the water.

"Yes, it is," Kayla said, her mind fuzzy with flashes of Cage and his date. Was Liz right? Did she have feelings for him? Whether she did or not, they worked together, and there was nothing she could do about it.

Paul turned to her. "Where are you from, Kayla?"

"Mobile, Alabama."

"I thought I picked up a deep southern accent."

"Look who's talking, Mr. Durham, North Carolina." She was grateful for the conversation; it kept her mind off Cage.

He bent his head slightly forward. "Born and raised."

"Any siblings?"

"Three brothers. No sisters."

"All boys. Your parents must have had their hands full. Where do you fit in?"

"I'm in the middle." He smiled. "I have two older brothers. One younger."

"Any in the army?"

He took a deep breath. "My oldest brother, Devin, is a tanker, stationed at Fort. Hood, Texas." He cleared his throat. "He told me this morning he's on his way to Iraq. He's shipping out next week."

Kayla noticed a look of sadness flash over his features. "I'm sorry, Paul." She wanted to reach out and hug him but decided against it.

"It's our job, right?"

Kayla heard the disappointment in his voice. Paul put on a brave face. She was sure he was concerned about his brother heading into harm's way.

"How long have you been at Walter Reed?" she asked, changing the subject.

"About six months."

"And where were you stationed before?"

"I transferred from Tripler in Hawaii. Before Hawaii, I was at Fort Knox, Kentucky."

Kayla raised a perfectly arched eyebrow. "Hawaii? I would love to go there. I always select it on my dream sheet. So far that's all it has been, a dream."

Paul chuckled. "I love being stationed there. Good duty station. Who knows, you may still get there."

Kayla sighed. "I should be so lucky. I have spent my entire first enlistment here. I'm ready for a change."

"If you had, you would have never met me."

Kayla smiled at him. She nodded in agreement. "True."

"So, what about you?" Paul inquired. "Any brothers or sisters?" He wanted to know everything about her.

"I'm an only child."

"I bet your parents weren't so happy about their little girl joining the army."

She grinned. "My mother took it better than I thought

she would. My father," she shook her head from side-to-side, "that's another story. He never served in the military and believes no one should serve, especially women. But he's coming along."

"You can't blame him."

"I guess not. I think it's because they can't interfere in my personal life."

Paul pepped up. "Did they do that?"

She smiled. "All the time."

"You didn't like that?"

Kayla giggled. "No. I didn't."

"A beautiful woman like you. I'm sure Daddy just wanted to keep the boneheads away."

The animation left her face. "My parents divorced when I was thirteen. I didn't see him much after that."

"Sorry to hear about your parents."

"It's okay. I have learned to deal with it."

Paul's heart went out to her. He couldn't imagine growing up without his father and watching his mother raise four knuckleheaded boys on her own. He was sure his mother could have done it. She carried out the bulk of the discipline in their household whenever they got out of line. Despite her strength, nothing could substitute a man's presence in the home.

"My father didn't like any of my dates," Kayla said.

"No man is good enough for his little girl."

"No, not at all." She remembered how her father would grill her dates with questions and threaten them with bodily harm if they got out of line with her. She didn't have very many second dates.

"What made you want to be a nurse?" Paul asked, looking directly into her face.

Kayla looked away, then returned her gaze to his. "I like the idea of being able to help people who can't help themselves. It's something I always wanted to do."

"Good career to go into."

"I think so." She crossed one leg over the other. She was tense under Paul's direct stare. "I remember you telling me that your cousin influenced you to join Special Forces. Who's your cousin?"

"Victor Sexton, co-owner of Cadence."

"Victor and Gerald are your cousins?"

"My mother and their father were brother and sister."

"That explains your presence at the club a lot."

He smiled that smile of his. "Yes, it does."

"And the free food," she added.

"Not because I'm chasing women."

Kayla leaned back. "Who said you were chasing women?"

"You did."

Kayla waved a finger side-to-side. "No, I said women throw themselves at you." She was enjoying the gentle amusement that flowed between them.

Her sparkling personality dazzled Paul. He was having a good time.

"Men don't make a run at you?"

Kayla blushed. "I do all right."

"Why are you single, Kayla?" Paul inquired. "Or am I assuming?"

"No. You are not assuming. I am single. Now is not a good time to be in a serious relationship. My main focus right now is going to school."

"There is never a bad time to be in a relationship."

"Then why are you still single?"

Paul's eyes locked with hers again. "Never met the right woman."

"Never?"

Paul took a deep breath. He thought about his former girlfriend, Dina. She was a subject he didn't want to discuss. "I thought I did once."

"What happened?" Paul seemed like such a nice man. The woman who let him go should have her head examined.

"Let's just say we had different definitions of the word 'infidelity.'"

"Oh," Kayla whispered under her breath. "It's her loss. You are handsome. You have your head on straight. Know what you want out of life. I have a feeling you won't be single for long."

"I hope not."

Kayla had no problem picking up on the meaning in his eyes.

"So, uh, you think I'm handsome?" Paul asked.

Kayla cocked her head to one side. "You look all right," she joked.

His voice became serious. "And I think you're very beautiful."

Kayla swallowed the lump in her throat. Her heart slammed in her chest a mile a minute. She had to get out of his presence.

"Why don't we head back?" she said. "Liz is probably looking for me."

Paul wasn't ready to leave. He was enjoying the time they were spending together and didn't want it to end, but he didn't want to push. "I'm sure Liz won't be angry when she finds out you are with me."

His brown eyes twinkled with mischief. She tried to

submerge the heat flaring in her stomach as he stood close in front of her. She felt a strange feeling in her limbs when he gently touched her bare arms.

"Chill bumps," he said, grateful for the opportunity to touch her. "Are you cold?"

"No," she managed to say. The heat radiating from his body was warming her through and through. She felt a tingling in the pit of her stomach.

"Lead the way," he said, extending a hand and gesturing for her to take the lead. "Do you have plans for tomorrow?"

"I'm going to church in the morning. After that, I will relax and get ready for work on Monday morning." She glanced over at Paul. "Why?"

"Just curious. What church do you attend?"

"James Martindale A.M.E Church. It's in Columbia, Maryland. Have you ever heard of it?"

"Yes, I have. Victor and Gerald are members. Matter of fact, Reverend Martindale is going to perform Victor's wedding ceremony."

"I heard through the grapevine that Victor was engaged." Marissa expressed interest in the handsome, older club owner. While he was flattered, Victor made it clear that he was taken.

"It's true. He has invited me on several occasions to the church. I just never got around to it."

"Have you been to church since you've been here?"

He looked embarrassed. "No, I haven't. Don't tell my mother. She would have a fit."

"Your secret is safe with me, but we can fix that by you coming to church with me tomorrow." They made their way back through the gate and along the short path to Liz's backyard.

"What time is service?" Paul asked.

"Bible study is 9 a.m. Worship is at 11 a.m."

"I will be there."

"Which service?"

"Both. We are at war. We need all the prayers we can get."

"Amen," Kayla chimed in.

Kayla found Liz in the kitchen looking for garbage bags to put trash in. Some of the guests had gone. Paul stopped to converse with Timothy.

"Liz, let me help you," Kayla announced, taking the garbage bags.

Liz straightened up. "Thanks." She looked past Kayla, hoping to see Paul. She was glad to see them hitting it off. They made a good-looking couple, just as she thought. She had never met two people more suited for each other. "Where's Paul?"

Kayla had to smile. She really enjoyed spending time with him. "He's outside talking to Timothy."

"This time it's you glowing," Liz squealed. "I saw you guys take a walk toward the lake. What happened? What did you talk about?" She fired one question after the other.

Laughing, Kayla answered, "Slow down! One question at a time. First, nothing happened. We just talked, general conversation. I asked some feeling-out questions."

"And?"

"Like, I said before, Paul is a nice guy."

"That's it?" Liz shook her head. "You are hopeless." They were interrupted when Timothy and Paul strolled into the kitchen.

"Ladies, I have to get going," Paul said, hugging and planting a kiss on Liz's cheek. "Congratulations on the baby. It couldn't have happened to a nicer couple."

Liz reached out, grasping her husband's hand. She grinned from ear-to-ear. "Thank you, Paul."

Paul turned toward Kayla, and her heart skipped a beat. "I will see you in the morning." He also kissed her on the cheek before heading out the door.

"What's happening in the morning?" Liz asked after he left.

"I invited him to church," Kayla said, as they started cleaning the kitchen. While they were putting food away, dumping paper plates and cups, Kayla filled Liz in on the conversation she'd shared with Paul.

Several hours later, after helping with the clean up, Kayla began her drive home. She couldn't help thinking about Paul. Despite her conversation about not getting involved in a relationship, she had a good feeling about him, and looked forward to seeing him again in the morning. It was going to be a long night.

Chapter Five

 ayla, Paul, and Marissa were seated at the end of the eighth pew of the James Martindale A.M.E. Church. Liz and Timothy were seated in the middle of the row behind them. Today the congregation was full because of the reverend's famous son, Garrett Martindale.

Ladies were dressed in their Sunday best, hoping to catch the attention of the R&B singer. When he did appear, Garrett often led the choir, sang solo, or played the piano. This morning, he moved the church members into a spiritual frenzy with his gospel single, "Witness," from his latest CD.

"Can I get an amen?" Reverend Otis Martindale said loudly from the pulpit, after the congregation calmed down from Garrett's solo. The tall, distinguished man in his early fifties had been preaching his entire life, like his father before him.

"Amen," Paul said. He turned to Kayla and whispered, "Garrett sang that song. I have all of his CDs." He was enjoying the service, glad Kayla had invited him.

"I have him in my collection, too," Kayla responded.

Reverend Martindale instructed the congregation to bow their heads in prayer.

When the service was over, they made their way

through the crowd, shaking hands with Reverend and Mrs. Martindale. Paul got a chance to tell Garrett how much he enjoyed his music.

Thirty minutes later, they headed over to Cadence for lunch. Gerald Sexton met them in the foyer. A polite smile curved his mouth when they arrived.

"Hello, cousin," he said, pulling Paul into a hug before greeting the rest of the group.

Taking a step back, Kayla looked up into the eyes of the tall, handsome man who still held her hand in his.

"How have you been, Kayla?" Gerald asked.

"I have been good. What about yourself?"

Paul felt a stab of jealousy at the way Gerald smiled at Kayla.

Gerald released her hand. "I've been good. I haven't seen you in the club recently."

"I was here Friday night," Kayla answered, smiling.

"I'm sorry I missed you," Gerald replied. He flashed Kayla a bright smile as his eyes took a quick perusal of her. He thought she was a beautiful young woman, the type of woman he would ask out.

"I was here, too," Paul added quickly, as he moved as close as he could to Kayla's side. He flashed Gerald a look that clearly stated he was treading in his territory. Gerald smiled, indicating he understood. "Sorry, I missed you, Paul. Table for five?"

"Yes," Paul answered.

"Let me get someone to show you to your table." Gerald waved to the host.

A young man wearing all black approached them, a friendly smile on his face. Gerald leaned over to whisper to the host.

"Enjoy your stay at Cadence," Gerald said.

"Thank you." Paul leaned over to Gerald. "I will talk to you later."

"Follow me, please," the host instructed.

The group trailed the host and meandered through the jazzy atmosphere that was Cadence—the soft conversation that flowed through the club, the sounds of a live band that mixed with the conversations. The host led them to a table next to the window, then gave them menus, took their orders, and left.

Several hours later, they headed to their cars in the parking lot. Marissa drove off first, followed by Liz and Timothy. Paul escorted Kayla to her car.

"I really had a good time in church today," Paul said.

"Your mother will be pleased."

"I will be attending more often."

"I'm glad to hear that. I'm so full; all I want to do is go home and go to sleep."

"Would you like some company?" Paul asked sheepishly.

Kayla playfully poked him in the chest. "Men."

He shrugged. "What did I say?"

"Get your mind out of my bedroom."

"Easier said than done."

She was challenging him. "Try."

Paul laughed. "Trust me. I *have* tried."

"So what you want to do is sleep with me?" Her lips pouted with annoyance. She turned away from him.

"I didn't say that."

"You didn't have to." They were standing next to Kayla's car. She rambled in the bottom of her purse for her keys. She disarmed the lock and opened the car door.

"Why are you being so defensive?"

"I'm not being defensive. What you said was inappropriate."

"I apologize." He took her hand in his. "I wasn't thinking. Whenever I'm around you, my mind goes off on its own. I didn't mean to offend you. Forgive me?"

Kayla knew she had overreacted. How could she be mad at Paul for the same sexual thoughts she had of him? He was just more honest about his feelings.

"Apology accepted."

Paul smiled. "Good." He opened the door wider, allowing her to slide behind the wheel of the car. "Drive safely. Call back to the club and let me know you made it home."

Kayla's head snapped up. "Call and let you know I made it home?"

Paul closed the driver's side door. "That's what I said."

"I don't have to check in with you."

Paul chuckled. "True. But you're a friend, a friend I care about. So when you arrive home, call me, and let me know you made it home safely. Can you do that for me, please?"

Kayla didn't answer. She responded by stepping down on the gas pedal, burning rubber out of the parking lot. She stopped at the red light. "Who does he think he is?" She tapped her fingers on the steering wheel. "Telling me what to do. On top of that he called me a friend." She thought about his invitation to share her bed. An opportunity wasted. She could only imagine what it would have been like. It caused a delicious shudder to wash through her as she sped through the green light.

CR ED

Paul watched Kayla's car make a left at the intersection. He smiled. He loved a strong, independent woman. Kayla was definitely that. Heading back inside the club, he made his way to his cousin's office. Victor was standing at the file cabinet. He turned around when Paul knocked.

"Come in, Paul."

Paul strolled in, taking a seat on the sofa across from the desk. He laid his head back, closing his eyes.

Victor watched him a moment, then turned back to what he was doing. He'd known Paul long enough to know when something was bothering him. When he was ready to talk about it, he would.

"As long as I live, I will never understand women."

Victor inwardly chuckled. "Here we go," he said to himself, as he continued searching for the form he needed.

Paul sat up straight. He spread his hands apart. "I can't figure this woman out. One minute she's sending me signals that she's interested. Then when I try to get close, she shuts me down. It's driving me crazy." He stood. "I don't know what to do."

Victor located the form, closed the drawer, and walked back to his desk. Paul began pacing in front of the desk. "Can I ask you a question?" he asked suddenly.

Victor looked at Paul in amusement. It had been a long time since Paul had been this worked up over a woman. The last one, Dina, his former fiancée, hurt him. It took years for him to get over her. Victor shook his head. He was happy to see him getting back into the dating scene. He hoped Paul would take things slowly.

Victor made himself comfortable in the large, leather chair. "You got the floor." He leaned back and clasped his hands together in his lap.

Paul began to pace in front of the desk again. "Here's the thing. I really like this lady. I believe she likes me, too."

Victor nodded his head. "What's the problem?"

"The problem is she doesn't want to have anything to do with me because we're going in different directions in our military careers. I have applied for Special Forces. She has applied to the Green to Gold Program, trying to go to nursing school."

Victor's brows rose in surprise. "Situation sounds like mine."

"I know. That's why I need some advice. You and Dominique met while on active duty. Service members do it all the time. What am I doing wrong?" Paul plopped down on the sofa again. "She won't give me any time.""

"Who's this woman that has you so twisted?"

"It's Kayla Perry."

"Beautiful. Intelligent. I can…" Victor cleared his throat, "…see your interest." Paul caught his meaning. "Tell me about it. From the moment I laid eyes on her, I was a goner. I can't get her out of my mind. I can't explain it. It's not like it was when I met Dina. This is different. It's like I know she's the woman for me." He placed a hand over his heart. "I can feel it here."

Victor shook his head. He was speechless. He'd never heard Paul talk about Dina the way he was talking about Kayla.

Paul stood. "What do I do?"

"Whether you like it or not, Paul, you have to respect her wishes." He didn't miss the look of surprise on Paul's face. He waved a hand in mid-air. "I know that's not what you want to hear."

Paul puffed his cheeks out. "No, it isn't."

"That's because you're thinking with the wrong head."

Paul threw him a look, then sat back on the sofa. "I can't help it."

Victor tapped a finger on the side of his head. "Think

about it. What if you're accepted to Special Forces? Then what? Where does that leave her? Leave you? There's no guarantee you will see her again."

Paul frowned. "I realize nothing is guaranteed right now."

"And on top of that, after nursing school, she may not remain in the area," Victor explained. "With recent deployments going on, who knows where either of you will wind up."

"I'm aware of everything you're telling me."

"She's worth it?"

"I think so. Look at you and Dominique. You met under similar circumstances. Separated. Got back together. Now you are engaged."

Victor placed both arms on the desk. "Dominique and I were lucky. After three years, we were stationed in the same area. It doesn't always work out that way for active duty members. I don't have to tell you that. Hell, even married couples sometimes have a difficult time being stationed together."

Paul glanced off, a faraway look in his eyes. "So tell me this, the way you and Dominique met, everything you went through. Was it worth it?"

Without hesitation, Victor answered, "Yes."

Paul seemed satisfied with Victor's response. He bounced his head up and down. The conversation ended when Gerald breezed into the office. He jokingly pointed at Paul. "I got your message about Kayla."

"I just wanted you to know what was up," Paul answered.

Confused, Victor looked from Gerald to Paul. "What's up?"

"Gerald hit on Kayla today. I had to get him straight."

"Kayla isn't Gerald's type anyway," Victor said with a chuckle.

Gerald frowned. "What's that supposed to mean?"

"She can complete a sentence," Victor answered. "And read."

Paul joined Victor in laughter.

"Funny," Gerald quipped. "As long as she can say the word, *yes,* that's all I need to hear."

"What did I tell you?" Victor replied.

Laughing and joking with his cousins reminded Paul of being with his brothers. His mind wandered to Devin. "I spoke with Devin the other day," he said.

"He's he doing?" Victor inquired.

"Not too good," Paul answered. "He received deployment orders for Iraq. He leaves next week."

The mood in the room suddenly plummeted as silence ensued.

"Damn," Victor finally said aloud.

C3 80

Kayla entered the apartment to the sound of a ringing telephone. She rushed over to the end table and picked it up.

"Hello?"

"Kayla, it's Liz. I was beginning to think you weren't in."

"Just came through the door. What's wrong?" She stripped the purse strap from her shoulder, throwing it on the chair cushion.

"I have in my possession two tickets to see Mary J. Blige Wednesday night at Wolftrap. I was going to surprise Timothy, but we can't use them."

"Why not?" Kayla knew how much Liz loved Mary. For her to give up a chance to see the Queen of Hip-Hop, there had to be a good reason.

"I'm going to a basketball game instead," Liz answered in a dry tone. Kayla could just see Liz's twisted face. She hated basketball, but Kayla knew that Timothy loved the sport. "I gave my word to Timothy the next time he bought tickets to see the Washington Wizards that I would go with him. Guess what? He bought tickets to the game this Wednesday. The Wizards take on the Lakers. I can't go back on my word."

Kayla tried not to laugh.

"I figured you could use the tickets."

"I don't have anyone to take," Kayla said, though her mind immediately went to Paul.

"I'm sure you have someone in mind." Kayla could hear the humor in her voice. "I'll give you the tickets tomorrow at work." Liz didn't wait for a response. Kayla heard a click.

Kayla punched in the numbers to Cadence. She found herself looking forward to speaking with Paul, hoping he was free to attend the concert. The phone rang several times before it was answered. She asked for Paul and was transferred. A moment later, Victor's voice came on the line.

"Just a moment, Kayla. He's right here," he said, before Paul came on the line.

"Hi, Paul."

"Kayla."

"I just want you to know I made it home safely."

"I'm glad to hear it. The way you burned rubber out of the parking lot, I didn't think I would hear from you." She could feel him smiling through the phone.

"I always drive like that."

"You should slow down. You could hurt someone and yourself."

Silence fell between them.

Paul was the first to speak. "Thanks for calling."

She didn't want him to hang up without inviting him to the concert. She had never asked a man out before. Tugging on the phone cord, Kayla asked, "Paul, do you have plans for Wednesday night?"

"Just staying home, watching the basketball game. Why?"

"The Wizards?" She was stalling.

"Yes. They're playing the Lakers. Why are you asking?"

Kayla bit down on her lips. "I was wondering if you would like to go see Mary J. Blige." She couldn't blame him if he said no, especially after the way she'd treated him earlier.

He chuckled. "With who?"

She loved his sense of humor. "With me, silly."

"Let me see, stay home and watch Gilbert Arenas and Kobe Bryant go at it or spend the evening with a beautiful woman. That's a difficult choice."

"It better not be."

"I'm only kidding, Kayla. I would love to go to the concert with you." He glanced up to see Victor and Gerald watching him closely. "I'll tape the game and watch it later."

"Great. We will discuss the arrangements later."

"I look forward to hearing from you." Kayla replaced the phone in the cradle and grinned. She was looking forward to Wednesday night. She marched over to her CD player, put in Mary J. Blige's latest CD, and listened to *Be Without You*. She turned the volume up and sang along. As she headed into her bedroom, the phone rang again.

Hell, who is it this time, she wondered.

"Kayla?" Paul's voice came through the line. She hoped he wasn't calling back to cancel. Maybe he'd forgotten about a prior engagement.

"Hi, Paul."

"You did ask me out Wednesday night?"

"Yes, I did. Is something wrong?"

"No," he said. "I just wanted to make sure I wasn't dreaming. I'll talk to you later, beautiful." He hung up.

Kayla looked at the phone and smiled. He got brownie points for that one.

CB EO

The next morning, Liz knocked on Kayla's office door. "Good morning."

"Good morning, yourself," Kayla said, returning the greeting.

Liz closed the door behind her and sat in the chair across from Kayla's desk.

"Is everything all right?" Kayla asked.

Liz smiled. "Everything is fine. I stopped by Dr. Maundry's office. He wrote a prescription for prenatal vitamins, and I scheduled my next appointment. Everything is going to be fine this time." She placed a hand lovingly over her abdomen.

Her motherly gesture caused Kayla to grin. "I told you not to worry."

Liz took a breath. "I'm due the last week in October."

"Something to be thankful for."

"I think so," she said, beaming. "So, did you ask Paul to the concert?"

At the mention of Paul's name, her heart thumped. She couldn't help but smile. "Who says I was going to ask Paul?"

"Don't play with me, gurl. What did he say?"

"All right. All right. He said yes."

73

Liz raised her hand, giving Kayla a high five. "Yes. I knew he would. Today is Monday. Will you be talking to him before Wednesday?"

"I'm sure I will, why?"

"Just asking."

"All up in my business," Kayla teased.

"Like I said, I just want to see you happy. You're a beautiful person inside and out. Always there for other people. Putting up with me and Marissa. You deserve someone to look after you for a change."

"Whoa. Whoa. Hold up. Where is this coming from? I'm doing just fine. Thank you."

"Cut the act, Kayla. You're a strong, independent woman. Your love life is on life support." She giggled. "No. It's dead."

Kayla loved Liz, but her habitual spiel about her love life had gotten old. "Paul and I have a date on Wednesday. That's all I can say for now."

A knock on the door caused both women to turn their heads. Cage came further into the office. He hadn't been in morning formation. This was Kayla's first time seeing him today. As usual, his uniform was impeccable, fitting him like it was tailor-made for his body.

"Good morning, ladies," he said, stopping in front of Kayla's desk.

"Good morning, Sergeant Cage," Liz said. "How are you this morning?"

Cage grinned. "I'm fine, Liz, what about yourself?"

"I'm good. Did you have a good time Saturday?" Liz didn't waste any time. Curious, she wanted to know more about Maria. So did Kayla.

"I had a great time. Thanks for inviting me. Maria enjoyed herself, too."

Liz arched an eyebrow. "Is Maria your *girlfriend?*"

Embarrassed, Cage glanced over at Kayla. She swallowed. Hard. "We just met," he explained. "I wouldn't call her my girlfriend."

"But you like her?" Liz inquired.

He nodded. "Very nice lady."

"I think you guys make a lovely couple."

A private person, Kayla was surprised Cage answered Liz's questions.

"As far as Liz is concerned," Kayla said, "every couple is a lovely couple. She's the company's official matchmaker. She's in the wrong career. She should open her own dating service."

Liz laughed. "Don't think I haven't thought about it." She returned her attention to Cage. "What does she do?" she asked. "Where is she from? Is she in the army?"

"Liz," Kayla gasped.

Liz shrugged her shoulders. "What?"

"Don't you have work to do?" Kayla replied.

Liz's mouth dropped. She stood. Trying to look hurt, she said, "Fine. I know when I'm not wanted. I was only trying to offer my dating expertise to Sergeant Cage and Maria, just like I did for you and Paul." She strolled toward the door. "If you don't want my help," she mumbled, as she walked out.

Kayla and Cage looked at each other. Both were trying not to laugh.

"She is something else," Cage said, shaking his head.

"I agree. She didn't mean any harm," Kayla stated.

"I know." Cage handed her a white sheet of paper. "Scores from the Physical Fitness test this morning."

"How did our personnel do?" Her eyes scanned the paper, anxious to read the scores. Kayla figured, Cage must have been one of the graders. In excellent shape, he always scored perfect on his Physical Fitness test; he was the perfect candidate to conduct the test.

"They all passed," Cage said.

Kayla breathed a sigh of relief. "Good. I was worried about Specialist Taylor. She worked so hard. I'm glad to hear all of her hard work paid off." She placed the folder in the box marked **IN**.

Cage pulled up a chair and straddled it. "Is Paul your boyfriend?"

Kayla stopped in mid-motion. "We're friends." She glanced into his eyes, allowing her gaze to slip to Cage's lips. She often wondered what her lips would feel like pressed on his. She quickly pushed her thoughts aside. Cage was forbidden fruit and off limits to her.

"He seems like a nice guy," Cage said.

"Maria seems like a nice woman," Kayla found herself saying. "Is she on active duty?"

Cage threw her a curious look.

Kayla threw her hands up. "It's only a question. I don't have ulterior motives for asking."

"Are you sure about that?" he asked, rising to his feet.

The statement caused Kayla to lean back in the chair. Her heart dropped into her stomach. "What do you mean?" she said, in a low tone.

His eyes remained locked on hers. "Nothing. I will talk to you later. I have a meeting with First Sergeant. You're in charge."

Speechless. She could only bob her head up and down in response.

Chapter Six

arissa had been nineteen years old when she'd moved into her own apartment two years ago. Therefore, she was living on her own when she met Randall. On their first date, they went to a movie and dinner afterward. She invited him inside after the date, and he never left.

The relationship had been full of ups and downs. Mostly downs the past few months. Whenever she attempted to talk about their relationship, Randall assured her everything was fine. Things got even worse after he withdrew money from her bank account. Though she was upset that he'd taken the money without permission, she forgave him. She still didn't know the reason he'd taken the money, and it didn't matter. She loved Randall and would do anything to keep her man happy.

She hoped to do that this evening and had planned something romantic. She stopped by the supermarket and purchased strawberries and whipped cream, two of their favorite aphrodisiacs. Combined with a new piece of sexy lingerie, she hoped it would be a night neither one of them would forget.

Marissa quickly put the items away and headed into the bedroom. She heard the sound of Randall's key in the lock and laid the lingerie across the bed. Heading down the hallway, she heard Randall's voice. Entering the living room, she found him standing in the middle of the floor. He was talking on his cellular phone. A young, white male around her age that she didn't recognize was with him.

Randall glanced up at her. "Give me about an hour," he was saying. "We will talk about it. No. I need to shower and change clothes."

Flipping the phone closed, he walked over and gave Marissa a soft kiss on the lips. "Hi, baby."

"Hi, yourself," Marissa said, trying to hide the disappointment in her voice. "What's going on?"

"I have to go back out," he stated.

"You just got home," she said calmly. She was trying not to aggravate him. They'd argued the entire weekend. She was in no mood to get into it with him again and in front of company.

"I know, but I need to take care of some things."

"What?" Her voice climbed a little.

"It's business." He sidestepped her and removed his uniform shirt. He was halfway down the hall when he said over his shoulder, "Marissa meet Jason Bain. Jason, this is Marissa."

Marissa focused her attention on the guy who stood in her living room—his slim build; long, dirty blonde, shoulder length hair; blue-eyes. He was casually dressed in a pair of baggy black jeans that hung loosely on his hips, a white John Lennon T-shirt, and a pair of black converse sneakers on his feet. He seemed thuggish. She could sense that he was nothing but trouble. "Nice to meet you, Jason."

Jason threw up a hand. "Hey." He spoke in a soft, awkward voice.

"You guys get acquainted. I'll be out in a minute," Randall shouted from the bedroom.

"Can I get you anything?" Marissa inquired.

"No. I'm fine. Thank you." At least he was polite.

"Excuse me a moment," Marissa turned and trekked into the bedroom after Randall. Randall was sitting on the foot of the bed, unlacing his tactical boots. "Where are you going?"

"I already told you, I'm going out. Jason and I are meeting some friends at Cadence." He removed one boot and then the other, throwing them in the walk-in closet. Then, he removed the rest of his uniform.

"Who are you meeting?" Marissa wanted to know. Randall didn't like when she questioned him. She'd hoped for a quiet evening for them. He was spoiling it. She wanted to know why.

Randall turned to face her. "Why all the questions?"

"I have the right to know."

"Since when?"

"I planned for us to spend a quiet evening at home."

"I have something I need to do." He headed into the bathroom, where he pushed back the blue shower curtain and turned on the hot water. Steam filled the small room. Removing the rest of his clothing, he stepped underneath the water, leaving Marissa on the outside without an answer. She sat down on the bed, pouting.

CR ED

"The doctor said everything is fine," Liz said, answering Timothy for the third time.

Washing dishes, she rinsed the glass with hot water and placed it in the dish rack. She had a dishwasher but preferred to do the dishes by hand.

"The longer I carry the baby," she added, "the better my chances are for a healthy delivery."

Unable to attend Liz's first doctor's visit, Timothy was concerned about her and their unborn child. Leaning in the doorway, Timothy strolled into the kitchen. "I just want to make sure everything is okay in case I'm deployed."

Liz stopped in mid-motion. Her face went blank. She swallowed the lump lodged in her throat. "Are you being deployed?"

To busy his hands, he helped her dry the dishes. They had never discussed him being deployed before. It was a topic neither wanted to talk about. "Nothing official. Just talk."

"Nothing official," Liz answered in a sad tone. She handed him a skillet.

"No." He could see the worried expression on her face. He bent down and placed the skillet in the lower cabinet. She had a right to be concerned. He'd received a tip from a reliable source in Headquarters that his unit was being deployed within the next couple of weeks.

"When will you know?"

Timothy shrugged. "I don't know," he lied.

"I don't want you to go." Liz's voice caught in her throat. "I need you here."

"I don't want to go. I want to be here. The way it looks . . ." His voice trailed off. "It will be a great way to earn extra money. They will pay me hazardous pay for being in combat. I can set up an allotment for you and the baby."

Liz threw the dishtowel on the counter and stormed out of the kitchen. Timothy followed. She sat on the sofa, bending one leg underneath her, and crossing her arms over her chest. Timothy slowly sat down next to her.

"What's the matter?" he asked.

"It's not about the money."

Timothy leaned forward. He laced his fingers with hers.

"I'm just thinking about you and the baby." He reached out, taking her in his arms. She leaned her head on his shoulders. "Try not to worry."

"I can't help it. What am I going to do without you here?"

"You will be fine. The army will take care of you while I'm gone," he assured her. "There's always my family." He kissed her softly on the forehead. She closed her eyes. "Honestly, I would feel better if you went to stay with my family in Fort Worth."

Liz sat up straight. "No. I'm not moving in with your family. I like them, but I don't want to live with them."

"I don't want you to be alone. What if something happens?"

"You mean what if I have another miscarriage."

Timothy's shoulders sagged. He took a deep breath. "That's not what I meant and you know it."

Liz felt bad about the comment. She knew Timothy was concerned about her and the baby. "I'm sorry. I didn't mean that." Her voice was softer. "I'm just so angry right now."

"I know, but we have to think about what's right for you and the baby if I am deployed."

Liz pointed at Timothy. "I'm not going to live with your parents and that's final."

CR ED

Paul pulled the vehicle into the empty parking space in front of Mr. Floyd's. He hoped the barbershop wasn't full. It was time for his weekly haircut. Wednesday would be here before he knew it. He couldn't wait to see Kayla, hear her voice. He even tried to think of a good reason to phone her before Wednesday. People who knew him wouldn't understand his reason for being hesitant. The conversation he'd had yesterday with Victor played in his mind. He'd thought about it all day. He could understand Kayla's reason for not wanting to begin a relationship, but he wanted to see her, be with her, even if on her terms.

"There he is," Floyd exclaimed when Paul entered.

The tall, elderly, white-haired man smiled from ear-to-ear. "My best customer." With a bum right leg, a result of paying his dues in Korea, Floyd limped over to a shelf and removed a stack of white towels. The sounds of Al Green vibrated through the speakers, along with laughing and chatting from the other male customers. Regulars, Slick and George, enjoyed their daily game of checkers. The board was never touched unless by those two men. They had been playing the same game for the past year.

"What do you know, young blood?" Slick said.

"You got it, Slick." Paul made himself comfortable in a seat across from Floyd's barber chair.

"You're next," Floyd explained, draping the black cloth around a young customer's neck.

Paul nodded in approval.

"Heard anything yet?" Floyd asked.

"Not yet," Paul answered. Floyd was aware of Paul's plan to get into Special Forces. When the two men met, they'd hit it off and became friends.

"Patience, my man. No need to rush."

"My brother, Devin, stationed at Fort Hood is being deployed," Paul volunteered.

Floyd's thin chest released a deep sigh. "Well, he will be joining my grandson. He's already over there. Left last week. Nineteen years old. Boy fresh out of high school. He don't know what's going on. If he had any sense, he would have gone to college like me and his mama wanted him to."

"Ain't that the truth," Slick chimed in. "We don't have no business over there anyway. Talking about the man is a threat," he said in an irritable tone. "If anybody was a threat, it was that Bin Laden. He's the one who planned those attacks. The president just opened up a whole can of trouble we don't need."

"Tell the truth and shame the devil, now," Floyd added. "I keep telling y'all this is about oil. Don't let nobody tell you different."

"Bush is the threat," George said, as he pushed a checker on the board.

Everyone in the shop agreed. A soldier in uniform, Paul kept his personal feelings about Iraq to himself. It wasn't his place to agree or disagree with the Commander-in-Chief's policies. His job was to carry out orders, plain and simple.

"I know you don't have much to say," Floyd continued, "about your boss, but I do. I'm telling you, he has gotten this country in a mess. Fooling around with those turban heads— those people are crazy. They can't wait to meet Allah."

"Like it or not," Paul replied, "my job is to obey the president."

"Typical answer," Floyd said. "I understand. The country is still emotional from what happened on September 11th. The president knows that. He's using that to go after . . . " He looked around for help, snapping his fingers in frustration. "What's his name?"

"Saddam Hussein," Paul volunteered. "The same man who tried to have his father killed."

"True," Slick agreed. "Sounds like a hit to me. He could have had Special Forces go in and take him out. He didn't have to take the whole country to war, but I guarantee you when our young men and women begin coming home in boxes," his voice raised an octave, "the people ain't going to like that."

"Special Forces don't take people out," Paul said with sarcasm.

"The hell they don't," Slick chipped in. "You know they do."

Paul chuckled. "The war may be over in no time." He picked up a sports magazine, flipping through it. He had to be optimistic, especially since Devin was leaving. He might not be far behind him. "Like the Gulf War."

Floyd grunted. "That was a different president. This is going to be another Vietnam."

"Special Forces or not," George said, "he's going over there. He may as well go with the best."

"I agree," Paul said.

Floyd removed the black cape. The customer stood and extended a hand to Paul. "Captain Ernie Crow, retired army and former Green Beret. Everyone calls me, Ernie."

"Nice to meet you, Ernie," Paul said, accepting his handshake.

"Don't let them give you a hard time," Ernie said on his way out the door.

"I won't."

◌ ◌

Paul left Floyd's shop and headed home. The truck quickly ate up distance along the interstate. His cellular phone rang, and he answered on the fourth ring.

"What's up, Paul?" Devin said.

Paul's heart sank. Normally, he looked forward to hearing from Devin, but this time he knew what the call meant. "Devin, what's going on?"

"Just calling to let you know we're getting ready to pull out. Wanted to touch base with you before I left." Paul could hear the strain in his voice.

"What time are you leaving?" Paul inquired.

"In the morning."

Paul was quiet.

"I have told the rest of the family. Don't worry about me. I'm going to be okay."

"That's easier said than done."

"You of all people know this is part of our job."

"Job or not, it doesn't mean your loved ones won't worry about you."

"Look, I have been thinking, maybe you should reconsider joining Special Forces. At least for now."

"Why?" Paul was surprised at Devin's request. Out of all his immediate family, Devin was the most supportive.

"Mom and Dad. They are taking it hard that I'm being deployed. I don't know if they can take it," his voice cracked, "if something happened to either one of us."

Paul closed his eyes a moment. "Nothing is going to happen."

"Get serious, Paul. You know what I'm talking about."

The conversation reminded Paul of when he was sixteen years old, and Devin caught him and his girlfriend making out. It wasn't so much what he was doing; it was because when Devin questioned him about using protection, he found out that he hadn't used any.

"War is serious business," Devin said. "People get seriously injured. Killed. I may not come back."

"You will make it back."

"Paul," Devin began to say, "I'm just worried about you. I don't want anything to happen to you."

Paul managed a fake smile. "You are always worried about other people beside yourself."

"I'm worried about me, too."

Silence crept in the line between them. As men, they were raised not to show fear. Be brave. Tough. Paul knew what Devin meant. He wasn't scared of fighting for his country. He was afraid of not seeing his wife, not seeing his kids grow up, and not spending time with the family.

Paul choked up. "That's why I need to hurry up, come over there, and kick some butt." He was trying to lighten the mood. It worked. He heard Devin chuckle.

"The Lake brothers doing their thang in Iraq. That will be something. Look, I hate to cut the conversation short, but I have to finish packing, so I can spend the rest of the evening with Jennifer and the twins."

Paul didn't want Devin to hang up. "Give the rug rats my love."

"I will do that. Call Mom and Dad. I know they would want to hear from you. I will phone when I can. Love you, little brother," Devin quickly added.

"I love you, too," Paul said, before the phone line went dead. He pulled the car over to the soft shoulder of the road and turned the warning lights on. He had to get his emotions under control before he made the phone call to his parents.

☙ ❧

"I think you're making too much out of it," Liz said, munching on a carrot stick. She reminded Kayla she was eating for two and insisted upon grabbing a chicken salad at Cadence before heading home. Kayla ordered a tuna on rye sandwich.

Kayla bit into the sandwich. "I saw him with Maria. I was a little bit jealous."

"I knew you had a crush on him. You always denied it."

"Seeing him with another woman made me realize that I do have feelings for him. It doesn't matter. We can't date."

"Yeah, but the things you can't have make it more desirable."

"Yeah, you're right," Kayla agreed. "But it's not worth it."

"Says who?"

"Can you imagine Cage and me getting caught for fraternization? That would be the talk of the unit."

Liz pointed a carrot stick at her. "The key is not to get caught."

Kayla tilted her head to one side. "I'm surprised you agree with me. I thought you wanted me to be with Paul."

"I do." Liz took a sip of water. "You have to make your own decision."

"I do like Paul."

"But?" Liz prompted.

"No buts. We're going out. I can tell you more after the date."

The remark brought a tight smile to Liz's face.

"What's wrong?" Kayla asked.

Liz twirled the straw in her water glass. "Timothy may be deployed."

Kayla sat up. "What? When?"

"He doesn't know yet. There's a rumor from Headquarters, but he thinks it may be true."

Kayla thought about the conversation they'd had a few

days ago when Liz was afraid that Timothy would be deployed, and she would be left alone to raise a child.

"I'm sorry, Liz." It was all she could say at the moment.

"It comes with the job, right?"

Kayla reached out, placing a hand on top of her friend's.

"Maybe the source is wrong," Liz said.

Kayla nodded in agreement. "He doesn't have orders. Nothing is official. Try not to worry about it. The stress is not good for the baby."

Liz reluctantly agreed. "I know. I know."

Both women had been around the military long enough to know that the rumor was probably true.

☙ ❧

The next morning, Paul exited the hospital elevators and was greeted by the receptionist, Laura Snow.

"Good morning, Sergeant Lake." Laura opened her top desk drawer, handing Paul the key to his office.

"Good morning, Laura. How are you?"

"I'm fine. Thanks for asking.

As Paul headed toward his office, he heard Timothy's voice. "You're late."

Paul frowned. He glanced at his army Swiss watch. He was ten minutes early. "What are you talking about? I'm ten minutes early."

"You're always thirty minutes early."

Paul chuckled. He placed the key in the lock and activated it. Entering the office, his hand automatically found the light switch. Timothy followed. Paul strolled behind the desk, placing his black bag in the seat of the chair. Timothy stopped at the desk. He appeared anxious.

"You ready to work today?" Paul teased.

"I'm always ready," Timothy said. "Friday is my last day in the unit."

Paul's eyes widened. "Why? What's going on?"

"My unit is on alert. I'm being pulled back."

Timothy didn't need to say anything else. Paul figured his friend was going to be deployed. "How is Liz taking it?"

Timothy's finger tapped the edge of Paul's desk. "Not too well with the baby coming."

Paul leaned his head to one side. "Man."

Timothy shrugged. "The president has awful timing. I don't want to leave Liz right now. She needs me. I will never forgive myself if something happens with this pregnancy and I'm not here." He shook his head. "I don't know how she will take it if she loses the baby. It may push her over the edge."

Paul was speechless. Timothy had confided in him about how devastated Liz was when she lost their first child. He couldn't imagine what they were going through.

"She puts on like she's tough," Timothy said, "but deep down she really isn't."

"You can't think like that. You have to believe that everything is going to be fine with Liz and the baby. From what I understand, all pregnancies are different."

"I know, but you understand why I feel the way that I do," Timothy added.

"Yes, but you have to believe in your heart that things will be differently this time." Timothy rolled his eyes upward. "I know it's easier said than done, but you have to be strong for the both of you."

Timothy let out a deep sigh and nodded in agreement. Paul came from behind the desk.

"As hard as it may be, while you're over there, you have

to think about doing your job and nothing else. You have to remain focused at all times."

Timothy ran a hand across his forehead. "I know I can't afford to slip up. I have a wife and child to come back to."

Paul slapped Timothy on the back. "And a lot of friends and family who wouldn't mind seeing that ugly mug again."

"You got jokes."

"No. No jokes. I spoke to my older brother, Devin, yesterday. He left for Iraq this morning."

"Ah man. How's the family taking it?"

"Not too good," Paul replied. "Especially since I may be following him. "What about your family?"

"As well as everyone else's family, I guess, nervous." Timothy shifted from one foot to the other. "To tell the truth, I don't mind going. The army has given me the best training as a medic. I'm ready to put it to good use."

Paul chuckled. "Yeah, well, don't forget to duck."

"I won't." Timothy grinned. "Liz tells me you have a date with Kayla. Going to see Mary J. Blige. I guess the two of you hit it off at the picnic."

Paul's smile widened. "I think so."

"Good luck. Kayla is a very nice lady. I hope it works out."

Paul sat on the edge of the desk. "The verdict is still out. The timing couldn't be worse."

"That's why you have to spend as much time together as you can," Timothy added.

Paul stood. "That's what I hope to do."

"That's my man." The two men dapped fists together.

"Come on, let's go to the dining hall and grab some breakfast," Paul suggested.

"Right behind you," Timothy said, trailing Paul out of the door.

Chapter Seven

"I'm tired of your mess, Randall," Marissa said, not loud enough for the people heading into the dining facility to hear. "I'm not going to take it anymore."

Randall closed the small gap between them. "What mess?"

He and Jason were out again late last night for the third night in a row. After work, Jason swung by the apartment, picked him up, and they didn't return until after midnight.

"Whatever you are up to, Randall, I will find out what it is."

"I told you last night," Randall threw back. "I'm not doing anything."

Marissa folded her arms across her chest. "If you were not doing anything, you would have had your butt at home last night, with *me*."

Randall tilted his head to one side. "It's not what you think."

Marissa pointed a finger in his face. "You better not be cheating on me." She clenched her teeth. "I mean it. I will go Lorena Bobbitt on you."

Randall leaned back, and with a wave of his hand, moved her finger from his face. "Why do women always threaten to cut if off?" His voice was serious. "That's not right."

"Because that's the only way we can get your attention, take away your manhood."

"I don't have time for this. You're talking crazy. I'm going to work." He turned and stomped off. "I will talk to you later," he shouted over his shoulder.

"I'm not through talking to you," she said to his retreating figure. He threw up a hand and kept walking.

"Is everything all right?" Timothy asked, coming up behind her.

Marissa turned to find him and Paul. Her face warmed from embarrassment. Clearing her throat, Marissa ran a hand through her blonde hair. "Yes. Everything is fine. Just a little misunderstanding. Are you headed into the dining hall?" she asked, changing the subject.

"Care to join us?" Timothy playfully bent at the waist. "Pretty lady," he said, pulling open one of the double doors.

Marissa blushed. "Thank you."

They headed to the grill-ordered food section and found a table in the middle of the facility. "We missed you at the picnic on Saturday," Timothy began, settling in the chair next to Marissa. Paul took the chair across from them.

"I doubt if all of you missed me." Marissa opened her container of orange juice and inserted a straw.

Timothy frowned. "What do you mean?"

Not sure of the reason behind Liz's verbal attack on her, she decided not to elaborate. She liked Timothy and didn't want to cause trouble. "Nothing. I already had plans. How is Liz? I haven't seen her in the last couple of days."

A large, sloppy smile covered his face. "She's fine. We're expecting a baby," he said proudly.

"Congratulations, Sergeant Shupe," Marissa exclaimed.

"Thanks. We're excited about it."

"I know you are," Marissa beamed. "It's your first one, right?" Marissa thought she saw a hint of sadness in Timothy's eyes for a moment, but it vanished quickly.

"Yes, it's our first."

"When is the baby due?"

"End of October."

"I won't be here, so you have to send me pictures."

Timothy lowered his head. "I won't be either. Liz has to send us both pictures."

A look of confusion crossed Marissa's face.

"I'm being deployed," he replied, in answer to her confusion.

"You're kidding," Marissa said in disbelief.

"I wish I was. My unit is on alert. We could leave at any time. I'm just waiting for the word."

Marissa glanced at Paul. "What about you?"

"No. But I know the hospital is shipping personnel." Paul bit into a biscuit. "My brother, stationed at Fort Hood, is on his way to Iraq."

"Every day it seems like everyone I talk to is leaving for Iraq or knows someone who's on their way to Iraq. It's beginning to scare me," Marissa said. "I began clearing post next week. I pray that I make it out of here."

"I don't see why they would stop you from leaving," Timothy added.

"The army has been known to do it," Paul threw in. "If they need your job skill, they will do it in a minute. What do you do?"

"I'm a pharmacy tech," Marissa answered.

"It's possible," Paul said.

"Thanks a lot," Timothy answered for Marissa, after he noticed the color drain from her face.

"I'm just telling the truth," Paul replied.

"I'm going to think positive," Marissa said. "I'm already sending some of my things home. I have given notice on my apartment. Household is coming next week for the rest. As far as I'm concerned, I'm already home."

"Hello, handsome," Liz said, as she popped up over Marissa's shoulder. She leaned down, kissing her husband on the right cheek. "I'm surprised to see you at breakfast."

"Sergeant Lake dragged me," Timothy said, as he pulled out the empty seat on the other side of him. Liz sat down. "Are you here alone?"

"No. Kayla is behind me." Liz smiled over at Paul. She waved Kayla over.

"Good morning, everyone," Kayla said. She plopped down in the seat next to Paul. He smiled at her. She returned his smile.

Paul felt warm all the way down to his toes. It was the first time he'd seen her in a military uniform. Civilian or military, Kayla looked good. She wore her hair pinned up in a French twist, off her face, and above her neck, according to military regulations. It allowed Paul to see her full, lovely face.

"Good morning, yourself, Sergeant Perry," Marissa said. "How are you this lovely morning?"

"I'm fine, Specialist. And you?" Kayla replied.

"One week and counting," Marissa boasted.

"Still counting the days?" Kayla inquired.

"You know it." Marissa stood. "I have to get going." She glanced at her watch. "I'm shadowing my replacement. I had to be there ten minutes ago. Sergeants Perry, Lake, and Shupe, I'll talk to you guys later." She slowly turned toward Liz. She flashed her a scowl. Marissa was ready for a remark. It didn't come.

Kayla hoped Marissa wasn't going to start another catfight this morning. She wasn't in the mood. On top of that, they would look ridiculous in front of Paul and Timothy.

"Congratulations on the baby, Liz."

Liz's shoulder sagged. She leaned back in the chair, surprised. She looked over at her husband who appeared to be in heaven. He lifted an arm around her shoulder and pulled her close. "Thank you, Marissa," Liz said, scowling. "I know you really meant that with all of your heart."

With a smirk on her face, Marissa picked up her tray. "I'll catch you guys later."

"She's a nice girl," Timothy replied, as they watched her walk away.

"Hey." Liz nudged her husband with an elbow. "Don't break your neck looking."

Kayla and Paul glanced at each other, then back at Liz and Timothy.

Timothy chuckled. "It's not like that. I just mean she seems to be all right."

"That's all you better mean," Liz snapped.

Timothy flashed her a surprised look. In the three years they had been married, there were two rules they lived by. One. Never go to bed angry. Two. No raising voices in their household. He sat down the glass of milk. "What is this about? You are not the jealous type. You have no reason to be."

That was all Kayla needed to hear to make her escape. "Paul, let's give them some privacy." He happily agreed. They found an empty table a few rows over.

"Never thought I would hear them argue," Paul replied, lowering himself in the chair across from Kayla.

"All couples argue," Kayla replied.

"I never heard my parents argue. Never knew them to raise their voices at one another."

"They just kept it behind close doors," Kayla said, remembering how her parents were always going at it. When they began talking about divorce, she still hoped they would stay together. As she got older, she realized it was the best thing they could have done. Both were remarried and were now the best of friends.

"I don't know about that. My mother ran the house. Whatever she said was law," Paul replied.

"She had your dad in check," Kayla teased.

Paul laughed. "She was the only woman in the house. She had us all in check."

He nervously looked her in the face. He felt like a giddy schoolboy. Clearing his throat, he said, "I'm looking forward to the concert tomorrow night. Mary J. Blige is one of my favorite artists. I'm glad you asked me."

"I'm just glad you were free on such short notice."

"For a chance to be with you, I would have made myself available."

Kayla leaned across the table and smiled. "Be careful, Paul. Fool around and I'll have *you* in check."

Paul didn't miss a beat. He winked. "You can have me any way that you want me."

℘ ℘

Kayla returned from breakfast and was informed there was a high priority meeting going on with the officers, staff sergeants, and above. Only a sergeant, she wasn't included. She paced outside the company commander's office door, hoping to hear a word or two. She didn't want to hear the word *deploy, Iraq,* or any place in the Middle East. She was so involved in eavesdropping that she jumped a mile when someone tapped her on the shoulder. She turned to find Liz giving her a pathetic look.

"You almost gave me a heart attack."

"You would have one if I was someone else. What are you doing?"

"I'm trying to find out what's going on in there. Everyone who's anyone is in the meeting."

"I know." Liz strolled back to her desk. "Whatever it is, they're keeping a tight lid on it. I didn't even know there was a meeting. I'm the secretary, I should know everything." She sat in the chair and rolled over to the filing cabinet. "I'm out of the loop." Opening the bottom drawer, she removed a new ream of printer paper. "Obviously, it's top secret."

"A trip to Iraq?"

Liz moved back to the desk. "I admit with everyone running around with their heads cut off this morning, it's the first thing that comes to mind."

Kayla walked over to stand in Liz's doorway. Her eyes zeroed in on the commander's door. Cage was in the meeting. Maybe she could get some information from him. They hadn't really spoken since he came to her office to inquire about Paul.

An hour later, with the meeting still going on, Kayla trekked back to her own office. She had soldiers' evaluations to complete. Entering her office, the low sound of jazz greeted her. She was doing her best not to think about what could be going on down the hall. She settled in the chair behind the computer and opened the folder.

"Good morning, Sergeant Perry," the familiar voice said from the doorway. Kayla looked up to find Cage walking in with a coffee cup in hand.

"Morning yourself." Discretely, she lowered her gaze and let her eyes travel up and down his physique. There was a tingling in the pit of her stomach. She was determined not to reveal her joy at seeing him. If she was going to find out what was discussed in the meeting, she had to be careful in asking her questions. "That must have been some meeting. You were in there for hours."

Cage sat in the chair across from the desk. He took a sip and sat the cup down on the desk's edge. Kayla turned in her chair, giving him her full attention. He crossed one leg over the over.

"You know how long-winded First Sergeant can be," he said.

"Did he talk about anything specific?" Kayla asked. There was a distinct nervous edge to her voice.

"Like what?" He knew what Kayla wanted to hear.

"Like, what the meeting was about," Kayla replied.

"Just the daily meeting."

"For three hours?"

"There's nothing to worry about." He managed a tight smile. He hated not being honest with her, but his hands were tied.

Kayla had worked with him long enough to know when he was being truthful; he wasn't. "I don't believe you. There's something going on that you're not telling me. That worries me."

Cage considered Kayla's dilemma. "Don't let the lower enlisted soldiers know that you're worried. It could be bad for morale." He stood, picked up his coffee cup, and walked out the door.

As Cage left, Liz ushered herself into Kayla's office.

She rolled her eyes. "I agree with you," she said. "A three-hour meeting? Something is up."

"Were you listening?"

"How else was I going to find out what's going on?"

"Well, as you heard, he didn't tell me anything."

"I think you should seduce him," Liz said, giggling. "Get it out of him that way."

Kayla cast her girlfriend a cool glance. "You trying to get us in trouble? What kind of woman do you think I am?"

"One torn between two men," Liz said.

"There's only one," Kayla replied. "I'm going to the concert with him tomorrow night."

"You have made up your mind?" Liz gave Kayla an impish smile.

"Sergeant Perry," Private First Class Ebony Springs knocked and stormed in the office without waiting for an invitation. Her dark-brown complexion was clean, flawless, and free of makeup, with the exception of a hint of brown lipstick. At thirty-two, she was the oldest private in the unit. From Chicago, Illinois, she possessed a laid-back persona that made the other soldiers feel at ease with her. Though she was easy to get along with, Private Springs was no pushover. She was quick-witted and funny, but she was quick to let people know when they had crossed her.

"I need to go on emergency leave," Private Springs replied.

"Why? What happened?" Kayla asked, zooming from around her desk. She glanced over at Liz, indicating for her to give them privacy.

Liz causally headed toward the door. She looked back before closing the door behind her. Kayla knew she didn't appreciate being dismissed.

"You know I'm involved in a custody battle with my husband," Private Springs continued when it was safe to speak.

Kayla nodded in an attempt to follow the story.

"He picked the girls up over the weekend from my mother's and didn't bring them back." Private Springs was struggling to keep her composure. "I need to go home and find out where my daughters are."

"What did your mother say?" Kayla inquired.

"Just that he picked them up Friday evening for his scheduled weekend visit. He was supposed to return them on Sunday at 6 p.m. When he didn't show up around 8 p.m., she phoned him. She didn't get an answer. She drove to his apartment. He was nowhere to be found." Tears began to flow. "My girls are gone."

Kayla's heart went out to her. She went over and stood next to her, comforting her. "I'm so sorry. I really am." She reached over and pulled out a Kleenex, handing it to her.

Private Springs dabbed at her eyes. "I can't lose my girls. I just can't. Besides the army, they're all I have left."

"Does your mother know for sure that he's taken them?"

Private Springs sniffed. "The apartment was empty. Mom said the landlord told the police that my husband, his girlfriend, and their two daughters finished moving out Saturday night. It's obvious the move was planned."

"Sounds like it."

Private Springs drew in a deep breath and closed her eyes. For a moment, she seemed to be in deep thought. "I can't do anything here. I have to go home. If they deny my leave, I'm going anyway."

Kayla flashed her a sympathetic look. She understood how she felt, but she couldn't condone it. "How do you know they will deny your leave? You haven't even applied for it yet."

"Because of what's going on in Iraq. Right now my little girls are more important than any war."

"Go ahead and submit your leave to Liz. They can always call you back if we're deployed." As Private Springs turned to leave, Kayla added, "I didn't hear the talk about going AWOL."

Chapter Eight

"I wish you and Marissa would try to get along," Kayla said to Liz, as she assessed herself in front of the three-way mirror of the boutique in Lake Forest Mall. Kayla was looking for an outfit to wear to the concert tomorrow night. She was looking for something bright, cool, and sleeveless.

"I don't think so," Liz said, holding up a floral print dress. "This would look great on you. The color goes well with your skin tone."

"Why don't you like her?" She did like the pink color with the V-neck. It was cut low enough to add a seductive flair.

"I have my reasons," Liz answered, pushing her friend toward the dressing room. "Go and try this on. I want to see how it looks on you."

"What are your reasons?" Kayla said over her shoulder, as she stepped through the double doors and removed her clothing.

"Let's just say, I know her type," Liz said, a little annoyed. "She's selfish and vain. She doesn't care about anybody but herself. Not to mention she's a phony. I can't stand her."

Kayla pulled the tank top over her head. "A phony?"

Liz moved closer toward the dressing room, speaking for only Kayla to hear. "I hate a phony. Didn't she say she only began to date black guys when she moved to Iowa?"

"Liz, what does that have to do with anything? Who cares about her dating preference? Marissa is a very nice person. She has always been nice to you. Tried to get along with you."

"I don't care. I just don't like her."

Kayla couldn't miss the serious expression on Liz's face. She pictured Liz to be an open-minded person. Something else had to be going on for her to dislike Marissa. "Because she dates black guys? Tell me that's not it, Liz. I believe you're a bigger person than that."

For a moment, Kayla thought Liz was going to answer, but instead she said, "I told you I can't stand her—now go ahead and try that dress on. You have to be looking fierce tomorrow night on your date with Paul."

◌ ◌

Marissa sat alone with a glass of wine in her hand as she glanced around Cadence. Soft conversations flowed through the club and mixed in with the sound of smooth jazz. Her gaze roamed the room, looking for Randall. He'd phoned her at work, asking her to meet him. She really was embarrassed about the way she'd behaved that morning and couldn't wait to tell him how bad she felt. Time was too short for arguing and fighting when they should be spending as much time together as they could before she left next week.

A moment later, her eyes rested on Randall. He shook hands with another man, then his head moved in slow motion as he searched the room. His gaze found her and he

104

headed in her direction. Marissa's heartbeat sped up. Tan dress slacks lovingly encased his muscular thighs and long legs. A short sleeve matching shirt stretched across his broad chest.

"Mmm. Look at the brother coming this way."

"He is fine."

Comments came from the table next to Marissa. The three women were rating every man in the club. This time they were talking about Randall.

"Looks a little thuggish."

"Just the way I like them. You ain't had good sex until you had a roughneck."

"I know that's right. Thug love."

They all burst out laughing. Marissa shifted uneasily in her seat. She was prepared for the stares and remarks they would get when Randall sat with her. She should have been immune to it, but she wasn't. She didn't understand why people were so hung up on race. A person should be free to date and fall in love with whomever they chose.

Randall leaned down and kissed her on the cheek.

"Uh-unh," was the comment that came from the table next to them. "Brother got jungle fever."

"Sorry I'm late. I got hung up," Randall said, settling into the booth across from her. He reached out and took her hand in his. "Have you been waiting long?"

"No. Not very long." She quickly glanced in the women's direction. They were staring and chatting amongst themselves. Randall appeared oblivious to what was going on. He always said that he refused to be concerned about small-minded people. She was his lady. That's all that mattered to him.

"I'm starving," he said. "Sergeant Cage had me and four

other guys moving office furniture all day. I only had a sandwich for lunch." He took a sip of water. "I worked that off."

"Moving furniture?" Marissa inquired. Randall was trained as an army medic, but because he was a troublemaker, he was always on some type of work detail.

"The weapons room is now downstairs and on the other side of the hallway." He reached for the menu and let out a sigh. "I think I'll have the fish." He closed the menu and signaled for the hostess. "I'll have the number two." He turned to Marissa. "Baby? What about you?"

"I'll have the number five." As soon as the hostess disappeared, Marissa reached for Randall's hand. Her blue eyes filled with love as she looked into his. "I want to apologize for this morning."

"No. I'm the one who should apologize. I haven't been the best boyfriend lately. You have a right to get on me for that." He squeezed her hand tighter. "Can you forgive me?"

"You know I do. I just don't want us to fight anymore."

Randall chuckled. "Sweetheart, all couples fight."

"But we have been doing it more lately."

"I know. You have to admit the makeup sex has been worth it." He winked. "Makeup sex is the best sex."

"This isn't about sex, Randall."

Randall's eyes stretched. "Speak for yourself."

Marissa leaned back in the cushion of the booth. She crossed her arms over her chest. "Will you be serious? We have to talk about our relationship, and you're acting like it's some kind of joke. The last couple of weeks, we have been arguing about everything. I'm leaving in about a week. We need to have some type of understanding."

Randall placed his arms on the table. He locked his hands together. "Marissa, you are overreacting. We don't need to discuss what we already know. You love me. I love you. When I get out, we will be together. What else is there to discuss?"

"Changing your ways, Randall. That's what."

Randall cocked an eyebrow inquisitively and raised a hand. "What about my ways?"

Marissa leaned forward. "I want you to treat me with more respect. When we first met, I was always receiving flowers, candy, phone calls, and being taken out. I couldn't get rid of you. Now I don't know where you are half the time. No more romance. We don't go anywhere together."

"What are you talking about? We're out now."

Marissa tilted her head to one side. "Only because we've been arguing the last couple of days and you want makeup sex."

"What's wrong with that?"

"Give me a break."

"One of the reasons we've been arguing is because you have been nagging me. *Randall, do this. Randall, do that,*" he mimicked in his best Marissa imitation. "*Where have you been? What have you been doing?* It's gotten old."

"That's because," she began to say when the hostess appeared with their dinner. As soon as she left the table, Marissa lit into him, her temper escalating with every word. "You have been hanging out at all times of the night with Jason. Coming and going as you please. You treat my place like a hotel, checking in and out, not paying any bills, and you expect me to say nothing."

"See, that's exactly what I'm talking about. Who wants to stick around and hear this all the time?"

"You're missing the point," she said through clenched teeth.

"What's the point?"

"You act right. I won't nag."

Randall spread his napkin across his lap. "This conversation is going nowhere." He bowed his head in prayer before shoveling a fork full of mashed potatoes in his mouth.

"Whenever the conversation is about you and your wrongdoing," Marissa said, picking up the saltshaker and sprinkling seasoning on her food with extra force, "you don't want to discuss it. I'm beginning to think I'm the only one interested in saving this relationship." She glanced up at Randall and saw him enjoying the dinner. "Randall, are you listening to me?"

He dabbed at his mouth with the napkin. "I told you when I came in I was starving. Can a man please eat in peace?"

Marissa knew that meant the discussion was over for now. There wasn't going to be any makeup sex tonight.

CR ED

Paul stood outside of Kayla's apartment, clutching a bouquet of red roses in one hand while ringing the doorbell with the other. To say he was nervous would be an understatement.

"Just a second," came the familiar voice he had come to look forward to hearing. A moment later the door opened, and a lump formed in his throat at the sight of her.

Kayla stood before him beaming brightly. Her hair was upswept to the top of her head, with two long curls hanging loosely on each side of her face. She was dressed in a floral print georgette dress with a surplice wrap, with pink matching sling back shoes. She topped the ensemble off with a pair of diamond studs and a gold bracelet.

"You're beautiful," Paul said. He leaned down and kissed her on the cheek. Then he presented her with the roses.

Kayla blushed. "Thank you, Paul. They're lovely." She was pleasantly surprised. "How did you know I like red roses?"

"A lucky guess." He smiled.

"Come on in. I will be right back. I have the perfect vase for them."

Kayla disappeared into one of the back rooms, giving Paul a chance to look around. He noted the hardwood floors and aqua-colored sofa with matching chair in the living room, the Van Gogh paintings on the wall, the wicker cocktail glass table holding a copy of *Ebony* magazine. She definitely had an eye for decorating. He had only seen the living room, and he hoped to see the rest of her apartment—especially the bedroom.

"Ready?" Kayla inquired.

"Let's go."

Paul gently touched her on the elbow, guiding her out the door. Once outside, Paul opened the door of the truck for her. *I hope the rest of the date goes as smoothly as this,* he thought.

Mary J's fans came out in droves to the concert, every one of them yelling and screaming and clapping and singing. Kayla joined in, clapping and singing along with every song that Mary J performed.

She looked over at Paul, whose smile was as big as hers. His body moved with the music. Kayla smiled. She leaned over, speaking loud enough to be heard over the loud music. "Enjoying yourself?"

He turned to her, their faces so close that all Paul had to do was lean forward and their lips would touch. His gaze traveled over her face. "Definitely," he said. "Mary's awesome."

Kayla tried to squelch the tingling in the pit of her stomach.

After Mary's encore performance, the crowd rushed from the theatre. To keep from being separated, Paul reached out and laced his fingers with hers. She made no effort to release his hand. His fingers were warm and strong. She felt safe and protected.

A few minutes later, they stopped at the International House of Pancakes for a bite to eat. They talked nonstop about their favorite part of the concert. Before she knew it, it was midnight. She had to get up in less than five hours.

At Kayla's apartment, Paul walked her to the door. Kayla removed the door key from the bottom of her small clutch bag. Paul took the key from her hand and unlocked the door.

"I really had a great time tonight," Paul said, handing her back the key.

Kayla smiled. "So did I."

He leaned forward. "Will you go out with me again?"

"Once is not enough, Sergeant Lake?"

"Not when it comes to you."

"I will see you around," Kayla said, being coy.

"You can count on it." He leaned forward and kissed her lightly on the cheek, promising to phone her the next day.

Kayla was impressed but disappointed that he didn't attempt to come inside.

As she prepared for bed, her thoughts were filled with Paul. There was a connection with him. She couldn't wait to see him again.

☙ ❧

"Extend to the left…march," Cage's voice commanded. Kayla was still half-asleep at five- thirty in the morning, getting only four hours of sleep. After stretching and calisthenics, she began to feel revitalized. Fifteen minutes later, Cage gathered the group together for the morning run. Though she didn't like running long distance, she was good at it and was always selected to run in front of formation, carrying the unit flag. Cage's soulful, rhythmic voice broke in an army cadence. The unit ran and sang along with him. Before she knew it, Cage was leading them back to the unit.

After a quick shower in the barracks, Kayla dressed and was on her way to her office when she ran into Marissa. She was dressed casually in a pair of jeans and a Penn State sweatshirt. Her makeup was flawless, and her long blonde hair hung past her shoulders.

"You look nice this morning." Kayla gave her a hug.

"Thanks. It feels good to get out of the uniform."

"What are you doing here?" Kayla inquired.

"Sergeant Cage asked to see me," Marissa answered.

"Shouldn't you be in uniform?"

"I'm clearing post," Marissa answered, with a dismissive flutter of her hand. "He knows that."

"Okay. Don't say I didn't tell you. You are not out of the army yet." Before Marissa could respond, Kayla added, "I went out with Paul last night."

Marissa's eyes beamed. "Really? Where did you go?"

Not wanting anyone to overhear the conversation, Kayla led Marissa into her office. Kayla took a seat at her desk. Marissa dragged the chair from in front of the desk and placed it next to Kayla. She didn't want to miss one word. "Don't leave anything out."

Kayla proceeded to tell her about the concert, going to eat afterward, and how he was a perfect gentleman when he escorted her home.

Marissa scrunched up her face. "No goodnight kiss?"

"No. Paul was a perfect gentleman," Kayla explained.

Marissa sucked her teeth. "Are you going out again with him?"

"Yes, I will," Kayla answered, without hesitation. "If he asks me."

"Oh, he will ask you out," Marissa said. "He didn't get a kiss. His curiosity is already up. You haven't seen the last of Sergeant Lake."

"Speaking of men, how are things between you and Randall?"

Marissa waved a hand in mid-air and shook her head. "I don't know anymore. We had a fight yesterday morning. We went to Cadence last night to smooth things over. We wound up getting into another fight."

Kayla listened with open ears.

"I believe I'm the only one interested in saving this relationship. He's not even trying," Marissa continued. "I've just about had it with him."

"You think it's because you're leaving?"

"I don't know what his problem is. I'm getting tired of it."

"Specialist Poe," Private Bean bellowed from down the hall. "Sergeant Cage will see you now."

"I gotta go," Marissa said. "I'll stop by your office on my way out. We will talk later." She gave Kayla a hug and rushed out the door.

CR ED

The morning seemed to rush by in a whirlwind. Marissa didn't stop by the office; it was just as well because Kayla didn't have time to talk. There was no sign of Cage. After lunch, Kayla wanted to follow up on the situation with Private Springs. She made her way to Liz's office. She arrived in time to see Liz coming out of First Sergeant Chambers' office. She had a worried expression on her face.

"What's going on?" Kayla asked.

Liz pointed toward the First Sergeant's closed door. "There's a Sergeant Kim in there from Personnel."

"She has some orders for the unit." Liz shot her a penetrating look. "I think the unit is being deployed."

Kayla stood rooted to the floor. "Are you sure?"

Liz's voice dropped. "No. But when I was leaving the office, I heard the words *orders* and *deployed* in the same sentence. What does that tell you?"

Kayla didn't get a chance to answer; First Sergeant's door opened and the mysterious Asian female sergeant emerged. She smiled politely at Kayla and Liz before exiting out of the double doors.

"The behind-the-door meeting earlier in the week. A visit by personnel," Liz echoed. "This doesn't look good."

Kayla suspected something was going on, but she was determined not to overreact, not just yet. "I won't believe anything until I hear it from First Sergeant."

"That's because you are in denial," Liz said. "Did you want something?"

For a moment, Kayla almost forgot the reason for her visit to Liz's office. "Oh, yeah. I wanted to follow up on Private Springs. She's having personal problems back home.

She wants to go on emergency leave. I'm just following up on whether or not she submitted her leave form, and where we are on that."

Liz went over to her file cabinet, removing a brown folder marked *Leave*. She flipped through the sheets of paper, locating Private Springs's form. She frowned, then handed the copy to Kayla. "Her leave was denied."

Kayla accepted the paper, looking at it for herself. "Why would they deny her leave? She needs to go home and take care of her children."

Liz shrugged. "I don't know."

"Does Private Springs know her leave was denied?"

"I don't think so. I haven't seen her today."

Kayla glanced up to see Cage strolling down the hallway. Sergeants Villegos and Duncan flanked him. She walked toward them.

"Sergeant Cage," she said, "can I have a word with you, please?"

As always, he looked directly into her face. "Sure." He addressed Sergeants Villegos and Duncan. "I will see you guys in the meeting," He refocused on Kayla. "My office or yours?"

"Your office is closer," she said.

"After you," he said, with a wave of his hand.

Kayla could've sworn she felt Sergeant Cage watching her as she walked in front of him; the thought made her skin tingle.

Entering the room, he closed the door behind them. The sound of classical music greeted them.

"Have a seat." He pointed to a chair across from his desk, then sat down in the large chair.

"No, thank you. I will stand." Kayla looked around the

immaculate office. It was cleaner than her apartment. The wall was full of awards and plaques signifying his outstanding military career. On the brown maple desk was a computer surrounded by family photos, including those of his two smiling children.

"What's going on?" He took a seat behind the desk.

"Private Springs is what's going on."

He clasped his hands together on the desk. "What about her?"

"She's having a problem with her husband and their two children. She applied for leave and was denied. I was wondering if you could talk to First Sergeant about allowing her to go."

"There's nothing I can do," he said quickly.

"Why not?"

"Because as of this morning all leaves are denied. Matter-of-fact, we may be canceling leaves of our soldiers already on leave. First Sergeant hasn't decided yet."

Kayla felt as if the ground had opened up and swallowed her whole. Her suspicions were correct. "Are we being deployed?" she inquired in a soft voice.

"First, I heard just certain key personnel, then I heard the unit as a whole. They don't know how they want to use us."

Kayla dropped her head. "I see."

"I'm sorry, Sergeant Perry," Cage said. "I don't know how this will affect your status of getting into school. Hopefully, it won't."

"That's not important at the moment," she found herself saying." I can always go when we return."

Sergeant Cage's eyes locked with hers. "Let's hope it doesn't come to that."

Kayla nodded. She was filled with mixed emotions. On

one hand, she wanted to go to nursing school. On the other, if the unit was deployed, she wanted to be with her fellow soldiers.

"You may want to speak with Specialist Poe," he added.

Kayla pepped up. "Why?"

Sergeant Cage's eyes skidded from hers. "Her orders were cancelled until further notice."

Kayla felt as if the breath had been zapped out of her.

After leaving Sergeant Cage's office, Kayla tried on numerous occasions to reach Marissa on her cellular phone. The home phone had been disconnected earlier in the week. No answer. All she got was her voice mail. She left several messages for Marissa to phone her as soon as possible.

Several hours later, the phone rang. Kayla hastily picked it up, thinking it was Marissa.

"Hello?" she said into the receiver.

"That is not the proper way to answer a military line," Paul said on the other end.

"Hello, Sergeant Lake," Kayla corrected herself. "I lost my military bearing. I thought you were Marissa."

"What going on with her?"

Kayla ran a hand through her hair. "She found out this morning her orders were cancelled. I have been unable to reach her. I'm thinking of stopping by her apartment after work to make sure she's okay. Would you like to come along?"

"Sure. No problem."

They spoke a few more minutes before making arrangements for Paul to meet her after work, then drive his truck to Marissa's. On the ride to her friend's place, she prayed everything was all right.

 C3 80

Kayla and Paul stood outside of Marissa's door. Kayla used the knocker once more, followed by the ringing of the doorbell. No answer. Then they heard the sound of someone heading toward the door. A second later, the door opened, and they were face-to-face with Marissa. Her hair was mussed. Her eyes were red and puffy. She had been crying.

"Can we come in?" Kayla asked finally.

Marissa nodded. She moved aside to allow them to come further into the room. They stood in the middle of an empty living room. All that was left was a rolled up sleeping bag, a folding chair, and a wood crate with a color television on top of it.

Marissa trailed them. She dabbed at her eyes with a white handkerchief. "I would offer you a chair, but as you can see," she twirled around in the middle of the floor, "I don't have one."

"This is fine." Paul dropped down in the middle of the carpeted floor. He stretched out his long legs casually before him. "This is better than some field exercises I've been on."

Kayla dropped down next to Paul, facing him. She folded one leg underneath her. Marissa joined them

"I guess you heard my orders were cancelled," Marissa began. "I'm part of stop loss."

Kayla reached out, covering Marissa's hand with her own. "Cage told me."

"I don't know why I'm surprised. Everyone tried to tell me."

"It looks like all of our lives are about to change," Kayla replied. "Cage told me the unit may be deployed. He doesn't know when or in what capacity,"

"So much for Penn State." Marissa was pouting.

"For now," Kayla added.

"What about nursing school?" Paul asked Kayla.

Kayla shook her head from side to side. "That may be out," she replied.

"You don't know that for sure," Marissa threw at her.

Kayla reached out and gently touched Marissa on the arm. "Have you told Randall yet?"

"No. I haven't told anyone. I'm going to let my parents have it," Marissa joked. "They talked me into joining the army. Look where it got me. As far as Randall," she waved a hand in mid-air, "he may be glad that I'm going. He won't have to listen to me nagging him all of the time."

Paul chuckled, tilting his head to one side. "I doubt if he wants his lady going off to war. No man would. I know I wouldn't." His eyes caught Kayla's. She smiled. Marissa looked from Kayla to Paul. She grinned in approval.

"So, Paul, Kayla tells me you're waiting to hear from Special Forces."

"I hope I get in. Now more than ever," Paul boasted. "Since all of my friends are being deployed."

"What about you and Kayla?" Marissa inquired.

Kayla gave Marissa an I'm-going-to-kill-you look.

"It's going to be hard to maintain a relationship," Marissa said.

Paul smiled at Kayla. "No matter where we are, Kayla and I will keep in touch with each other. I will see to that."

"That's what I like to hear." Marissa beamed. She pointed at them. "I just have a feeling there is something special between you two."

Kayla blushed. "Thank you, Oprah."

"You're welcome," Marissa teased.

Kayla couldn't help but glance over at Paul. He was still grinning. "We just met," she said. "We don't know where we're headed."

Paul's grin slipped.

"We have to wait and see," Kayla added.

"That was cold," Marissa said.

"Wasn't it though." Paul's lower jaw twitched.

"Let's talk about something else," Kayla said to no one in particular. She could feel Paul's eyes on her. "I'm starving," she said, in an attempt to change the mood. "Why don't we go grab something to eat?"

"Count me out," Marissa said, standing. She stretched. "I'm going to wait for Randall. We have a lot to talk about."

Kayla turned to Paul. "What about you?"

"Sure. Are you cooking?" Paul asked.

Marissa threw her head back and laughed. "Cook? Are you serious? You will never find this woman in the kitchen cooking."

Paul stood. He stretched a hand to Kayla, pulling her to her feet. "You can't cook?" he asked.

Kayla was so embarrassed. She was a bumbling klutz when it came to cooking. She was the daughter of a career mother and never learned to cook. Her dinners usually consisted of sandwiches, frozen dinners, or restaurant food.

"No," Kayla answered. She turned to Marissa and added, "Neither can you." Looking at Paul, she added, "My mother never taught me how to cook."

"I can cook," Paul said. "My mother made sure all of her sons knew their way around the kitchen in case we were bachelors or we married women who didn't know how to cook. Which she suggested," he said, smirking, "we don't do."

Marissa arched an eyebrow at Paul's remark. "A man

who likes to live dangerously and can cook. You are one of a kind."

"Keep telling Kayla that," Paul said.

"Oh, I will," Marissa answered, amused.

"So, Kayla, if you'd point me in the direction of your kitchen," Paul said, clasping his hands together, "I'll see what I can whip up."

"Sounds good," Kayla said.

Marissa placed a hand on Kayla's right shoulder. "I want to thank both of you for coming by to check on me. I was a wreck when I left the unit earlier. I'm a little better now."

Kayla gave her a tight hug. "You know I had to come and check on my girl. I wanted to make sure you were okay."

"I am. Now you two better get going." Marissa followed Paul and Kayla to the door. She allowed Paul to exit first. "Paul seems like a nice guy," she whispered when he was out of earshot.

"Everybody keeps telling me that," Kayla teased.

"Everybody can't be wrong. Give it a chance." She playfully pushed Kayla out of the door.

∞

"You were only going to pick up a few items." Kayla watched Paul place two plastic bags in the cab of the truck. They stopped at the army commissary when Kayla admitted she didn't have the ingredients he needed to prepare homemade chili. It was his favorite dish. It didn't take long to prepare, and he wanted to share it with her.

After loading the bags, Paul walked around the truck. He opened the door for Kayla.

As Paul pulled out into traffic, the conversation between

them flowed nonstop. If he was still angry about the comments she'd made at Marissa's, he didn't show it. Before they knew it, they were back at her apartment building. He grabbed the grocery bags while Kayla walked ahead of him, unlocking the door. She pointed him in the direction of the kitchen, where Paul placed the bags on the counter.

"Make yourself at home," Kayla said. "I will be back to help with the groceries."

"No. I got this," he said. "You just do what you normally do when you come home from work." He began removing the ingredients from the bags. "The difference is today you have a handsome chef…me. I'm going to cook a delicious meal for a beautiful lady…that's you."

Kayla blushed. Paul knew the right words to say. No man had ever cooked for her before. It was a lovely gesture that made her feel warm throughout her body.

"You don't need my help?" she found herself saying to his back, as he began opening cabinet doors. "What are you searching for?" she asked, as he bent down to open the bottom cabinet door. "Aha, found it." He placed an aluminum skillet on the stove.

"I guess you don't need me."

Paul looked toward Kayla and smirked. She was so cute. She was pouting. "I do need you, baby." He smiled that smile of his. "Just not in the kitchen."

Kayla shook her head. "Oh, you got jokes" She turned and strolled down the hallway to the bedroom.

"I'm not joking," Paul said to her retreating figure. She heard him chuckle.

"He never gives up," she said to herself. She began stripping off her uniform. The shirt, pants, and boots were followed by the tan T-shirt. Once the clothing was gone, she headed into the bathroom for a quick shower. She emerged a few minutes later to the aroma of meat frying in the kitchen. It was tantalizing her taste buds.

Kayla applied lotion on her body. She walked over to her high chest, removing a white tank top and a pair of black sweat shorts. She removed the bobby pins from her hair, allowing it to flow freely past her shoulders. Stepping into a pair of black flip-flops, she was ready for a casual dinner.

She strolled back down the hall and into the kitchen. Paul was busy at the sink, with his back to her. She couldn't help but notice that he'd removed his army shirt and tactical boots. She observed how snug his T-shirt fit on his lean, muscular frame. She resisted the urge to sneak up behind him and embrace him around the waist. He was always flirting; she didn't want to give him more motivation.

"It smells good in here." She walked over to the stove, lifting the lid off the pot.

"Yeah. My own recipe or should I say my mom's." Paul quickly glanced over and had to do a double-take. She was wearing her hair down for the first time in front of him.

"What?" Kayla said, nervously running her fingers through her hair. The way he was staring made her uneasy. She was beginning to think that inviting him back to her place for dinner was a bad idea.

"Just never saw you with your hair down."

She shrugged. "I always wear it up. Habit. Being in the military. You like it?"

"You know I do. I like long hair. You should wear it down more often." He cleared his throat, then stirred the pot.

"I see you made yourself at home." She sauntered closer to him. Watching his hands skillfully slice up green peppers was a turn on.

"I believed you when you told me to make myself at home. Can you hand me a bowl, please?"

"Sure." She reached up, opened the cabinet door overhead, and handed him a small black bowl. "And I did mean it."

"So, removing my shirt and boots wasn't overdoing it," he quickly added. "I mean, I don't want to wear out my welcome." He moved back to the stove and added the peppers with the other ingredients.

"No. Everything is fine."

"Glad to hear it. I don't know how to take you sometimes."

"What do you mean by that?" Kayla's voice rose a little.

Paul looked at her. She was wearing her serious expression. He wished he hadn't said anything. "Relax, Kayla. I didn't mean anything by it. I just didn't want to overstep my boundaries with you." He continued stirring the chili and adjusted the flame. "We just have to let it simmer." Things were going good between them. He didn't want to ruin it. "Would you like to set the table?"

"Sure." Kayla happily strolled over to the cabinet, grateful to be needed. She felt useless not being able to help prepare dinner. She removed two glasses, bowls, and silverware, setting them in their appropriate places on the dining room table.

"Got everything?" Paul asked out of the blue, washing his hands at the sink.

"I think so." Kayla admired her handiwork. Whenever she visited her father, she helped her stepmother set the table for dinner.

Paul dried his hands on the dishtowel. He came and stood in front of her, looking her directly in the face.

Nervous from his open glance, she folded her arms across her chest. Her eyes skidded away.

He dropped his head and chuckled. "Why do you do that every time I look at you?"

"Do what?" she asked. She knew what he meant.

He reached out, tilting her chin up to look at him. "Look away. Do I make you nervous?"

She felt a heat wave wash over her. Of course he made her nervous. Very nervous. She was more attracted to him than she cared to admit. She was nervous about what was happening between them now.

Kayla shrugged. "No. I'm not nervous," she lied. Not sure what to do with her hands, she hugged herself.

Paul closed the small gap between them.

Determined to prove that he wasn't having an effect on her, she boldly looked up into his eyes as his tall frame towered over her. He reached out, embracing her in his arms. "There's no need to be nervous," he whispered, gently pulling her to him.

Despite Kayla's effort to put up a brave resistance, her body automatically leaned against him. Her heart rate sped up. She watched as his lips slowly descended to meet hers.

The soft touch of his lips on hers was as tender and light as a summer breeze, then his tongue traced the fullness of her lips; the sensuous gesture sent the pit of her stomach into a wild swirl. He moved his mouth deeply over hers, tasting her, feeding her.

Kayla's defenses broke all the way down. She wanted, needed to deepen the kiss. Her hand slid around his waist to his nice, firm bottom, cupping it and pulling him closer. At the same time, she thrust her tongue deeper into his mouth. Their tongues mated, hotly, hungrily. She could hear his ragged breathing, and it caused her to moan as she enjoyed the sweetness of his kisses. She could feel the heat of her center as it came in contact with his manhood pressing firmly against her.

"Paul," she said, breaking off the kiss and trying to push him away. This isn't what she needed, especially with everything in her life up in the air.

"Yes," Paul whispered huskily; his lips brushed against her ear.

She shivered.

He tightened his hold on her. He reached up and traced his finger along the curve of her cheekbone. His gaze locked with hers. "You can't deny what's happening between us."

She returned his gaze with eyes filled with desire. She placed a hand to his chest to put space between them. "I have to deny it."

"No you don't. It's not going away." His finger moved from her cheek down to the curve of her neck.

"But we are, Paul," she said, her voice shaky.

"Then we need to enjoy each day that is given to us. Don't be afraid," he said, recapturing her soft lips again. "I know what I want. I want to be with you. We…"

"We are going in different directions, Paul. Can't you see that? Timing for us is just all wrong."

Paul knew she was lying. He could see it in her eyes, feel it in her passionate kisses. She was emotionally afraid of him. "I don't give a damn about the timing."

"Look at what's going on." Her voice was shaky. "First it was school and now the war. I just don't think we were meant to be."

"You are making up excuses." He recaptured her lips again.

He just wanted her to think about what was going on between them at the moment and not the future. He made the kiss deeper and hotter than before, allowing his tongue to make slow, sensual love to her mouth.

He finally broke the kiss. "All I care about is us, right here, right now." She had to smile. "Neither one of us was interested in meeting anyone. But we did meet. We can't pretend like nothing is happening between us." Kayla began to speak, but he cut her off. "I won't let you do that to us. You will see me again and again. Give us a chance." He reached out and laced his fingers through hers. "I believe our meeting was meant to be. One way or another, I'm going to prove that to you."

He lowered his head and placed another kiss on her lips. His mouth curved into a warm smile. "Now, let's eat. Dinner is getting cold."

Chapter Nine

*M*arissa clapped her hands and moved her body as rapper The Game performed onstage at Cadence. His surprise appearance and performance worked the young Friday night crowd into a frenzy. She wished Randall was there with her to catch his favorite rap artist. But earlier in the evening, after she'd informed him that her orders were cancelled, he became upset and mumbled something about needing time to absorb the news and stormed out the door.

Marissa was still reeling from the news. She expected Randall to be more understanding and consoling though she shouldn't have been surprised that he was the complete opposite. "Hey, Specialist Poe," a voice yelled next to her.

Marissa looked over and recognized Private Springs, dancing and singing to the music. She held a drink in her hand. She was clearly enjoying herself.

"Private Springs, what are you doing here?" With over 125 personnel in the unit, the two women knew each other but didn't hang out.

"Just trying to enjoy The Game," she answered, with slurred speech.

Marissa leaned back as the scent of alcohol hit her full force in the face. "What do you know about The Game?"

She giggled. "I don't know anything about him. I certainly don't understand anything he's saying." She staggered a little. "I like the old school rappers, you know, like Heavy D, LL Cool J, Grand Master Flash, and the Furious Five. Rappers whose words you can understand." Private Springs looked toward the stage. "He's cute though. I guess it doesn't matter what he's saying."

Marissa chuckled. "No, it doesn't."

"I heard they cancelled your orders." Private Springs leaned back again. "They rejected my request for emergency leave." She took a sip. "I can't go see about my babies. They don't care about them."

Marissa frowned. "Your babies?"

Private Springs's eyes closed briefly. "Never mind." She spilled a bit of her drink from the glass as she waved it in mid-air. "What am I telling you for? You're Sergeant Perry's friend. You don't care either. You can't help me. No one can help me." She turned to walk away. "I have to help myself."

Marissa didn't know what Private Springs was talking about, but she was concerned about her condition. "Are you headed back to the unit?"

"Not right now." Private Springs made a beeline toward the bar. Marissa trailed her.

Marissa stood next to her. "You don't need another drink."

Private Springs threw her a mind-your-business look.

Marissa threw her hands up in a surrendering gesture. "I know it's not my business."

Private Springs braced both of her hands on the bar for support. "No, it isn't. So back off," she exclaimed.

"I'm just saying," Marissa continued, "whatever is bothering you, alcohol isn't going to solve it."

Hunnicutt, the bartender, glanced up at Private Springs and then Marissa. He watched them closely. Marissa shook her head from side to side.

Private Springs slowly sat on the stool, facing Marissa. "Who are you?" she snapped. "My therapist?"

"I'm just someone who cares about you."

Private Springs laughed. "Hah. We have been in the same unit for almost a year and you have never said two words to me. Now, all of a sudden, you care. Go on, Becky, leave me alone."

Marissa's face turned beet red. She took a deep breath. "My name isn't Becky," she said. She knew Becky was just a nickname for a white girl. "Don't make me pull rank."

Private Springs laughed even louder. "What are you going to do? Order me not to drink?"

"If I have to," Marissa replied.

"Too late."

"It's time to go before you get yourself into trouble," Marissa chimed in.

"There will be trouble if you don't leave me alone."

Marissa turned back around on the stool.

"Hunnicutt, another scotch," ordered Private Springs in a loud voice, causing several patrons to turn around and look.

"Listen to your friend. You have had enough."

Private Springs giggled. "She's not my friend. We just happen to be in the same army unit, that's all."

Hunnicutt shook his head no. "You have had enough."

"Come on, Hunnicutt," Private Springs pleaded. "Just one more drink. I promise to leave."

"I am your friend. You're leaving now," Hunnicutt replied. He nodded at Marissa to remove Private Springs from the bar. "Do you need help?" he inquired.

"No. We will be okay." Standing around 5'4" and slim, Marissa was several inches taller than Private Springs. "Come on, let's go." Marissa attempted to help her from the barstool. Private Springs pushed her away.

"I said, leave me alone," Springs said. "I'm waiting for my drink."

"There are no more drinks," Marissa explained. "It's time to go."

"No." Private Springs pushed her again. This time, Marissa fell upon a young man standing behind her. He looked, didn't comment, and walked off cursing. Marissa was not only embarrassed by Private Springs's behavior but also angry. Her instincts told her to leave Private Springs at Cadence, but her heart wouldn't let her leave a fellow soldier in need.

Marissa gripped Private Springs firmly on the arm. "If you don't get off that barstool," she said through clenched teeth, "I'm going to ask Hunnicutt to have the bouncers escort you out."

Private Springs must have understood because she awkwardly slid off the barstool. Marissa helped her stand up straight. As they headed for the entrance of the club, Marissa looked up and recognized two of the African-American women who were eyeballing her and Randall the other night. The taller of the two, a light-skinned, medium built woman, stared Marissa up and down before making a face and leaning over to her friend to whisper in her ear.

When she passed Marissa, she bumped into her. Marissa believed the incident was on purpose, but she wasn't going to instigate.

"Excuse me," the woman said with attitude, rolling her head to one side.

Before Marissa had a chance to answer, Private Springs

chimed in. "Why don't you watch where you're going?"

"Why don't you?" the woman threw back.

"You bumped into us," Private Springs snapped.

"I didn't bump into you."

Private Springs stepped toward the woman. Her petite frame had to look up into the woman's face. "You bumped into my friend, you bumped into me."

Marissa could see the situation beginning to get out of hand. Sensing something was about to kick off, she watched the woman's friend come and stand next to her.

"Is that right?" the first woman said.

Private Springs waved a finger in the woman's face. "You heard me."

The woman reached for Private Springs's finger, but missed. "You better get your hand out of my face," she snapped.

Marissa stepped between the two women. "She didn't mean anything. She had a little too much to drink."

"You better get your friend."

"Or what?" Private Springs peeped around Marissa and asked. It was obvious the alcohol had made her braver than usual. "Ain't nobody scared of you."

A crowd was beginning to gather upon hearing the exchange between the women.

"You may be bigger than me, but I ain't scared," Private Springs said.

"What do you want to do then?" the woman challenged.

"She doesn't want to do anything," Marisa chimed in, holding Private Springs back. "We were on our way out. Like I said, she's drunk. She doesn't mean any harm."

The woman seemed to be satisfied with the answer. She grabbed her girlfriend by the hand and turned to walk off.

In the blink of an eye, Private Springs hit the woman in the back of the head, knocking her off balance. As the woman was falling, Private Springs used her right foot to push her to the floor. The woman landed on her abdomen. Private Springs took advantage of the situation, slapping her repeatedly in the back of the head. The woman's friend attempted to pull Private Springs off, but Private Springs pushed her away. The woman's friend quickly regained her footing, striking Private Springs across the face and dragging her off her friend. Marissa noticed the bigger woman was now on her feet, and it would now be two women against one. Both women began hitting Private Springs along the body as the young crowd cheered them on.

Marissa's adrenaline kicked in. She pulled the bigger woman off Private Springs by the hair. The woman squealed and let out an expletive. The woman managed to turn around. As she was about to strike Marissa, several bouncers appeared and separated the four women. The taller woman continued to throw out expletives and finished the tirade by threatening to call the police and file charges. To top it off, Marissa looked up to see a very unhappy Victor Sexton staring her in the face. She hung her head in embarrassment as the bouncers led them away.

α β

"You have a variety of DVDs," Paul said, flipping through Kayla's large selection of movies. "How many do you have?" He picked up *John Q* and flipped it over to read.

"About one hundred and fifty," Kayla boasted proudly. After dinner, she suggested they watch a movie. Paul agreed. To be honest, she wasn't ready for him to leave.

"Kimberly Elise has come a long way since, *Set It Off*," Paul said. "Do you mind if we watch *John Q?*"

"Not at all. I can watch Denzel anytime." Walking to the armoire, Kayla opened the double doors to the television and DVD player. Turning both on, she took the DVD from Paul and slipped it into the player.

"It's because Denzel is famous, isn't it?" Paul joked. "Because I'm cuter."

Kayla laughed. "Much cuter." She gently touched the side of his face. "And you make some awesome chili. You really put your foot in it."

Paul laughed, too. "My mom did say the way to a woman's heart was through her stomach." He winked.

Kayla sat on the sofa and patted the space beside her. Paul joined her, sitting close.

"I thought it was the other way around," she said.

"It works both ways."

Kayla slipped off her shoes. She put one leg underneath her and leaned back into the cushion. Paul wrapped his arm along the back of the sofa. Kayla leaned in closer to him.

Touched by the gesture, Paul snuggled close. She felt good next to him. He tilted his head to look into her face. "Comfortable?" he asked, as the movie began.

"Very comfortable." Kayla looked to Paul, and he gave her a quick kiss.

"Mmm," she cooed. "You are a great kisser."

"So are you." His hand began moving up and down her arm. He turned, concentrating on the television screen.

Kayla felt disappointed that she was no longer the center of Paul's attention. She stretched out her legs, placing her head in his lap.

"Sleepy," he asked, running his fingers through her hair.

"I'm just relaxing," she answered. Her heart began beating a mile a minute when his hand began massaging her back. She felt moisture between her thighs. She could only imagine what his hands would feel like all over her body. She hoped to find out soon.

They must have dozed off because she awakened to the sound of the doorbell. Sitting up, she wiped her mouth with the back of her hand. Paul was still asleep. She hoped she hadn't snored or drooled on him. She glanced at the digital clock on the VCR. It was 10:15 p.m. The doorbell rang again. She wondered who it was. Slowly, she rose and trekked to the door. Peeping through the peephole, she saw Cage. He'd never been to her apartment before.

She checked her appearance in the wall mirror. Her hair was meshed a little on one side and she looked tired. A quick run of her fingers through her hair and she was presentable. She opened the door.

"Hello, Sergeant Perry," Cage said. "I don't mean to stop by so late. Did I wake you?" He appeared agitated.

"I dozed off watching a movie," she replied. She glanced over her shoulder to see if Paul was listening. "What's going on?"

"We have a problem."

Kayla straightened. "What kind of problem?"

"Specialist Poe and Private Springs are in jail."

"What? Jail?" Kayla exclaimed. "For what?"

"Assault."

"Who is it, Kayla?" Paul asked, coming up behind her.

Cage's eyes stretched in surprise. "I didn't mean to disturb you. Specialist Poe phoned me from jail. I was on my way to bail them out. I thought maybe you wanted to come along."

"Of course," Kayla answered quickly. She waved Cage inside. "Come on in." He stepped further into the room. Kayla closed the door behind him. She quickly reintroduced the two men, and relayed the information to Paul.

"Would you like for me to come along?" Paul asked. He didn't miss the look Cage gave him upon his request.

"That's okay. You have been an angel once today. I couldn't ask you to go out of your way again for my friends."

"It really is no problem," Paul answered. "You know that."

"I know, but Cage is going to drive me. I will be fine."

Paul didn't like it. He had to keep an open mind. Marissa was in trouble and the two ladies were friends. He glanced at Cage. He looked pleased. Though the Sergeant outranked him, he wanted to knock that smirk off his face.

"All right," he said with a sigh. "Let me grab my things. I will be on my way." Paul reluctantly went into the living room. He slipped into his uniform shirt and grabbed his tactical boots. He was miffed. He stepped down into them without lacing them, then turned around to face an upset Kayla. Embracing her in his arms, he whispered in her ear, "It's going to be all right. I'm sure it's nothing serious."

"Thanks," she whispered back. "I will call you later." She kissed him on the cheek and wandered over to the entertainment center, flipping off the DVD and television. "Let me freshen up a bit," she said over her shoulder to Cage.

"Take your time," Cage said. He walked into the living room and took a seat on the sofa.

"I'll see you later," Paul said, looking from Kayla to Cage. He was letting the sergeant know he was going to be around.

A few minutes later, Paul settled inside the cab of his truck.

He turned the key in the ignition with extra force, then stepped down on the gas pedal and burned rubber out of the parking lot. He made a left turn onto the main street. When he stopped at the red light, his mind couldn't help but think about Cage. Paul thought he noticed Cage's standoffish demeanor toward him at Liz's cookout. Tonight, he didn't imagine it. Cage was interested in Kayla.

⊰ ⊱

"Sergeant Perry," Marissa exclaimed, running down the steps of the DC Police Department. She flung her arms around Kayla's neck. Cage had posted bail for the women.

On the ride to the Police Department, Cage was talkative but steered away from asking about Paul. Kayla was disappointed. She wanted him to be jealous. There was no question about it; Paul was bothered by Cage's appearance. Why couldn't Cage react the same way?

Marissa was pale. "I can't believe I was in jail," she said, flustered. "I just can't believe it. It was awful and disgusting. I was put in handcuffs like a common criminal and put in the back of a police car." Her face twisted. "The place stinks, and it's dirty."

"Oh quit crying," Private Springs said, moving slowly down the steps, carefully taking one at a time. "I told you I wasn't going to let anything happen to you."

Marissa pointed at her. "You stay away from me. You're crazy."

"I was taking up for you," Private Springs shouted, and the two women began arguing.

"At ease," Cage commanded. The two women became quiet on cue.

"What happened?" Kayla managed to ask.

Marissa ignored Kayla's question and lit in on Private Springs again. "It's your fault that I was arrested in the first place. If you would have just kept your mouth shut and left like I asked, none of this would have happened."

Private Springs frowned. She ran a hand across her forehead. She looked tired. Her clothes were disheveled. "Quit talking so loud," she said. "I have a terrible headache. I'm going to have a horrible hangover."

Marissa made a move toward Private Springs. "You're going to have more than that."

Kayla grabbed Marissa by the hand to calm her down. "Why were you arrested?"

"Because G.I. Jane here got into a fight at Cadence," Marissa said. "The women pressed assault charges against us."

"Everybody just calm down," Cage said. "Let's just get in the car and get out of here." He opened the car door and motioned for Kayla to sit in the passenger seat. Private Springs and Marissa occupied the back.

"What were you fighting about?" Cage asked Marissa once they were on the interstate. Private Springs was asleep, snoring loudly.

Marissa filled them both in on everything that happened at Cadence.

"I couldn't stand by and let it be two against one," she said. "That wouldn't be right. She's a fellow soldier."

"A fellow soldier that was in the wrong. I'm glad that you looked out for each other." Cage looked at Marissa through the rearview mirror. "The punishment won't hurt as much. You will share it together."

Marissa's mouth dropped. "Punishment? What punishment?"

"The punishment you will get for your conduct this

evening. You can't go around beating up people," Cage explained. "You're a soldier in the U.S. Army. You're supposed to set an example, be an example, and not a bad example."

Marissa leaned forward from the backseat. "I didn't beat up anybody. I was just trying to help Private Springs, that's all. She was the one who started it. She was the one getting beat down, not me."

"The women pressed charges against you and Private Springs." Cage exited the interstate and made a right turn at the light. "It makes you look guilty. Ever heard of guilt by association?"

"Just because they said it, doesn't mean that it's true."

"You're right," Cage said. "We will see what comes down when CID investigates. Until then, save all that aggression for the Iraqis, all right?"

Marissa dipped her head. She leaned back in the backseat, wondering how she could have such a roller coaster week. Her relationship with Randall was hanging by a thread, the army rescinded her orders, and Private Springs helped get her a trip to jail. Someone had her number. She hoped they'd lose it because she couldn't take much more. She leaned her head back on the cushion and closed her eyes.

CR Ᏸ

Kayla gave Marissa a hug and watched as Cage escorted her to her apartment door. Marissa was greeted by an upset Randall. Cage spoke with him a moment, then strolled back to the car. Private Springs was still fast asleep in the backseat.

"What did Randall say?" Kayla asked, watching Cage settle in the seat. He refastened his seatbelt.

Cage took a deep breath. "He wanted to know what happened. I just told him that Marissa phoned and asked me to bail her out of jail. Anything else he will have to get from Marissa."

"Sounds like another fight to me," Kayla replied.

"I'm willing to bet on it."

Cage steered the car back out onto the highway. It was after midnight. Not much traffic was moving.

"Marissa says they are in love," Kayla said. "Fussing and fighting comes with the territory."

Cage glanced over at Kayla. He grinned. "In love, huh?"

"That's what she told me."

"If that's what she wants to call it, who am I to question it?"

Kayla looked out of the passenger window. The lights of the local businesses twinkled as the vehicle moved along the street. "Who wants that kind of love?"

"I don't know." Cage gripped the steering wheel. "Works for some people. Makeup sex is the best kind of sex."

She snapped her mouth shut, stunned by his remark.

He chuckled at her reaction. "Don't forget, I was married. I know quite a bit about makeup sex."

Kayla forced a smile. "I bet you do. How long were you married?"

"Eight years."

"What happened?" Kayla asked.

"The army happened." Cage focused back on the road. "Early in my career, I was assigned to a field artillery, then infantry. I was always on some type of field exercise, thirty or forty-five days at a time. My wife didn't take to loneliness too well."

Kayla knew what he was going to say before he said it.

It was a common theme for a lot of married couples, spouses stepping out on each other. The divorce rate was high among soldiers.

"I came home from a training exercise, and she had moved another man into my house—a house I was paying the mortgage on every month." Bitterness laced his tone. "She tried to tell me she wasn't happy. I wasn't listening. I found out the hard way."

Kayla could hear the sadness in his voice. "I'm sorry," she said.

"Things happen. What about you and Paul? I hope I didn't cause a problem between you two."

"No. Don't be silly."

"He looked upset."

With a small chuckle, she shook her head and said, "He wasn't upset. He was a little disappointed that the evening was interrupted."

"Can't blame him for that."

Silence fell between them. The windows were lowered midway to take advantage of May's cool night breeze. Cage leaned forward and turned on the radio. The soft sound of smooth jazz filled the vehicle's interior. He cleared his throat and asked, "How are things going between you and Paul?"

Kayla glanced at Cage. "Not much to talk about right now."

"It's wise to take your time. Not rush into anything. Especially with everything going on with the unit now."

"We have talked about the timing."

Cage nodded in agreement.

"He's waiting to hear if he's accepted to Special Forces," she continued. "Then there's nursing school." Kayla's hair blew against her face. She pushed it aside.

"What did he say about the timing?" Cage inquired.

"He believes we should take advantage of the time we have together," Kayla said.

"He's a man. What did you expect him to say? He wants what he wants. He's never going to see the big picture."

Cage turned left onto Kayla's street. He stopped the vehicle in front of her apartment building, turned off the ignition, and turned in his seat to look at her. "How do you feel about Paul?"

Kayla's heart dropped into her stomach. Her eyes locked with his, pleased with the inquiry. "Paul's a good friend. I like him."

"Just a friend?"

"Just a friend," she answered, forcing him to understand what she was saying. She experienced a tingling in the pit of her stomach. "Why are you asking?"

She studied his profile to see what impact her question had on him. She watched as he leaned his head back in the headrest and glanced over at her. "I just wanted to know."

She didn't let him off the hook so easy. "Why?"

He opened his mouth to speak, but nothing came out. He peeped in the backseat. Private Springs was still asleep. Without another word, he got out of the car and walked around the vehicle to open the door for her.

They walked up the sidewalk in silence. He hoped he hadn't overstepped his bounds. He hoped Kayla felt something for him, as he did for her. He was sure she did, but he couldn't do anything about it and it was killing him inside.

Being with her now, he wanted to tell her how jealous he was of Paul. So many things he wanted to say, but couldn't.

"You think Private Springs is all right?" Kayla asked.

Kayla's soft voice interrupted his thoughts. His gaze took her in and slowly dropped to her lips. He dreamed of kissing those lips. "Private Springs will be fine. She has proven that she can take care of herself. I'm going to drop her off at the barracks in a few minutes. Make sure she gets to bed."

He watched as Kayla nervously swept her tongue over her lips. "It's been an interesting evening," she said, reaching into her purse to retrieve her door key.

"You're right about that," Cage said.

Kayla stared at him for a long minute. She hoped he would finish the conversation they'd begun in the car. He wanted to tell her something, and she had a feeling it was something she wanted to hear.

"You were going to tell me something," she said, after a long, deep breath.

He arched his right eyebrow. "No, I wasn't," he said in a husky whisper.

"I believe I know what you were going to say." Taking a deep breath, she calmed her racing heart.

He closed the small space between them. His tall, slim frame looked down at her. "How do you know what I was going to say?"

She looked up at him, her brown eyes filled with desire. "I just do."

"We're in an awkward position."

She nodded, realizing the position they were in.

He shifted from one foot to the other. "You working for me and everything."

"I won't always work for you."

"I know." He became quiet a moment. "I...uh was

wondering if you would like to go out with me sometime. No pressure," he quickly added. "Just two friends getting together. Having a drink or something."

Kayla's mind was tossing back and forth. She'd been waiting for this moment for so long. She wanted to scream *yes* at the top of her voice.

"Do you think that's a good idea?" she asked, thinking it didn't matter. She just wanted to hear him ask her.

He smiled. "I think it's a great idea. We're friends and colleagues. I should have asked a long time ago." His smile warmed her through and through. "Think about it."

"I will." She returned his smile.

"Like I said, no pressure." He took the key from her hand and slipped it into the lock and activated it. She walked inside her apartment. Cage followed her in. She strolled over to the end table and switched on the lamplight.

"I have to get out of here. Drop Private Springs off," he said, coming up behind her. He turned her around to face him.

Her body automatically leaned into his and felt his arms tighten around her.

"I'll see you in the morning," he whispered, as his mouth softly covered hers. She felt transported on a soft and wispy cloud.

Chapter Ten

The next morning, Paul parked the truck in the parking garage. He was running late for work, something he'd never been since arriving at the hospital. Punctuality was a strong trait of his.

He bolted from the vehicle and activated the alarm. His long legs stretched into a jog. If it wasn't for Kayla, he thought to himself, he would be on time. He'd tossed and turned all night, finally dropping off around 2:30 only to wake around 6:00, thirty minutes late.

The elevator doors opened before Paul. His mind drifted to Kayla and Sergeant Cage being together. He became angry all over again. When the elevator doors opened a second time, the female's voice indicated he was on the fifth floor. He stepped off and strolled briskly toward his office.

"Good morning, Sergeant Lake," a voice said, creeping into his thoughts. He looked over to find Laura grinning at him. "You're not speaking this morning?"

"I had something on my mind."

"I can tell."

"Sorry." He turned and trudged down the hall to his office. He unlocked the door, then bent down to pick up a note from Timothy. He said he'd stopped by and would be back later. Paul hated that he'd missed him. He needed to talk and hoped to spend time with him before he left for Iraq.

Sighing, he walked over to the window and opened it wide. Fresh morning air circulated around the room. He took a deep breath, taking in the view of the morning traffic as it moved hastily along Georgia Avenue. His mind shifted to Kayla. He thought about how good she'd felt in his arms last night. The soft touch of his lips on hers. He grinned. A delicious thought drifted through him. She was a good kisser. She had a set of full lips just like he liked them. He could feast on them all night. The evening had been going well until Sergeant Cage made an appearance.

Despite Cage, Paul wasn't going to be deterred. Anyone who knew him knew he was very persistent. He didn't get where he was without determination. He was determined to have Kayla in his life.

He turned to a soft knock on the door, followed by Timothy's head peeping around it.

"Running late again this morning?" Timothy walked further into the room. He was dressed in a tan desert army fatigue with matching hat.

"Yeah, long night," Paul answered.

Timothy frowned as he stared at his friend. "I can tell. You look like crap."

"Thanks for pointing that out." Paul narrowed his eyes.

"Just telling the truth. What's going on?"

"Kayla is what's going on."

Timothy smiled. "Oh, it was that kind of night."

Paul shook his head. "I wish."

Timothy spread his hands apart in confusion. "I don't understand."

"What do you know about Sergeant Cage?"

Timothy arched an inquisitive eyebrow. "Not much. He seems like an alright guy." He shrugged. "I have only met him a couple of times. What about him?"

It surprised Paul that although he had only known Timothy for a short period of time, he felt comfortable enough to discuss his personal life with him.

"He showed up at Kayla's last night."

Timothy tilted his head to one side, giving Paul his undivided attention.

"It seems Specialist Poe and Private Springs went out and got themselves arrested after an altercation at Cadence."

Timothy straightened. "I hate to hear that."

"Yeah, me too," Paul agreed. "Anyway, he says he came by so that Kayla could accompany him down to the police station to bail them out of jail."

"Seems harmless," Timothy said. "What's the problem? Marissa and Kayla are friends. Private Springs works for Sergeant Cage. It would make sense for them to look out for their soldiers."

Paul ran a hand down his face in frustration. Maybe it was just him. Maybe he was bent out of shape because their evening was interrupted. Maybe Cage didn't have any interest in Kayla besides being a fellow employee. "You're right, I'm trippin'."

"Something got you rattled. What happened last night?"

Paul proceeded to tell Timothy about the evening he and Kayla were enjoying, the appearance of Sergeant Cage, and the exit he'd had to make.

"Are you upset because he ruined your evening, or do you think Cage is your competition?"

"Both," Paul admitted. He plopped down in the chair

behind the desk. "I know he's interested in Kayla. He made that obvious to me."

"What did he do? Did he say something to you?"

"He's smarter than that. It was the looks he gave me," Paul answered. "It was the way he was looking at her. Even the way he acted around her and reacted toward me last night. Oh, he's interested."

"I don't know," Timothy said, shaking his head. "What are you going to do?"

"There's not much I can. She's not my lady, yet."

"So, you're going to do nothing?"

Paul looked Timothy directly in the eye. "You know me better than that."

A slow smile crept across Timothy's mouth. 'That's what I'm talking about. Never walk away from a battle."

"Especially one that's worth fighting for. I see you're dressed for the desert," Paul said, changing the subject. "When are you leaving?"

"Day after tomorrow. I'm packed and ready to roll out."

"We have to hang out before you go," Paul suggested.

"It has to be tonight," Timothy said, his eyes full of mischief. "Tomorrow night, I plan on spending a romantic evening with Liz. Going to try to get enough to last for eighteen months."

Paul laughed. "One night isn't going to get it done."

"I said try." Timothy joined in the laughter. "That is the fun part."

෴ ෴

"He kissed you?" Liz asked over the phone. Kayla phoned her at home after Liz called in ill. She wanted to

148

make sure mother and baby were fine. Liz promised that other than a severe case of morning sickness she was all right. Still in bed, Liz held the phone to her ear with her shoulder. "Hold on a second." Liz adjusted the pillows and sat straight against the backboard of the queen-sized bed. "Okay, I'm back."

"I couldn't believe it," Kayla muttered.

"But you wanted him to, right?"

"I think I did. It happened so fast. I don't know what I'm feeling right now."

"How was it? Is Sergeant Cage a good kisser?"

Kayla beamed. She was sure Liz could feel her grinning through the phone line. "It was nice, real nice."

Liz let out a whoop. "Okay. Okay. Who is the better kisser? Sergeant Cage or Paul?"

Kayla was flabbergasted. She shouldn't have been surprised that Liz would ask such a question.

"Come on, Kayla, answer me," Liz prompted. "Who's better?"

"Okay, honestly, the kiss was nice, but Paul does it for me. I swear I felt my toes curl in my shoes after Paul kissed me."

Liz squealed. "I knew it. Paul just looks like he knows what to do. He gets my vote."

"I know." Kayla smirked. "Whenever Paul and I are together, we have a great time."

"Hmm," Liz said. "And he's a good kisser. You can't forget that."

Kayla agreed. "He's a good kisser."

"But you don't want him."

"I never said that. Right now, at this point in my life, I don't know what I want."

"Or who, but you can't have both of them."

"Who says I can't have both? Men do it all the time. I'm not committed to Cage or Paul."

"That's just nasty. You're not scandalous like that, and you don't have that type of game."

"It's not about game. It's about commitment. I don't have one. I can see who I want to see."

"Go ahead, Miss Thang. A week ago you didn't have a man, now you got two."

They both chuckled, then spoke a few minutes more before hanging up.

❧

Kayla didn't know how to react when she ran into Cage later on in the day. She was glad to see him, but she tried to act like she wasn't.

"Good afternoon," Cage said, as they met in the hallway.

"Someone has been busy." Kayla nervously tapped a ballpoint pen against her right leg.

"A staff sergeant's job is never done." He stared at her a moment, taking in how beautiful she looked. His glance fell to her lips, and his mouth softened. After kissing her last night, he found it difficult to think about anything else. "Have you thought about what we talked about last night?"

She smiled. "I have." She fell in step with him as they moved slowly down the hall.

"Well?"

"I'd love to go out with you sometime."

He grinned back at her. "Yes." He clasped his hands together. "You just brightened up my day. Look, I have to get going. I have a meeting with First Sergeant. Specialist

Poe and Private Springs will be going up before him this afternoon. I'm going to speak on their behalf. See if I can recommend extra duty instead of an Article 15."

"That would be good if you can do that," Kayla added.

"Stand by in case I need you." He tapped her on the shoulder and hurried down the hall with a little spring in his step.

Kayla strolled back to her office. The sound of Mary J. Blige playing on the radio greeted her. She thought of the night she and Paul went to the concert. She'd had a great time on the date and a greater time last night. Two men had kissed her, but it was Paul's lips that had made her tingle inside. With all the uncertainty going on around her, she was sure now more than ever that it was wise not to get seriously involved with either man.

ℭ ℂ

Paul and Timothy stood at the bar and placed their orders with Hunnicutt, then took their Heinekens to an empty booth. Smooth R&B music filtered through the club's speakers. The dance floor was crowded with couples, and there were a few bold women dancing and singing along to the music.

"I'm going to miss this place," Timothy said, taking a sip.

"You will be back before you know it," Paul added.

"I hope so."

Paul bounced his head to the music and turned to Timothy. "None of that talk."

Timothy took a long swallow of beer. "That's all I think about," he said. "How is Liz going to get along without me? What if she has complications and I'm not here? Too much can go wrong. It's enough to drive you crazy."

"Is she staying in the area while you're gone?"

"Yeah. She doesn't want to leave."

"What about her family?"

"She doesn't get along with her mother, and her grandmother is dead." He took another sip. "I tried to talk to her about staying with my family. She didn't want to discuss it."

"I know how stubborn women can be."

"With Kayla possibly being deployed, there won't be anyone to look after her. I just don't know what to do. I can't make her go."

"No, you can't," Paul said, looking at Timothy's solemn expression. "That's the worst case scenario. Everything will be fine. Your homecoming will be Liz and a new baby. You can't beat that."

Timothy managed a tight smile. "There are numerous family support groups for service members deployed. She has the church, her job." He took another sip. "I can understand why she wants to remain in the area." He looked down in the empty glass as if looking for the answer to his dilemma. "What about you? Any news on Special Forces?"

"Still waiting," Paul answered, noticing how his friend was struggling to keep his composure.

"I hope you hear something soon. I'm going to need you so I can make the trip back home safely."

"I know," Paul said.

"Thought about Kayla?" Timothy asked.

"Not until you brought her name up." Paul took a sip.

Timothy chuckled. "Liar."

Paul leaned back. Any other time, he would have disagreed, but not this time. Timothy's observation was dead on. Kayla filled every crevice of his brain.

"I don't want to talk about Kayla," Paul said. "Tonight, it's just two brothers hanging out. Let's not spoil it." He took another sip and raised his bottle. "Let's make a toast. To your safe return."

"And to yours," Timothy added. They tapped bottlenecks.

◌◌ ◌◌

"Good evening, Kayla," Victor said, as she and Cage strolled into Cadence's waiting area.

"Good evening, Victor. It's good to see you again."

Victor tilted his head to one side. "Same here, Kayla." His eyes shifted in the direction of the stranger standing next to the woman his cousin wanted to get to know. He couldn't help but wonder what the relationship was between the two and if Paul was aware of the situation.

Kayla's glance followed Victor's. "Victor, I'd like for you to meet Staff Sergeant Maurice Cage. We're in the same unit. Staff Sergeant Cage, this is Victor Sexton, one of the co-owners of Cadence."

Cage extended a hand to Victor. "It's a pleasure to meet you, Mr. Sexton."

Victor accepted his handshake. "Same here, Sergeant Cage. Call me Victor."

"Only if you call me, Maurice," Sergeant Cage replied.

"It's a deal."

"I just want to let you know," Cage continued, "that I enjoy coming to Cadence. It's nice, classy, respectable, and has the best food in the district."

Victor smiled. "Hearing compliments like that makes my brother and me proud of Cadence. Thank you very much. We appreciate it."

"No problem."

"Well, enough of that." Victor nodded to Kayla. "I'll get someone to show you to a table. Any preferences?"

"Somewhere close to the stage," Cage suggested.

Victor waved to the host. The tall, medium-built male, dressed in black slacks, white shirt, with a black bowtie, put on a wide smile for Kayla and Cage. Cordell stopped in front of Victor. Victor leaned over and whispered something in his ear. Cordell nodded.

"Follow me," Cordell said to Kayla and Cage.

"Enjoy your evening," Victor said after them.

Cordell led them to a table adjacent to the stage. The sound of Troop's *Spread My Wings* filled the room.

"I hope this is all right," Cordell said. "If not, I can try to move you a little closer."

"This is fine," Cage answered. He pulled the chair out for Kayla. After she was settled, he moved around the table and sat. Cordell handed each a menu.

"Would you like to order your drinks?" Cordell asked.

"I'll have a Heineken," Cage said, before glancing at Kayla.

"Sprite. Light on the ice," she replied.

"Give us a few minutes to order dinner," Cage instructed Cordell.

"Okay. I'll be back with your drinks." He quietly walked away.

"Like I was saying in the car," Cage said, "I managed to talk First Sergeant Chambers into giving Specialist Poe two weeks of extra duty and garnishment of one-half a month's pay. Private Springs will receive one month of extra duty, garnishment of a whole month's pay. Both are restricted to the post."

"Kind of harsh, isn't it?" Kayla said.

"I think the punishment fits the crime. It's better than the stockade. Let's hope the women don't file a civil suit against them."

"I guess you're right," Kayla agreed. "Thanks for everything you did for them."

Cage reached out and covered her hand with his. "No need to thank me. Just doing my job. They both are good soldiers. Never have been in any trouble. Those are the soldiers you don't mind going out on a limb for. Besides, as wrong as it was for them to be fighting, I admire Specialist Poe for stepping in and doing what she did. Never thought I would see that kind of camaraderie out of her."

"I'm not surprised," Kayla said, slightly offended. "Specialist Poe is a good friend. She's a person who has your back no matter what's going on."

"She's just naive on matters of the heart," Cage said. "Everyone in the unit knows the situation surrounding her and Randall."

"I have to agree with that."

Silence fell between them. Kayla glanced up to find Cage staring at her. Her eyes skidded away. She was enjoying herself, but was nervous. When Cage phoned and suggested coming to Cadence, she tried to talk him into going somewhere else for dinner. She knew just about everyone from the unit visited the club, including Paul.

"Nervous?" Cage asked.

Kayla's eyes found his. "A little bit."

"Everything is fine. We are just two friends, co-workers out having dinner."

Kayla allowed her body to relax. She was too uptight. She just hoped they didn't run into Paul.

"Ready to order?" He opened the menu.

Kayla picked up the menu on the table. She was grateful that it gave her something to do. "I'm starving. What about you?"

"I will eat anything as long as it's not broccoli." He made a face. "I'd eat dirt before I eat that stuff."

"I like broccoli." Kayla giggled. "It's good for you."

"That's what my mother kept telling me." His eyes continued to scan the menu. "She kept trying to get me to eat it when I was a kid. She even attempted to keep me at the kitchen table for hours to see if I would give in."

"Really?" Kayla asked, surprised. This was the first time he'd ever shared anything with her about his childhood. "Did you eat it?"

"No. She made me go to bed."

Kayla shook her head.

"That was after she spanked me. On top of that, she fed me the same broccoli the next day."

"What?" Kayla exclaimed in disbelief.

Timothy chuckled. "But I stood my ground. I refused to eat it."

"How old were you?"

"I was about eight or nine," Cage said.

"What finally happened?" Kayla inquired.

"She tried to spank me again, but my father intervened. They got into a big fight, which wasn't unusual for them," he added. "They fought a lot."

Kayla could identify with Cage. Her parents fought all the time, too. She remembered many nights when it seemed as if the arguments went on for hours.

"Are your parents still together?"

A somber expression crossed his face. He leaned back into the chair. "My father is dead."

"I'm sorry for your loss," Kayla said.

"He was murdered. Stabbed to death when I was twelve."

Kayla's heart went out to him. It must have been hard to lose a parent so young and in such a tragic way. "Did they catch who did it?"

"Yes. The person responsible was a juvenile. He was sixteen at the time. Stayed in jail until he was twenty-one, then his records were sealed. No one will ever know what he's done except the victim's family."

"Why did he do it?" Kayla inquired. Before he could answer, Cordell approached, placed their drinks on the table, and proceeded to take their dinner orders. Both decided upon steak, medium rare.

"He did it to get initiated into a gang," Cage continued. "My father was the first person he saw. He killed him. My father was at the wrong place at the wrong time." He took a sip of beer.

Kayla gulped.

"I will never forget it," Cage added. "It was my birthday. My dad had gone to pick up my present. A black and gold bicycle that I had been admiring." He managed a slight grin. "He worked all summer at a second job to get it for me." He shook his head as if to erase the thought.

Kayla's eyes misted.

"He was a wonderful father. I hope to be like him with my children."

"You will. You had a great role model."

"Taken from me early in life. I have nothing but great memories of him. What about your parents? Are they still together?"

"No. They divorced when I was thirteen. But they remained good friends."

"You were lucky. Divorces can be ugly."

"I don't think luck had anything to do with it; you never had to spend time between the two of them."

Cordell appeared with the food. Cage waited until he disappeared before he replied, "You were lucky that although your parents separated, they cared enough about you to remain in your life. A lot of parents divorce, and they divorce the kids, too."

"I didn't mean to sound insensitive. I know I'm one of the lucky ones."

"It's okay. I know you didn't mean anything by the remark." He picked up the knife and fork. "I don't think you have a mean bone in that pretty little body of yours."

Kayla blushed. "I don't know about that."

"I disagree." He began cutting into his steak. "You're beautiful inside and out. One of the things I like about you."

"One of the things?" she questioned.

Cage smiled. "Besides being a good kisser, I don't know how good you are in bed. But if you move your body as good as you kiss, I can't wait."

Kayla almost choked on a piece of bread. She knew Cage was forward, but she thought with intimate matters, at least he'd be more discreet.

She took a sip of water. "You don't hold back, do you?"

"I always say what's on my mind." He locked eyes with hers again. "I hope I didn't offend you."

Kayla was uncomfortable. She lowered her eyes. "No. Not at all," she lied.

"My wife," Cage began to say, then caught himself. "My ex-wife couldn't deal with it. She often said it was the military mentality. I hope it won't be a problem with you."

Kayla shrugged. "I don't know."

"I'm different. Anything you want to know about me, just ask."

"Okay. I have a question."

"Shoot." Cage shoveled another piece of steak into his mouth.

"What's going on between you and Maria?"

Cage finished chewing his food and wiped the corners of his mouth with his napkin before replying. "We're friends."

"You're not a couple?"

He reached out, covering her hand again. "If we were, I wouldn't be here. We went out on a couple of dates. We had a good time. It didn't work out. Sort of like what happened between you and Paul."

ରୀ ଛ

Paul had to do a double take. He couldn't believe his eyes. Kayla and Cage were having dinner together. He felt like someone had kicked him in the chest. His suspicions were correct; there was something going on between them.

"What are you looking at?" Timothy asked, craning his neck to see what had Paul's attention.

"Kayla and Cage having dinner together."

Timothy's beer bottle froze mid-air. "What? Where?"

"To your left, nine o'clock."

Timothy turned his head, getting a view of Kayla and Cage. He let out a sigh of disappointment. "They could just be having dinner together. It doesn't mean anything is going on between them."

"Then why were they holding hands?"

Timothy didn't have a response.

"Why don't I just go over to say hello." Paul stood and headed toward Kayla and Cage before Timothy could stop him.

He ran straight into Victor.

"Where are you going?" Victor halted him with a firm grip on the elbow.

"I'm going to say hello to Kayla."

"No, you're not," Victor replied, steering Paul in the opposite direction.

"I just want to say hi." Paul attempted to remove Victor's hand, but he held on tighter.

"I said no." Victor's voice rose an octave. Several customers glanced up, including Kayla. Her mouth gaped.

"Let's go into my office." Victor pushed him toward the back of the club and gestured for Timothy to join them.

Upon entering the office, they found Gerald stretched out on the sofa. He sat up from the commotion, a look of confusion on his face. "What's going on?"

"What's going on is Cousin here was about to fight over a woman," Victor said.

"I was not about to fight over a woman," Paul argued. "I was just going over to say hello and find out what was going on."

"I bet you were," Victor answered in a sarcastic tone.

Gerald stood. "So, he was going to say hello to a woman. What's wrong with that?"

"The woman is Kayla Perry," Victor explained. "She's in the club with another man."

"Oh," Gerald said on a long breath. "Just let it go. She's not worth fighting over."

Paul knew Gerald was telling him the truth, he should just let it go, but there was just one problem. He couldn't. He was in love with Kayla.

Chapter Eleven

s soon as he arrived home, Timothy undressed and stepped into the bathroom to take a shower. He was careful not to awaken Liz. A few minutes later, he turned off the shower and toweled off. Reentering the bedroom, he found Liz sitting up in bed, propped up on one elbow. She smiled.

"I was trying not to wake you," he said, as he opened the middle chest of drawers and removed a pair of boxer shorts. As he slipped them on, his gaze was drawn to the wedding photo of he and Liz, reminding him of the happiest day of his life.

"I just dozed off." She stretched and yawned. "Did you have a good time?"

He strolled over to the side of the bed. Turning down the sky-blue comforter, he slid in bed next to her. "Yes and no."

Liz looked confused. "What do you mean?" She grabbed his pillow, fluffed it, and positioned it behind his head.

"Paul and I were having a good time until he spotted Kayla and Cage having dinner together."

Liz looked guilty. "Oh."

"When did they become a couple?" he asked. "And why didn't you tell me?"

"They are not a couple."

"You mean they're not supposed to be a couple. Talk about unethical. He's her boss for Christ's sake. I thought Kayla was much smarter than that."

"There's nothing going on between them. They were just having dinner. You're jumping to conclusions."

"It didn't look that way to me. Paul is very upset."

"Did he speak to Kayla?"

"He didn't get a chance to. Victor prevented him from speaking to her."

Liz closed her eyes. "I'm glad Victor was there. I know Kayla likes Paul. It's just that at this moment, she isn't interested in getting involved with anyone, especially with talk about getting deployed. She's trying to get into nursing school. She has a lot on her plate right now. She doesn't know what she wants."

"You would take up for her," Timothy said, shifting in bed to face Liz. "But that's no excuse for treating Paul like that."

"Kayla doesn't need me to take up for her. She hasn't done anything wrong."

"You think leading Paul on is all right?"

"How did she lead Paul on? She told Paul exactly how she feels. She is free to date whomever she wants."

"I thought you wanted her to date Paul?"

"I do, but Kayla is her own woman. What's wrong with her dating other men? Men do it all the time. No one thinks twice about it. The moment a woman does it, it becomes an issue."

"I never said it was an issue," Timothy said, sounding defensive. "I just don't want Paul to get hurt. He really likes Kayla. You should have seen him. If Victor hadn't stepped in, it would have gotten ugly. Maybe you can talk to Kayla," he added softly. "See where her head is. Going out with Sergeant Cage is not the right answer."

Liz sighed. "There's nothing to talk to her about." She reached out gently and stroked the side of Timothy's smooth, brown skin. He grabbed her hand, kissing one finger at a time, then inched closer to her.

"Okay," he said, his voice dropping an octave. "I'm through talking about Kayla and Paul."

Liz rolled onto her back, allowing her husband to position himself between her legs.

He looked down into her eyes, simultaneously running his fingers through her hair. Looking into his eyes, Liz could see the sadness of him leaving her and the love he had for her.

"Am I too heavy?" he asked. "I don't want to hurt you and the baby."

Liz grinned from ear-to-ear. "No. I'm fine. I love you, Timothy."

Timothy wasn't a man who spoke the four-letter word often. He allowed his actions to express his feelings. He was a good man, and Liz had no doubts about his love for her. "You know how I feel about you. I know I don't tell you often enough, but I do love you with all of my heart."

"I know you do, Timothy." Liz's eyes misted. "I know." She reached up and enclosed her arms around his neck. Pulling him close to her, she pressed her lips to his. "You are still talking." She continued nipping at his lips, thrusting her tongue deep into his mouth.

Their tongues began a mating dance. No other words were spoken or needed the rest of the night.

❦

Paul sat in his car across from Kayla's place. He couldn't believe what he was doing. He glanced at his watch again.

Eleven o'clock. He'd arrived ten minutes ago—plenty of time to allow Kayla to settle down for the evening after Cage dropped her off.

He wanted to hear from Kayla's own lips what was going on between her and Cage. He got out of the truck and strolled toward the building. The light was still on in the foyer. He was so engrossed in his thoughts that he didn't notice the vehicle moving toward him. He jumped when the driver blew his horn. He allowed the car to pass, then jogged across the street.

Paul had been made a fool out of once by a woman. He wasn't going to allow that to happen again. If Kayla didn't want to be with him, she should be woman enough to say so to his face and not make him look foolish.

A moment later, he was staring at the door. He took a couple of deep breaths to calm his nerves. He knocked. A moment later, he came face-to-face with a surprised looking Kayla.

Just as he'd suspected, she was dressed for bed. Her hair was pulled back into a long, flowing ponytail. She was wearing a silk purple robe with matching slippers. Paul cleared his throat. "I know it's late," he mumbled.

Kayla pulled the ties of the robe together with extra force. "Do you know what time it is?"

"Yes, I do, but we need to talk. Can I come in?"

Kayla didn't move for a moment. For Paul it felt like a lifetime. Finally, she stepped to one side and allowed him to cross the threshold. He waltzed into the living room, standing in the middle of the floor. Kayla trailed after him, taking a seat on the sofa.

"I'm going to get right to the point, Kayla," he said. "What's going on between you and Cage?"

"There's nothing going on. We were just having dinner, that's all."

Paul gave her a look. "Does it look like I have stupid written across my forehead?" He spread his hands apart. "The look he gave me at the picnic, at your place the other night, and now you two having dinner, looking very cozy." He raised a long, thin finger at her. "No, Kayla, something is going on. I want to know what it is."

Kayla wasn't used to answering questions. The way she saw it, he didn't have the right to ask about her personal life. "I don't owe you an explanation."

"So you're not going to give me a straight answer?"

Kayla lifted her chin. "No. I'm not."

"Maybe you have something to hide."

"Maybe because it's none of your business."

The comment caused Paul to lean back. "None of my business?" he repeated. "Well, excuse me for thinking that we were trying to get something going."

"What gave you that idea?" Kayla threw back at him.

The moment the statement left her lips, she regretted it. She didn't mean it. She didn't like the fact that he'd showed up unannounced and began to question her. *Who did he think he was?*

Paul stepped closer to her. "So you were playing games with me? Is that it?"

Kayla straightened. She couldn't believe Paul thought that about her. "No. That's not it."

"Then what do you call it?" He placed a hand to his chest. "We had been spending time together. I thought we were vibing on each other. The next thing I know, you're stepping out with Cage. What's up with that?"

"It's going out and having a good time. Sergeant Cage and I are *friends*. Just like you and I are friends."

Paul stood rooted to the floor. He cared deeply for Kayla. She knew it. He'd never fallen so hard for any woman. For her to use the word friend to describe their relationship was hard to take.

"Friends, huh?"

"We've already discussed this."

Paul once believed that there was a chance he could change her mind. But this made him realize that he would never have Kayla; it was time for him to move on.

"You don't have to repeat yourself," Paul said, in a low voice. "I get it loud and clear." He turned to walk away. Kayla grabbed him by the arm.

"Paul, don't leave," Kayla pleaded. "Let's talk."

"There's nothing to talk about. You made everything clear."

"Don't leave like this."

"Let me go, Kayla." Paul attempted to free his arm from her grip, but she held tighter. She could see the hurt in his eyes, but it didn't match the sadness she was feeling at the moment.

Kayla wasn't going to let him go—she couldn't. Instead, she pulled his body close to hers. She heard him gasp when her body meshed with the contours of his.

"What are you doing?" he asked, in a much softer tone. His eyes skidded away from hers. He couldn't look at her without breaking down.

"When I said I don't want you to leave, I meant it."

He slowly turned to look in her eyes. "I'm not in the mood to play any more games with you."

"This is no game," Kayla assured him. She reached up to touch the side of his face. Paul leaned back, as if protecting himself from a snake. Kayla's heart dropped from his response.

"A few minutes ago, you said we were friends. There is nothing left for us to talk about," he said. "I told you I understood. That's the end of it."

"It's not the end of it." Her voice dropped. "I was angry because you came in here demanding answers." She tightened her hold around his waist. "I didn't mean any of those things I said."

Paul's handsome face softened. He took a deep breath, and she could feel his body relax. "I'm sorry, too, Kayla. You're right. I don't have the right to march in here and ask you about Sergeant Cage or any other man. You are free to see whomever you like."

Kayla laid her head to one side. "You really mean that?"

"No," he answered, with that smile of his that warmed her inside. "I'm not going to lie. When I saw you with him, I didn't like it. I don't want you to go out with any other man but me."

Kayla blushed.

"I know how you feel about a serious relationship," Paul continued, "but I can't help the way I feel about you."

She reached up and gently touched the side of his face; this time he didn't move away.

"I don't know what it is about you," he said. "You are like no other woman I have ever been with. I feel this closeness to you. There's a connection, a bond I have never had with any woman. I can't explain it. We just met, but I feel like I have known you all of my life."

Kayla held him tighter, laying her head on his chest.

"I know you're probably thinking, *This man is crazy. He can't possibly feel this way about me.*" He cupped her chin and searched her upturned face. "But I do."

Kayla watched as he leaned forward and pressed his lips to hers. Forcing her lips open, he thrust his tongue deep in her mouth. The kiss sent a delicious sensation throughout her body. His tongue began to explore the recesses of her mouth. She returned the kiss with a special intimacy that only they shared. She heard herself purr with pleasure as their tongues mated over and over again. She couldn't get enough of him. She tilted her head to the side, wanting more.

She felt his manhood bulge against her. She began moving her hips against his in a circular, slow, agonizing motion. He wrapped his arms around her waist snugly to match the motion she was giving him.

Paul opened the front of her robe. It fell open, exposing a black bra and panty set.

Kayla reached out, removing his shirttails. Reaching around his back, her hands touched his smooth, warm skin. She felt his body quiver.

Taking him by the hand, she led him to her bedroom. Standing next to each other, they quickly undressed each other. Paul stood a moment, looking at her beautiful, brown flesh in the moonlight that streamed through the half-pulled curtain. She was just as exquisite with her clothing off as on. He reached out. His hands began exploring one breast and then the other. She closed her eyes, enjoying the feel of his hands on her body.

The mere touch sent a warming sensation through her. She wanted him to take her and put an end to her erotic agony.

Paul was only the second man she had seen naked. His physique was in excellent shape. His broad and muscular chest extended into a flat, hard abdomen. Not an ounce of flab anywhere on him. Her gaze slipped down his midsection. Her glimpse revealed that he was well-endowed. She licked her lips in anticipation of what was going to happen between them. It was almost unbearable.

Paul clasped her body tightly to his. Her soft curves meshed to his lean body. He recaptured her lips again. This time, the kiss was more aggressive.

A moment later, Paul swept her into his arms, placing her in the middle of the bed. Kayla positioned herself so that he was nestled between her thighs. He began to touch and kiss her in places no man had before, causing her to raise off the bed. Her body was set aflame.

Paul lifted his head, his breathing ragged. "You sure you want to go through with this?"

Kayla's eyes widened in surprise. She made a fist and shook it at him. "I will kill you if you don't finish."

Paul chuckled. "I'm just checking. I want you to respect me in the morning." He ran a hand across her flat abdomen. He moved to the side of the bed, picked up his slacks, and removed a condom from his wallet.

After protecting himself, he slowly eased his manhood into her inviting body. She gasped in sweet agony and lifted her hips to fully envelop him.

Their bodies began to move in perfect harmony with each other. His hands roamed intimately over her breasts, down her thighs, returning to her breasts as he thrust deeper inside her. Wave after wave of ecstasy coursed through her body. She moaned when the involuntary tremors of love flowed through her like warm honey. A moment later, she felt Paul's hardness expand, followed by the sound of his breathing quickening.

The scream that was at the back of her throat exploded, and she found herself calling his name. Paul had taken her to a place she had never been before.

Paul's heart pounded in his chest as he struggled to hold onto the passion that radiated from the core deep inside of him. Before the explosive rapture took him over, he called Kayla's name over and over before collapsing on top of her. Paul had never been so satisfied with a woman. It didn't take him long to realize that it was because he had fallen in love with her.

He placed a kiss on her swollen lips, then found the strength to roll over. Snuggling her close, Paul held her until she fell asleep. With a smile on his face, he dozed off.

ঙ ৪০

Kayla woke up the next morning to Paul gently caressing her right ankle. Turning over on her back, she noticed that he was fully dressed. He sat on the edge of the bed.

"Good morning, beautiful."

"Morning, handsome," she said groggily. "Why didn't you wake me when you got up?"

"I wanted you to get an extra hour of sleep." Staring at her, he wondered if she was aware of how captivating she looked this morning. He loved everything about Kayla that made her who she was.

She sat up, holding the white sheet tightly against her chest. Paul lowered it. Her naked body exposed, she blushed at the raw passion she saw in his eyes.

"There's no need to cover up," he said. "I have seen your body. It's beautiful." He leaned forward, kissing her. "I like what I see, what I saw, felt, and touched. The picture is etched in my mind. It will keep me going all day until I see you again. I will drop by after work."

"You better," Kayla said, then nipped at his lips, moved over, and thrust her tongue in his ear.

His entire body quivered. He moaned. "You know we have to go to work." But Kayla's response was to pull him closer. She kissed his eyes and the tip of his nose. Her hands gently began touching, memorizing his handsome face before thrusting her tongue in his mouth.

"We still have a few minutes," she whispered in his ear. Her breath was hot against his neck.

Paul's response was to begin taking off his army shirt, a task Kayla was more than happy to help him with.

◯₰ ₰◯

When Kayla arrived at the unit several hours later, she was still floating on cloud nine. "What are you grinning about?" Liz asked.

She came and stood next to Liz's desk, wearing a large, sloppy grin. Liz placed her purse in the bottom desk drawer. "Timothy told me what happened last night."

After Kayla and Paul made love this morning, they'd had to scramble to make it to work on time. It was worth it. She could get used to that type of spontaneous lovemaking with him. "Paul and I made up," she said. "Everything is fine."

Liz flashed her a surprised look before sitting down in the chair. Although she was barely showing in her pregnancy, she wore a maternity dress. Her hair was pulled back in a long ponytail. She looked radiant. She did a once over of her workstation to make sure everything was where she'd left it the day before.

"When did that happen?" she asked. "Tim told me Paul was pretty upset. What were you thinking? You know Paul hangs out at Cadence."

"Paul was upset last night." Kayla leaned over the counter and whispered loud enough for only Liz to hear. "But, uh, he was fine this morning." She purposely strolled off. She knew she couldn't make a statement like that to Liz and leave her in suspense. She'd want more information. By the time she made it to her office door, Liz was hot on her trail.

"Uh, huh, you know you can't drop news like that on me and not give details," Liz said, her hands flailing. "What do you mean, this morning? What happened?"

Kayla giggled. "Just what I said." She headed to the wall shelf and turned on the radio. "He stopped by my place last night. We talked. Worked things out and everything is fine." She thought about how his lips and hands loved her so passionately last night, this morning, and squelched a desire to moan.

Liz ran a hand across her forehead in confusion. "Wait a minute. I understand you guys talking and working things out, but how did it lead to him spending the night?"

Kayla smiled and inclined her head to one side.

"Okay. I know how it happened," Liz replied. "The last time we spoke, you said that you were not committed to either one of them. And you were going to see them both."

"When Paul was threatening to walk out on me," Kayla said, "it made me realize how much he means to me." She picked up a spray water bottle and squirted water on the plants positioned on the desk and windowsill. "We decided to see where things may lead."

"Sounds like you did more than talk." Liz giggled.

Kayla was thankful that her back was to Liz. She couldn't stop blushing.

"So how was it?" Liz inquired, bursting with excitement.

Kayla slowly turned around. "It was good," she said, joining in the laughter. "Reaaal good."

"Well, all right," Liz squealed. "What about Cage?"

Kayla sat the water bottle in the window next to the plants. She turned and faced Liz. "What about him?"

"Are you going to see him again?"

Kayla moved over to the desk, steadying the chair behind her. She sat down. "I don't think so. I really want to see where things go with Paul."

"Good," Liz said

Kayla laced her perfectly manicured fingers together. "The whole time I was out with Sergeant Cage, I felt like I was cheating on Paul. I will never forget the look on his face when he saw us together. I felt so bad."

"Sounds like love to me."

Kayla sat up straight. "Don't be ridiculous. It's not love. I just care about Paul, that's all it is."

"Hmm," Liz responded.

"Don't you have a desk with your name on it?"

"Okay, I'm going," she replied, closing the door softly behind her, then sticking her head back inside. "It's love."

After Liz left, Kayla thought about what her friend had said. Was she in love with Paul? "Of course not," she said to herself. She cared about him. Definitely was attracted to him. But it didn't mean she was in love with him.

She took a glimpse at today's training schedule to take her mind off Paul. It didn't work. They were friends. She found herself grinning. Very special friends.

"I hope I put that grin on your face," a voice said.

Kayla looked up to see Cage sauntering through the door. She gulped.

"Good morning, Sergeant Cage." She was doing her best to answer in a normal voice.

"How are you this morning, Sergeant Perry?" Cage was smiling. He appeared more upbeat than usual this morning.

"I'm good," she answered. Her eyes scanned the schedule again to hide her nervousness. "What about you?"

"I'm feeling better now that I have seen you." He looked over his shoulder to make sure no one was around. "Were you thinking about me?"

"You could say that," Kayla answered carefully.

"I was thinking about you," he said. "I thought about you all night." He strolled around the desk, reached out, and took her hand in his.

Kayla gently pulled her hand away. "You can't do that," she whispered. "Remember, we are at work. Someone may see you."

"You're right. It's difficult being this close to you and not being able to touch you."

She turned around in the chair to face him. "We need to talk."

Cage propped a hip on the edge of the desk, giving her his undivided attention. "Sounds serious."

"It is."

He gestured with one hand. "You have the floor."

"It's about Paul," Kayla began.

Cage straightened. "Why am I not surprised?"

"Last night, he saw us together at Cadence."

"So?"

"He was upset. He dropped by my place last night. We talked." She left out the intimate details.

Cage was looking her straight in the face. He didn't blink. His face was blank.

"We decided that we want to see where things go between us."

"You talked?" Cage inquired. He dipped his head. "I see."

"I just want to be honest about everything," Kayla explained. "I don't want there to be any type of misunderstanding or friction between us."

"There is an attraction between us."

Kayla blinked.

"A physical attraction," he answered. "You feel it just as much as I do. Why do you keep denying what's between us?"

Kayla leaned back. "It would never work between us. Sneaking around. Afraid someone would find out about us. I can't be in a relationship like that."

"So you solve the problem by being with Sergeant Lake?"

"I like Sergeant Lake," Kayla admitted.

"The other day you liked me," Cage threw back at her. "Honestly," he said, standing, "I don't think you know who or what you want."

Kayla dropped her eyes. "I know this isn't what you wanted to hear."

"And this isn't the place to talk about this. Why don't I drop by your place after work and we can talk about it?"

"I can't. I'm meeting Paul later."

Cage didn't attempt to mask the disappointment on his face. He was quiet a moment, then turned to leave. Before he left, he turned to face Kayla. "You didn't give me a chance. Give us a chance. We could have been good together." He left, not bothering to close the door behind him.

Kayla placed both her elbows on the desk and held her face in her hands.

"This is awful," she mumbled. "It was just one kiss, one date. How could it cause so much trouble?"

She sat a few minutes trying to collect her thoughts. The one thing she feared most about getting involved with Cage had come true. As untouchable as it was, she would have to deal with it. She clasped her hands together and sighed.

Kayla looked up when she heard a knock on the office door. "Yes?"

A frowning Private Springs breezed in. "Good morning, Sergeant Perry."

"Good morning, Private Springs," she said, displaying a somber mood. "What can I do for you, today?"

Private Springs stopped in front of the desk and executed the position of parade rest, her hands clasped together behind her back.

"Stand at ease," Kayla commanded.

"Sergeant Perry, I finished cleaning the female latrine. Sergeant Cage instructed me to come and let you know when the detail was completed so that you could inspect it." Cleaning the female latrine was one of the extra duty details that Private Springs had to do for the next month. They were to make themselves available before and after the normal duty work hours.

"I'll be there in a moment," Kayla replied.

"Yes, Sergeant," Private Springs answered in an irritable tone before snapping to parade rest again and exiting the office.

A few minutes later, Kayla carefully inspected the latrine. It was spotless. The sinks, commodes, and shower stalls were glistening. The knobs were highly polished. The tile floor was mopped, buffed, and smelled of clean disinfectant. Kayla ran a finger along one of the sink edges.

"Looks good, Private Springs. Looks real good."

Private Springs glared at her, frowning. "I worked hard on this bathroom, Sergeant. I think it deserves more than a *looks good,* she said with an attitude.

Kayla gave her a look, surprised by the insubordination. "Is there a problem, Private Springs?"

Private Springs' eyes stretched. "I'm sorry, Sergeant Perry. You didn't deserve that."

"You'd better watch yourself," Kayla said in a firm

voice. "I will overlook it this time. I know you're going through a lot right now, but I'm not the enemy." Her face softened. "Any news on your husband or the kids?"

Private Springs dropped her head. "No."

"Things will work out." She reached out and touched her hand in a comforting manner. You will see."

"Sergeant Perry, can you talk to Sergeant Cage about approving my leave?"

Kayla looked stunned at her suggestion. "The withdrawal has nothing to do with Sergeant Cage. No one in the unit is allowed to go on leave."

Private Springs shook her head regretfully. "I know, but I need to go home to see about my kids, my babies," she pleaded. "There has to be something someone can do."

"I'm sorry," Kayla replied, "but all leaves are cancelled until further notice."

Private Springs sighed. "Yeah. I'm sorry, too." She turned and ran out of the latrine.

"What's wrong with Private Springs?" a bewildered looking Marissa asked on her way into the latrine. "She almost knocked me over."

"She has a lot going on," Kayla answered.

"Tell me about it." Marissa rushed into the first open stall and closed the door. "Did I tell you I moved back into the barracks?"

"No, you didn't. How are you getting along?"

"It's different, but I will get used to it. I have to." Marissa flushed, left the stall, and moved over to the sink to wash her hands. "It's noisy. I'm in a room alone. That's good." She dried her hands with a paper towel.

"Have you heard from Randall?" Kayla asked carefully.

"I haven't seen Randall in two days. I don't know if he

knows I'm back in the barracks. Not that it matters."

Kayla didn't have a comment.

"Go ahead and say it." Marissa threw the paper towel in the trashcan.

"Say what?" Kayla asked.

"That you warned me about Randall. That he was no good. A user."

"I'm not going to get on you about Randall. What you need right now is a friend and a big hug." Kayla reached out and gave Marissa a tight hug. "You're going to be alright. You will see."

Chapter Twelve

Paul dropped by that evening after work, as planned. It began a daily ritual of him and Kayla spending time together. They felt like they were working against time and wanted to spend as much time together as they could. It was as if they couldn't get enough of each other. They began to eat lunch together. Paul would bring his work to her place to complete. Kayla would work on her reports. She would ask his advice on how to handle certain issues and situations. Most of the time, they would just snuggle on the sofa, watching a movie and listening to music, or they would be in the bedroom making love. Everyone thought they made a handsome couple.

They could talk about everything and were good friends. Kayla was comfortable with her decision to be involved with Paul.

Paul's conversations no longer involved being selected for special operations. There was no further word about the unit being deployed. Paul's cousins, Victor and Gerald, began to affectionately call Kayla sister-in-law. Still she couldn't help but wonder what would happen if one of them received orders to leave. Those thoughts plagued her mind day and night.

CR ∾

"How's baby Shupe?" Kayla asked Liz one morning, as the pair strolled through Toys 'R' Us. Liz was looking at baby furniture and toys.

Things were going so well with Paul that her maternal instincts began to evolve. She wanted to become a wife and mother one day. Something she'd never thought before.

"Baby Shupe is fine," Liz replied, beaming. "I felt him…or her move last night." The glow that resonated from her face dimmed. "I wish Timothy was here. I miss the way he would rub my stomach and talk to the baby. He believed the baby heard and understood what he was saying."

Kayla knew it was difficult for Liz since Timothy left a month ago. She and Paul stepped in to help as much as possible. Kayla accompanied her to several doctor's appointments.

"Have you spoken to your mother?" Kayla asked. She knew conversations about Liz's mother were off limits, but with Timothy gone and her deployment status unsure, she didn't want Liz to be alone.

"No," Liz replied, her face turning hard, "I haven't spoken to her." She picked up a heart-shaped photo frame.

Kayla flashed a careful glance her way before saying, "I don't want to get in your business."

"But you are."

Kayla blinked. She held her chin high with defiance. "I'm only trying to help. I don't want you to be alone. Paul, Marissa, and I may be deployed. You will need someone with you. I was hoping you would call her and ask her to come down."

"Like I told Timothy, I can look after myself. I don't need nor want her here."

"Liz, you're being stubborn." Kayla lowered her voice. "You only have one mother. Whatever happened between you two, I'm sure you can work it out. She should be here for the birth of her grandchild."

Liz gave her a hard look. "I wouldn't ask her to come here if she was the last person on earth. Now let's go grab something to eat," she said, to signal a change in conversation. "I'm hungry."

They started walking, taking in the sights of the other stores in the mall.

"What did she do that was so terrible?" Kayla asked.

They stood in front of Ruby Tuesday and were quickly escorted to a table with a window view.

"It's a long story," Liz said, picking up the conversation again. Her voice faded, losing some of its steely edge. She opened the menu, scanning the items.

Kayla leaned across the table. "You can talk to me about anything, you know that. We are girls. What happened?"

Liz relayed how her mother, Toni, was pregnant with her at the age of sixteen and was an alcoholic. Her drinking eventually evolved to drugs. She was addicted to crack cocaine. To support her habit, she began to sell her body. Men were in and out of their home like a revolving door. One man in particular, a white man named John Stanley, became a permanent fixture at their house. He was an ex-convict who'd served time for armed robbery. Liz softly explained how she never felt comfortable around John. There was an eerie and evil spirit about him.

"What happened?" Kayla asked. She had a feeling she already knew.

"I tried to tell my mother." Liz had a painful, faraway look in her eyes. "She didn't believe me. She thought because I didn't like John that I'd made it up. She took his word, a criminal's word over mine."

Kayla's eyes misted. She'd never dreamed her friend had gone through such a terrible ordeal at such an early age. Maybe it explained her feelings toward Marissa.

"He was always drunk. In the beginning," her voice cracked. "He would touch me. I guess that wasn't enough."

"Liz, no," Kayla shrieked in horror.

Liz dropped her head in shame. "I was thirteen at the time. I didn't bother to tell my mother. She wasn't going to believe me. I ran away to a friend's house. They phoned my grandmother. She drove up from Baton Rouge to get me. She won custody of me and raised me."

Kayla took a bit of her salad. "That's how you wound up living with your grandmother?"

Liz nodded.

"I'm glad your grandmother was there for you."

"My grandmother was great right up to her death ten years ago. I really miss her. It's so sad she has a sorry excuse for a daughter."

"Is that the reason you don't like Marissa?"

Liz cut Kayla a deep look. She avoided the question. "The last thing I heard was that she was still with him. What he did to me left permanent scars. It's the reason for the miscarriages. Now, you know why I never want to lay eyes on *that* woman."

Kayla shook her head in disbelief. She sympathized with Liz. She'd heard about women like Liz's mother who were in denial and looked the other way. In her case, she was sure the drug addiction had a lot to do with it. She was just glad that Liz was able to get out of the environment. "Does Shupe know about what happened to you?"

Liz shoveled a fork of baked potato in her mouth. "No one knows," she mumbled. "I want to keep it that way. Tim may not understand. It took years of counseling to deal with what happened."

"You're not giving Timothy credit." Kayla pointed her fork at Liz. "You were just a child. That man was a predator. Your husband won't blame you for what happened. He loves you."

"I know Tim loves me," Liz said. "I'm trying to keep him out of prison for murder."

"Even more reason why you should tell him," Kayla chimed in. "That man deserves to be six feet under."

ʘ ʀ

The weekends were the hardest to be stuck in the barracks. It was Friday night, and Marissa fumed as she watched her comrades get dressed and head out on the town. The building was eerie and quiet.

She rolled over in bed and curled up on her side. That old sinking *she should have known better* feeling rushed over her. The next week for her was going to be difficult. She groaned at the time left on her restriction. She knew how a prisoner felt. The fast-talking, tongue-swagging women in the unit were all basking in her situation, but she wasn't going to give the haters the satisfaction of getting to her.

Marissa forced herself out of bed; her bare feet padded across the tile floor. She walked into the small adjoining bathroom. Peeking at her reflection in the bathroom mirror, she had no doubt that she was attractive. She could get any man she wanted. She looked closer to see if the name *Sucker* was written across her forehead because that's the role she played in her relationships. Men like Randall, who always wanted to use her, walked all over her like a doormat. Maybe she should begin dating Caucasian men. She was sure a man of her own race would be more acceptable to take home to her strict Catholic parents. There was only one problem: she believed she had more in common with African-American men. She liked the way black men walked, talked, carried themselves, and their sexual prowess was the best she'd ever had. But at the moment, she wasn't thinking about how a man performed between the sheets. She wanted and needed a man to treat her like a woman. She wanted to be loved.

She headed back in the room and sat on the edge of the bed. Picking up the remote control, she pointed it at the television. *Friends* appeared on the screen. She made a face and continued surfing through the channels until she landed on BET. Videos of her favorite artists aired one after another. She sang along. She recalled when she was at Cadence a couple of weeks ago and caught The Game's performance. She should be out having fun. She was beginning to feel like the barracks walls were closing in on her. She was used to being free to come and go as she pleased. While on restriction, she was only allowed to venture on post.

"I can't do this," she mumbled. She headed to the locker and opened it. "I have to get out of here. I will take whatever punishment comes to me."

She quickly dressed and boldly walked past an unattended CQ desk. Ten minutes later, she walked through the door of the International House of Pancakes located a few miles from the post. The place was busy as usual; nearly every booth was occupied. She started to leave. Oh, God, in the barracks it had seemed like a good idea. She would be in a lot of trouble if she were caught. Her stomach rumbled, reminding her that she hadn't eaten since lunch. She was here now; she may as well stay and have something to eat. She spotted a seat in the back next to a window.

Ignoring the, *You can sit with me remark*, from a white guy sitting alone in a booth, she headed for the empty seat. "Don't be like that," he added, as she kept walking.

Now she remembered why she didn't like going any place alone, but the food was great. She picked up a menu. She wanted to be ready when she gave her order.

"Well, look who's here," someone said.

Marissa looked up into the face of Jason Bain, Randall's friend. He was dressed in a waiter's uniform. She swallowed the lump in her throat.

"Jason," she finally said. "What are you doing here?" She knew it was a stupid question, but she couldn't think of anything else to say.

A confused look crossed his face. He spread his hands apart. "What does it look like? I'm working."

Marissa's face turned beet red. "That was a stupid question, wasn't it?"

They both laughed.

"Yeah, it was," Jason added. "But I won't hold it against you."

"I have a lot of things going on in my head right now."

"Randall?"

Marissa gave a give-me-a-break-look. "No. I'm not thinking about Randall," she replied irritably.

"Sorry, I was just asking. Didn't mean to get in your business. Are you ready to order?"

"It's okay." She watched as he prepared to jot down her

order. As she looked at him, it was like she was seeing him for the first time. Dating Randall, she'd never noticed how handsome Jason was. Her heart skipped a beat. He reminded her of Justin Timberlake. He had a baby face, yet his body was all grown up. The uniform top he was wearing defined the muscles in his chest. But it was his blue eyes that captivated her. She tried not to stare. He was a close friend of Randall's. What was she thinking? Going out with Jason would get under Randall's skin. She smiled to herself. It would serve him right the way he mistreated her.

"Marissa?" she heard him say. "Your order?" He was smiling at her from ear-to-ear, looking at her as if she were wearing her birthday suit.

Her eyes slowly traveled over his frame. She wondered what he looked like naked. She placed her order for pancakes, sausage, eggs, and orange juice. Ten minutes later, he sat the plate in front of her. All of a sudden, she didn't feel hungry. She picked over her food, finally pushing the food aside on the plate. She got up and paid her bill at the counter. Before she walked out, she found Jason. Using the excuse that she wanted to talk to him about her relationship with Randall, she exchanged phone numbers with him. When she walked out to her car, she imagined the look on Randall's face when he found out she'd spoken with Jason about him. He hated it when she discussed their relationship with her girlfriends, let alone his best friend.

When Marissa returned to the barracks, they were still quiet. The parking lot was still empty. She parked her vehicle in the same space. She hoped the CQ was out making the rounds.

She was in luck. She opened the double doors, peeped her head around the corner, and discovered no one at the desk. She made a beeline up the stairs and down the hallway to her room. She removed her clothing in record time, slipping into a black army sweat suit. As she put her feet down into a pair of bedroom slippers, a knock on the door startled her. Was it CQ? Did they know she'd been out? She was careful not to let anyone see her leave and return.

"Specialist Poe?" the unfamiliar voice inquired.

She nervously cleared her voice before answering, "Yes."

"CQ."

"What is it?" she said toward the door.

"You have a phone call downstairs," he replied.

Her shoulders sagged in relief. "I will be right down."

⊗ ⊗

"Your blood pressure is down," Dr. Mahmoud Maundry said, removing the blood pressure cuff from Liz's arm during her monthly obstetrician visit. The silver haired, fifty-two-year-old doctor had come highly recommended from a co-worker whose daughter had also gone through a high-risk pregnancy. He didn't have much of a sense of humor, but Liz loved his bedside manner.

"I know you have been through a lot with your husband being deployed," he continued, "but try not to worry." He patted her gently on the hand. "Everything will be all right, okay."

"I have to think about the baby," Liz said. "It's not easy, but I have friends who have been supportive. Everyone wants to make sure the baby arrives in good health."

Dr. Maundry smiled. "So do I. I will do everything in my power to make that happen. I'm glad to hear you have a support system in place. You're going to need it. If we can't keep your blood pressure under control, I will have to put you on bed rest."

Liz's smile slipped. "Bed rest? Dr. Maundry, you can't do that."

Dr. Maundry pointed a finger at her. "I can and I will. My concern is not only for you, but also for the baby. If your blood pressure continues to fluctuate or if your feet begin to swell, I won't take any chances," he scolded.

Rita Camp, a young African-American nurse, came into the room. "Mrs. Shupe, don't forget to stop by the front desk to schedule your next appointment."

Liz slowly turned to face her. She was still dazed by Dr. Maundry's statement of putting her on bed rest. "Sure."

Dr. Maundry picked up her prenatal chart and began jotting down notes. Liz slowly stood. She collected her belongings. He turned to face Liz. "You mentioned that you had friends that are very supportive."

"That's right," Liz put on her black sweater. "Why?"

"If you are placed on bed rest, you are going to need someone to stay with you, look after you. If you didn't have anyone available, I'd have to admit you into the hospital."

Liz stopped in mid-motion. She realized that now that Timothy was gone, she didn't have family in the area. Kayla was a friend, but she would not be able to stay with her if she were placed on bed rest. She couldn't imagine being admitted into the hospital.

She filed out of the doctor's office and gazed up at the clear blue sky. She placed the shades over her eyes. She couldn't help but think that if her mother were in her life things would be easier. Deep down inside, she wished things had turned out differently between them. But the hurt was too deep. She wasn't able to forgive or forget. She never would.

CR ℘

Paul took a deep breath and knocked on Captain Anne Bjorowski's office door. She summoned him in. He stopped in front of her desk and clasped his hands behind his back. He had never been in trouble since he'd been at the command. From the way she was waiting for him outside his office, he believed something had happened to change that. Captain Bjorowski ran a tight orthopedic ward. She stood only 5'1", but what she lacked in stature, she made up for in character. She was tough but fair.

"You wanted to see me, ma'am?"

"Stand at ease," she commanded. She laced her fingers together on top of a manila folder.

Paul allowed his body to relax, still wondering why she wanted to see him.

"Sergeant Lake, I know you are probably wondering why I wanted to see you."

"Yes, ma'am. Has there been a complaint about my work?"

Captain Bjorowski frowned. "I have never had a complaint about you or your work. You're an excellent soldier, Sergeant Lake."

"Thank you, ma'am," Paul replied.

"That's the reason why what I have to do is so difficult. You're one of my best workers. Never gave me a problem. I hate to lose you."

This time it was Paul's turn to frown as the light bulb went off in his head. The captain handed him the brown folder. A grin crossed her face. "Congratulations, Sergeant Lake. You have been accepted to Special Forces."

Paul's heart dropped in his stomach. He didn't move for what seemed like an eternity.

"Sergeant Lake?" the captain prompted. "This is what you have been waiting for, right? Orders for Special Forces."

His mind instantly shifted to Kayla. Things had been going so well between them, Special Forces had taken a backseat. She'd been on his mind night and day. He didn't want to leave her behind. Not now. Not ever.

"Yes, ma'am," he finally replied, reaching for the orders.

"Don't jump up and down," she said, eyeing him closely.

"Things have changed since I applied."

"Oh." Captain Bjorowski stood. She walked around the desk and stopped in front of him. "What things?"

Paul's face split into a wide smile. He dipped his head.

"You don't have to say anything else. The smile on your face says it all." She grasped her hands together. "Looks like you two have a lot to talk about."

"Yes, ma'am, we do."

☙ ❧

Several hours later, Paul was sitting on a barstool at Cadence. He stopped by to grab a bite to eat for lunch and to inform Victor and Gerald that he'd been selected for training.

"I'm having second thoughts," he said.

"Seconds thoughts?" Victor repeated, as he slid onto the barstool next to him. "Special Forces is all you have been talking about for as long as I can remember," he continued in disbelief. "Is it because of Kayla?"

Slowly, Paul nodded. "Who else?" He took a sip of water.

"Have you told her yet?" Victor asked.

Paul shook his head. "You're the first." He shrugged. "It's not like I didn't know it was coming. I knew we were on borrowed time, but now that it's here, I don't know."

Victor placed his forearms on the bar counter. "I understand how you feel, but you have to look at the bigger picture. One, do you think Kayla would not allow you to go? Two, can you live with yourself if you didn't go? I mean like you just said, you both knew that the time would come when one or both of you could leave. It just happened to be you."

Paul ran a hand over his head in frustration. "Thanks a lot, cuz, rub it in."

"C'mon, Paul." Victor playfully slapped him on the back. "You have to think this through. Think logically. I know how you feel about Kayla, but you shouldn't allow this opportunity to slip away. It may not come around again."

"I have been thinking about it. I haven't done anything but think about it since I found out this morning."

"The first thing you have to do is tell Kayla. See what you are up against. The only thing you have to worry about now is if she's accepted into nursing school. If she's not accepted, you may be able to work something out. After training, you may be able to go on leave."

Paul made a face. "Her unit may be deployed."

Victor lifted an eyebrow. "That does make the situation difficult. When do you leave?"

"I have to report to Fort Bragg in two weeks." Paul stood. "I'd better get going. Kayla and I have a lot to discuss."

As Paul headed to his truck, he tried to think of how he was going to tell Kayla he was leaving in two weeks. No matter how he tried to prepare her, there was no easy way to do it. He could think of only one way to ensure that they spent the rest of their lives together. He pulled out of the parking space and pulled out into traffic. He had one stop to make before heading to Kayla's place.

ᘉ ᘊ

"Hey, baby," Paul said into the cellular phone. He was only a few blocks from her apartment.

"Hi, yourself," Kayla said, in a low, sensual voice. "I have been thinking about you."

Paul's middle tightened. "And what were you thinking about?" His voice matched her sultry, low tone.

"Thinking about what we're going to be doing later this evening."

Paul chuckled. He stepped down on the gas pedal, crossing the intersection. "I'm on my way to your place. I'm only a few blocks away. We have a lot to talk about." He didn't give her a chance to inquire. The phone went dead.

ᘉ ᘊ

Kayla glanced at the phone still clasped in her hand. Paul didn't sound like his usual self. Usually the mention of them together got a more heated response.

A few minutes later, he stood on her doorstep. Looking at his serious expression, she knew something was amiss. She stepped aside, allowing him to come further into the room. As he passed her, he reached out, taking her hand in his. Leading her to the sofa, he sat down. Kayla attempted to sit next to him, but he positioned her so that she was sitting on his lap.

Kayla looked up in his handsome face. "What is it?"

Paul took a deep breath. "Captain Bjorowski called me into her office this morning." He felt her body stiffen.

"Why would the captain want to see you? Are you in some kind of trouble?"

"No," Paul replied.

Kayla looked confused. "Then what did she want to see you about?"

Paul embraced Kayla tighter. "She called me into her office to tell me that I was accepted into Special Forces."

Kayla's lips formed words to speak, but nothing came out. She jumped out of his lap and crossed the room, turning her back to him. She hugged herself to head off the shiver from the news.

Paul just sat on the sofa. He didn't move. He couldn't. He didn't have the energy to try to explain things to Kayla. There was nothing left to say. Silence filled the room.

"When do you leave?" Kayla finally asked in a hushed voice.

"I report to Fort Bragg in two weeks." He noticed Kayla's shoulders sag in defeat.

"We can't say we didn't know this day would come," Kayla threw over her shoulders.

Paul moved from the sofa. He walked over and embraced Kayla from behind. "It's going to be all right," he said quietly.

"How can you say that?" Kayla asked.

Paul turned her around to face him. It was then that he noticed that her eyes were misty. "Oh, baby, don't cry." He pulled her body close to him, giving her a tight hug. He stroked a hand up and down her back in comfort. He felt her body trembling.

"I thought I would be able to handle this," she said in his ear. "I can't."

"I know, baby." Paul looked deep into her eyes. He saw the fear that resided in them. "I don't want to lose you."

Kayla managed a tight smile. "I feel the same way, Paul. I don't want to lose you either. What can we do?"

He reached out, taking her hand in his. Bringing her hand to rest on his chest, he said, "There's only one thing we can do."

"What?" Kayla prompted.

"Let's get married."

Chapter Thirteen

Kayla leaned back in surprise at Paul's proposal. She was crazy about Paul, but not enough to marry him.

"What did you say?" Her mouth fell open. She stared at him as if he'd lost his mind.

"I asked you to marry me." Paul led her back to the sofa and got down on one knee in front of her. He grabbed her left hand. With his right hand, he produced a diamond engagement ring and looked deep in her eyes. "Kayla Perry, I love you. I want to spend the rest of my life with you. Will you marry me?"

Returning his gaze, Kayla saw love there. She dropped her eyes from his. She had hoped to be proposed to one day, but not on a whim. She believed the only reason Paul was proposing was because he was leaving.

Kayla reached out to him.

Paul held her close. "We will be happy together," he said.

Pulling away from Paul, she stood and walked to the window. She looked out the window, nonchalantly staring at the rows of cars in the parking lot. She turned back to Paul. "I can't marry you." She didn't miss the stunned look on his face. "I'm crazy about you. We have a good relationship, but not enough to get married. Not like this."

Paul strolled toward her. "Like what?"

"You only proposed because you're leaving for training." The more she said it, the more she believed it.

"That's not true."

Kayla began to pace. "Yes, it is. I know about soldiers who get married because of that reason…because of deployment." Her hand movement demonstrated her frustration. "The majority of those marriages end in divorce or worse." Her voice trailed off. She turned back to Paul. "No. I can't. I won't marry you under these circumstances."

"I asked you to marry me because I love you." He put his hand to his chest. She opened her mouth to speak. Paul cut her off with a wave of her hand. He'd known from that day at Cadence that Kayla was the woman for him, and nothing would ever change that, not even the war. "You're the part of me that has been missing. I want you to be my wife and the mother of our children. Don't allow what's going on around us to ruin our future together."

Kayla believed in fairy tales. Believed she may have found her Prince Charming. She closed her eyes a moment, visualizing herself and Paul as husband and wife. She pictured them with children running and playing around. She began to imagine what their children would look like. Would the children be light in complexion like her or pecan brown like Paul? Would they be medium height like her or tall like Paul? Would she have all sons like Paul's side of the family? She managed a smile. A family of three was what she conjured up. Growing up, she was an only child with no one to play with. She told herself if she ever married that she wanted more than one child.

"We have to fight for what we have, Kayla," Paul continued.

"By getting married?" Kayla turned to face him.

"Yes. By getting married." He would beg if he had to. "Do you love me?"

The question seemed to catch Kayla off guard. She didn't know why. It was a legitimate question. She wanted him in her life, but wasn't sure of becoming his wife. She didn't know how to explain it to him without hurting his feelings.

A tear rolled down her cheek. "Paul, you know I care about you."

Paul shook his head from side-to-side. "What are you saying? You don't love me?"

"That's not what I'm saying, Paul."

"Then what are you saying, Kayla? Either you love me or you don't."

"It's not that simple, Paul." She choked back a sob. "I don't know if what I feel for you is enough for marriage. I—I need time to think. Marriage is a big step."

"I don't have time, Kayla. If we are getting married, it has to be within the next two weeks." He didn't miss the look of surprise on her face. "I know marriage is a big step, but we can make it work. You will grow to love me. I will make sure of that," he said, with no shame. "I know about couples who get married because of deployment. But I promise you it's not the reason I'm asking for your hand in marriage. I love you, Kayla."

Kayla buried her face in Paul's chest. "I don't know."

"I'm scared, too, Kayla."

Kayla's head popped up, looking him in the face.

"I can't say yes, Paul. I've got to think." She took the ring off and gave it back to him. "Save it for me."

Paul threw up his hands in a surrendering gesture.

"Forget I asked, Kayla," he said, backing away from her.

"I don't want to forget it," she replied, moving after his retreating figure. "Paul," she called, as he bolted for the door. He opened it and slammed it behind him. "Paul," she cried, hot on his trail.

He ignored her, climbing into the cab of the truck. He refused to acknowledge her knocking on the window. "Let's talk about this," she screamed. Turning the key in the ignition, he put the vehicle in drive and sped off.

Kayla watched in disbelief as the truck disappeared from view. Standing there a few minutes, she hoped he'd turn around and tell her they were okay. He didn't. After five minutes of waiting for him to come back, she slowly made her way back into her apartment.

Not bothering to remove her clothing, Kayla crawled in bed and into the fetal position. The tears began to flow. Her thoughts scattered from Paul's proposal. He wouldn't listen. She never said she wouldn't marry him, only that she needed time to think. Why couldn't he understand the position in which he'd put her? She gulped hard. Hot tears slipped down her cheeks. The relationship was in trouble. She missed him already. Unable to shut off the pain, she took the phone off the hook, switched off the lamplight, and closed her eyes.

CR 80

Paul sat at the bar of Cadence. He was still seething from Kayla's rejection.

How could she turn me down? he wondered to himself. The way he saw it, he was doing everything he could to keep them together. Why couldn't she see that? She was just like all the other women he'd been with. They use you up, break your heart, and move on. He was through with them. How could he think she was different? No other woman was going to hurt him again.

"Give me a Scotch, straight," Paul instructed Hunnicutt.

Hunnicutt stopped washing down the bar and flashed Paul a concerned look. "Don't you mean watered down?"

"No. I mean straight and leave the bottle."

Hunnicutt pepped up. He wasn't put off by Paul's remarks. "Listen, I don't know what's bothering you," he said, as he began pouring the liquid in the shot glass, "but the answer isn't in the bottle." He placed the bottle of Scotch on the counter.

"Hunnicutt, I'm not in the mood to hear that right now." Paul threw the warm liquid down his throat without hesitation. It felt good sliding down the back of his throat, trying to calm the storm raging inside him.

"I'm just trying to help," Hunnicutt replied.

"Don't," Paul quipped. Hunnicutt gave him one last glance before quietly moving onto another customer.

Paul didn't know how long he was at the bar or how much he drank. All he knew was at the moment, he was feeling no pain.

"Remember me?" a sweet female voice asked over his right shoulder.

Paul looked over and tried to focus as much as he could. There's no way he could forget the face of the young woman from the exchange who had sold him a computer a couple of months ago.

His eyes traveled up and down her body. He smiled in approval. "Of course I remember you. How could I forget?"

She returned his smile. "Okay. What's my name?"

Paul chuckled. At the moment, he could barely remember his own name. He threw his hands up in a surrendering gesture. "You got me, sweetheart. I don't remember, but I never forget a lovely face or body."

"With a compliment like that, I can't be too mad at you."

"Please don't be mad at me." Paul's speech slurred a little. "Everybody is mad at me today. I don't know why. I'm a good guy."

"I'm not mad at you." She smiled another award-winning smile. "By the way, my name is Cheryl. Cheryl Whitehead."

Paul tilted his head to one side. "That's right." He pointed at her. "You told me. I'm sorry. I'm not good with names, but I never forget a face—especially a pretty one." He extended a hand. "I'm Paul. Paul Lake."

Cheryl accepted his large, firm handshake. "I remember you very well. A brother as fine as you are is hard to forget."

Paul's grin spread wide across his face. At the moment, Cheryl's flirting was just what he needed to soothe his bruised ego. "I bet you say that to all the men."

Cheryl pushed her large D-cup breasts, which were snugly encased in a low-cut, white blouse, toward Paul.

"Just the one I'm interested in," she replied, tipping Paul's chin up with a well-manicured finger.

Paul's eyes couldn't miss what Cheryl was serving him tonight. "I hear ya, baby."

"What are you doing here all alone?" Cheryl placed her nice round bottom on the stool next to Paul.

"Drinking," Paul answered.

"I can see that," Cheryl replied. "What or who's driving you to drink?"

"Don't want to talk about it," Paul answered hastily.

Cheryl's face dropped a little. "I didn't mean to get personal. Just thought maybe you wanted to talk about whatever is bothering you. I'm a good listener."

Realizing he may have been a little hard on Cheryl, Paul softened his tone. "I'm sorry, it's not you. It's just me and my lady had a falling out."

"I figured it could be something like that."

"Yeah, well, what are you doing here alone?"

"Several of my girlfriends and I decided to hang out tonight." Cheryl turned around, waving to three women sitting at a table. The ladies giggled and waved back.

"No men?" Paul inquired. "Or did you leave them at home?"

Cheryl smiled, batting her eyelashes at him. "I don't have a man," she said, in a seductive voice. She looked Paul up and down. "I'm working on it."

"This could be your lucky night." Paul leaned in closer to Cheryl. Tonight he was determined to erase all thoughts of Kayla from his mind.

Cheryl licked her lips. "I hope so."

CR BO

Kayla awakened to the constant ringing of the doorbell. Thinking it may be Paul coming back, she almost fell out of bed as she rushed to the door. She swung it open wide to find Liz standing on the doorstep. She couldn't hide the look of disappointment on her face.

"Oh," she said. "It's you."

"I love you, too," Liz said, closing the door. She trailed Kayla into the living room. "What's wrong with you? You look awful."

Kayla took a seat on the sofa. She folded her legs underneath her. Liz dropped down beside her. She turned to Kayla. "Have you been crying?" she asked, after a closer examination.

Kayla nodded. "Paul stopped by earlier." Her voice was broken.

Liz looked her directly in her face, attempting to follow what Kayla was trying to say. "Okay. What happened? Did you guys have a fight?"

"Yes. Paul is leaving. He was accepted into Special Forces. He's leaving for Fort Bragg in two weeks."

Liz reached out, covering Kayla's hand with her own. "I'm sorry, Kayla."

"It hurts, Liz. I should have known better. This is what I didn't want. I didn't want to feel like this."

Liz reached out and hugged Kayla. "We can't control who we fall in love with."

"That's only part of it." Kayla pulled back.

Liz frowned. "What?"

"Paul asked me to marry him."

Liz's mouth gaped open. Speechless. She leaned back on the cushion of the sofa. "You're kidding?"

"I wish I was." Kayla stood.

"What did you say?"

"I turned him down."

"What?" Liz rose to her feet in disbelief. "Girl, I have to sit back down. This is too much for me." She placed a hand to her chest.

"Look, he only asked because he's leaving."

Liz cocked an eyebrow. "You don't really believe that, do you?"

"Yes, I do." She strolled into the kitchen. Liz trailed her.

"Kayla, Paul loves you. You know it."

Kayla reached up in the cabinet, removing a glass. She strolled over to the refrigerator, opening the door. She grabbed a bottle of water. As she poured, she said, "I'm so confused right now. I have so many thoughts, emotions going through my head. I don't know what I'm feeling right now. I don't want him to go. I think I have lost him."

"Not really," Liz said. "You can go to him and tell him you will marry him. Explain to him that his proposal caught you by surprise. I know Paul will listen."

"I can't," Kayla stammered out. "I can't do that, Liz."

"Why not?" Liz pleaded. "Do you want to lose him?"

"You know I don't, but I don't know if marriage is the answer," Kayla explained. "We barely know each other. This is insane."

"True love is never insane. Most people will kill for what you and Paul have."

Kayla ran a hand across her forehead in frustration. "I can't think about this. I'm getting a headache."

"It's not going to go away. You have to deal with it, Kayla, before Paul leaves."

"I know. I know I have to deal with it."

"Do you love him?" Liz asked.

Kayla stopped in mid-stride. "I think the world of Paul. When I'm with him," she did a flip-flop with her hands, "I feel good, loved, special, and safe. When I'm away from him, I think of him all the time. I get all giddy inside, knowing I'm going to see him again. I can't wait to see him." She grinned. "Oh, Liz, what am I going to do?"

"You can answer my question. Do you love him?"

Kayla took a deep breath. "I think so." She changed her answer when she saw the expression on Liz's face. "Don't look at me like that."

"I'm not looking at you like anything." Liz placed a hand on each of Kayla's arms. "Your face lights up whenever you talk about him. From what you described to me, it sure sounds like love to me. You're just afraid. Marriage is a big step. I want you to be happy. Paul makes you happy."

Kayla's eyes gleamed. "That he does," she said in a soft voice.

"I want you to go and work this out with Paul before it's too late."

Kayla opened her mouth to blurt out the truth. That she was afraid of marrying Paul. Afraid that if she married him, the separation from the war would destroy what they had. She couldn't conceive of a life without Paul. He meant everything to her. Still she didn't want to marry him, wondering if he'd proposed for the right reason. Once the war was over, maybe they could be together.

Kayla closed her mouth and swallowed the lump in her throat. "You're right. I do need to talk to Paul." Picking up the phone, she punched in the numbers for Paul's cellular phone. She didn't get an answer. He probably recognized her number and refused to answer. She left a message on his voicemail, hung up, and quickly dialed his home phone. "No answer," she said aloud.

"Maybe he doesn't want to talk right now," Liz replied.

"Maybe," Kayla repeated. She slowly replaced the phone in the cradle. She was worried about him. He had been upset when he left hours ago. She hoped he was all right. "I'll try Cadence." She quickly punched in the number to the club. Victor answered on the third ring.

"Hello, Victor. It's Kayla. Can I speak to Paul?" She really wanted to hear his voice. She had to know he was okay. The desperation reflected in her voice.

"Hi, Kayla. Paul isn't here. He left several hours ago."

"Oh, I see," she mumbled in disappointment. "Did he say where he was going?"

"No, he didn't. It's a weeknight. He probably headed home. Is something wrong?" Victor inquired, detecting stress in her voice.

"Did he talk to you?" Kayla inquired.

"Before or after the news about Special Forces?"

"After."

"No. I haven't had a chance to speak to him. It's been hectic around here. Why? What happened?"

Close to tears, Kayla took a deep breath and said, "We had a big fight. When he left, he was very upset. I just need to clear things up between us."

Victor wasn't going to push for details. If it was something Paul wanted to discuss, he would've spoken to him about it. When he was ready, he would. "Kayla, when I hear from him, I will let him know you're looking for him."

"Thanks, Victor, I appreciate it."

"No problem," Victor said, before the line went dead.

"Well," Liz prompted. "What did Victor say?"

"Paul left the club several hours ago." Kayla headed into the bedroom. She stormed over to the chest of drawers, grabbed a pair of underwear and a matching bra. "He's not answering his cellular or house phone. I'll just speak to him face-to-face."

Kayla stripped and headed into the shower. A few minutes later, she quickly dressed in a pair of jeans, a UM sweatshirt, and brown loafers. She picked up her purse and keys off the nightstand. She walked down the hallway and into the living room. Liz was nowhere to be found. Noticing the sliding glass door open to the balcony, she walked outside and found her friend admiring the starry night. "Liz, I'm on my way to see Paul."

"Okay," Liz said, turning around. "I'm leaving, too. If you need me, call me."

"I will," Kayla said and hurried out the door to her car. Before it was too late, she had to make Paul understand that she needed more time to think over his proposal.

Twenty minutes later, Kayla exited the vehicle and briskly walked up the sidewalk to Paul's high-rise apartment. She entered the revolving glass doors and into the lobby. She pressed the elevator button to take her to the fifth floor. As she waited, she thought about all of the things she needed to say to him.

When Kayla arrived on the fifth floor, she strolled down the hallway to apartment 517. She knocked on the door and waited anxiously for Paul to come to the door. Adrenaline pumped through her. Her heart pumped a mile a minute. She didn't get a response and knocked a little louder. She heard movement inside and grew excited.

"Who is it?" she heard Paul ask, but before she could answer, he opened the door. "I said who…" His voice trailed off when his eyes landed on her. "Kayla, what are you doing here?"

"We need to talk. I tried phoning. I didn't get an answer." Kayla attempted to push past him, but he blocked her entrance.

"Let's talk later."

"I know you're upset, but we can work this out."

"Kayla, you made it painfully obvious that you didn't want this relationship to go any further."

"Paul, listen to me." She choked back tears.

"No."

Kayla leaned back in surprise. She couldn't miss the fact that Paul smelled of alcohol. His eyes were red. He staggered slightly. "You don't know what you're saying. You're drunk."

"So what if I have been drinking. It's none of your business."

"Let's talk inside." Once again, Kayla attempted to sidestep him. Once again, Paul blocked her entry. Kayla flashed him a skeptical look. She didn't miss the annoyed look on his face. She attempted to glance over his broad shoulders. "Why can't I come in, Paul? Is someone here you don't want me to see?"

"It's just not a good time."

"Paul, who is it? I'm getting lonely." A tall, busty woman appeared wearing nothing but one of Paul's shirts. She smiled and waved at Kayla. "Hello."

Kayla whirled around to Paul, who looked like he just wanted to slink away.

"Kayla," he said, to her retreating figure. "Let me explain."

Kayla ignored him, pushing the elevator button with extra force. She wanted to get as far away from him as possible. She didn't want him to see her break down.

"Kayla, talk to me, please." He grabbed her arm when she didn't respond.

She jerked her arm away from him. "Go to hell, Paul," she screamed at him. "All that talk about how much you love me, you want to marry me, and how we can work things out." She was on the verge of tears. "I came here to try to work things out. Instead, I find you with that...that...hoodrat. I wouldn't marry you if you were the last man on earth."

"Kayla, I'm sorry." He attempted to take her in his arms.

She pushed him away. "Stay away from me," she yelled. Almost on cue, the elevator doors opened. Kayla turned to get on, but Paul grabbed her by the arms again.

"Nothing happened," he tried desperately to explain.

"Stop lying. You think I'm a fool? You were just caught with another woman in your apartment, wearing nothing but your shirt."

"Kayla, I love you. I—" He was silenced when Kayla reached out and slapped him across the face.

Satisfied by her action and the look of surprise on Paul's face, Kayla entered the elevator and pushed the close button. She looked away as the door closed in his face.

Chapter Fourteen

"This isn't about you and me," Marissa said, as she selected a Sarah Lee French Cheesecake and placed it in the small shopping cart. She stopped by Giant Supermarket on the way to Kayla's place. It was Kayla's favorite dessert. She hoped the gesture would put a smile on her face. "I don't know what to do. She's really down in the dumps. Nothing I say or do seems to work." The urgency in her voice and the situation forced her to call the one person she didn't get along with, but desperate times called for desperate measures. She moved to the next aisle, switching the cellular phone to her other ear. She picked up a container of strawberries. "Liz, what can I do?"

"Just be there for her. It's all we can do right now," Liz said.

Normally, Liz wouldn't have two words to say to Marissa. Not feeling well, she'd been out of the office for several days. It was good to know she had someone to talk to, even if it was Marissa.

"It hurt her, finding Paul with *that* woman," Marissa said, chatting on. "Wearing nothing but his shirt. She blames herself for not accepting his proposal."

Liz sighed. "I told her it's not her fault. She shouldn't blame herself."

"I told her the same thing." Marissa headed for the checkout line. "But right now it's like talking to a brick wall. I wonder who the other woman is."

"A better question would be, was Paul seeing her all along. It seems suspicious that the same day Kayla turned him down, she was at his place." She cradled the phone between her shoulder and ear and paid for the items.

"I don't want to believe that about Paul," Liz said, calmly defending her friend.

Marissa balked. "You would defend him. Our friend is hurting, and you're taking his side."

Liz took a deep breath. She was trying to get a grip on her emotions, for herself, and for the unborn baby. She had no desire to get into an argument with Marissa about her delusional ranting. She slowly released the breath she'd been holding.

"I'm not defending Paul," she said. "What he did to Kayla was wrong. From what I know about him, he's crazy about Kayla. It's out of character for him to do something like that."

"Well, he did do Kayla like that. He's just another man always thinking with his lower anatomy." Marissa grabbed the plastic grocery bag and sauntered outside to her car.

"All the guys you know," Liz quipped. She knew their little peace treaty wouldn't last long. She paused to turn up the volume on CNN News. Since Timothy left, she was glued to the television for any news she could get on the war. She was frustrated. She had spoken to her husband twice since he left, but he was forbidden to tell her about his mission. She relied on the news to try to get some answers. All she knew for sure was that he was stationed in Baghdad.

According to the news over the past couple of days, the

violence had increased, and soldiers were involved in heavy fighting with insurgents.

Liz was frightened out of her mind. She cared about Kayla and the situation going on between her and Paul, but at the moment, she was more worried for her husband and unborn child.

"Like you said earlier," Liz said, "this isn't about you. It's about Kayla and Paul."

"Who are over." Marissa settled behind the wheel of the vehicle. "Good riddance to him. Kayla doesn't need someone like that. She deserves better."

"I understand what you are saying. I agree with you to a certain extent, but let's get real. She turned him down, she hurt him, and that may have had something to do with what happened. Men react differently to heartache than women. He did what he did because he was hurt."

"It doesn't make it right," Marissa said.

"Don't get mad at me for telling the truth. I'm just saying that Kayla's rejection led to what happened. I don't agree with it, but it happened."

"Hmm. Well, regardless of how it happened, Kayla is wiped out." Marissa pulled the vehicle out in traffic. "Have you spoken to Paul?"

"No."

"Don't you think you should give him a call? Find out what's going on?" Marissa replied.

"I will talk to Paul in my own time. I don't need you telling me what to do," Liz said in a dry tone. She'd tried to get in touch with Paul, but didn't get a reply. She left several voice messages for him to call her as soon as he could.

Marissa huffed. "I wasn't trying to tell you what to do. Just suggesting."

"Anyway," Liz said, "I gotta go."

"How's the baby?" Marissa suddenly asked, catching Liz off guard.

Liz managed a small smile. She placed a hand over her abdomen. "The baby is fine. Thanks for asking."

"Yeah, well, I know you have been out of the office the past couple of days," Marissa said softly. Although they didn't get along, she hoped for a healthy delivery. "I just want to say I hope everything is okay."

"As long as I take it easy, everything will be fine," Liz explained awkwardly.

Marissa cleared her throat, not sure how Liz would take the sincerity of her words. "Well, if you need anything," she muttered, "give me a call."

Silence greeted Marissa.

After a second, Liz said, "I'll talk to you later, Marissa."

Marissa pushed the *End Call* button. She made a right turn at the light. She couldn't help but think about how she'd offered friendship to Liz. She really wanted to mend fences. She'd offered her assistance; the next move would be on Liz.

昆 昇

"I'm going to be fine," Kayla said. She took a seat in the oversized chair in the living room. Cage had just placed the last of last night's dishes in the cabinet. He'd stopped by to check on her and had been very supportive, insisting there were no hard feelings between them. They agreed to remain friends, nothing more.

"You're a very strong woman," he said. "You will get through this." He opened the refrigerator door, removing a can of cola. He strolled into the living room.

"I never saw it coming," Kayla replied.

"Speaking from a man's point of view, you didn't see it because men are masters at covering up things like that."

"Tell me about it." She decided to change the subject. "Have you heard anything about being deployed?"

He took a sip. "Not a word. I'm hoping they have forgotten about 32nd CSH."

"Me and you both."

"You will be able to attend school without being worried about being deployed."

Kayla sighed. "I haven't thought about school lately." She'd pushed the ideas of leaving Paul to the back of her mind. She couldn't fathom it a month ago. But now she couldn't wait to leave. There was nothing here for her now.

"Well, think about it. It will be good for you to concentrate on something else. Take your mind off Paul."

Kayla glanced up at Cage. "Thanks for being here. I appreciate it."

"You know it's no problem." Cage's response was followed by a knock on the door and Marissa's voice.

"Open the door," Marissa yelled. "My hands are full."

"I'll get it." Cage eased his long body out of the chair and headed for the door. "If I know Specialist Poe, she probably has one bag."

He opened the door and Marissa breezed in and quickly handed the bag to Cage.

"What did I tell you?" He chuckled, carrying the bag into the kitchen. "Drama Queen."

"I heard that," Marissa said, placing her hands on her waist, pouting.

"It's not heavy," Cage threw over his shoulder.

"Whatever, Sergeant Cage." She focused on Kayla. "Sorry I'm late." She leaned down, giving Kayla a big hug. "How are you doing?"

Kayla nodded positively. "I'm fine."

Marissa leaned back in disbelief. "Kayla, I know what you must be going through. You don't want to believe that your man cheated on you, but you will get over it."

Kayla knew Marissa was just trying to be supportive, but sometimes she got on her last nerve. She held up a hand. "Marissa, I don't want to talk about Paul right now."

"Okay. I understand you don't want to talk about that no good clown."

Kayla flashed her an irritated look. "What did you buy at the store?" She changed the subject.

"I picked up your favorite dessert, cheesecake. I thought it might cheer you up."

Kayla grinned. "Thanks. I definitely need it the way I'm feeling."

"I have been there too many times with Randall. Cheesecake always does the trick. I'll go and get us a slice."

"Already done." Cage appeared from the kitchen. He placed a slice of cheesecake in front of each of the women. "I figured you could use a slice. I know how women like to drown their pain in sweets."

Both women chuckled.

"Oh, I love you." Marissa beamed, shoveling the dessert in her mouth. "Delicious."

"You can run it off in PT tomorrow morning," Cage stated. "Well, ladies, I'm going to get out of here, so you can dog men out." He focused on Kayla. "I will call you later." He nodded toward Marissa. "Specialist Poe."

Kayla found herself looking forward to Cage's call.

"And yes, we are going to talk about you men when you leave," she said.

Cage chuckled and sauntered to the door, closing it behind him.

"Things heating up between you two?" Marissa asked.

"What makes you say that?"

"Just an observation. I know how he feels about you and so do you. I just don't think it's wise for you to be spending time alone with him."

Kayla leaned back in the sofa cushion. "Thanks for the advice, Oprah, but I can handle Cage."

"That's what I'm afraid of. Just be careful."

"Yes, ma'am," Kayla joked, but she knew Marissa was right. She became serious. "Love isn't for me. I finally get what you were trying to tell me about love. What you went through with Randall." She waved a hand in mid-air. "I'm done. Love hurts too much."

"You can't write off love because things didn't work out with Paul." Marissa took another bite of cheesecake.

"I'll leave love to you and everybody else."

"You're just hurting right now. You will get over him and meet the right man." Marissa knew Kayla was in pain and needed time. "Why don't we talk about something else?"

"Like what?"

"I spoke to Liz a while ago."

"How is she?"

"She says she's fine. Just going through the aches and pains of being pregnant."

"If that were true, she wouldn't have been home the past couple of days. I'm going to go see her later." Kayla placed the empty saucer on the coffee table. She was worried about Liz. She knew from Liz's last office visit that her blood pressure was high. The doctor insisted she try not to worry and rest as much as she could, but she couldn't help but worry. She'd been feeling uncomfortable the past couple of days as she had dizzy spells, experienced vomiting, and complained of a headache. She made an appointment to see Dr. Maundry. He checked her over, ran some tests, and insisted she get some rest. Kayla made it a daily priority to check on Liz.

"I told her to call me if she needed anything," Marissa chimed in.

"That was nice of you." Kayla leaned forward, knowing how difficult it was to offer. "She needed to hear that."

"She didn't say so."

"You know Liz," Kayla defended. "To proud to ask for help. That's why we have to check on her, make sure she's okay."

Marissa smiled coyly. "Even if she doesn't want my help."

"Come on, Marissa, be the bigger person."

"Yeah. Yeah." Marissa joked to cover her uneasiness. "Did I tell you I met a new guy?" Marissa smiled as she thought about Jason. Since giving him her number, they'd spoken for hours on end everyday. Their conversation began with discussions of Randall, but then the topic switched to them going out. They'd been on a couple of dates, and she was looking forward to their date Friday night.

She couldn't help but see Randall around the unit, but with sheer willpower, she hadn't spoken to him. He hadn't tried to speak to her. She didn't know how she felt about his sudden turn off.

"No," Kayla replied, "you didn't tell me. Who is he?"

"His name is Jason Bain."

Kayla frowned. She tried to place the name and drew a blank. "Where did you meet him?" She was glad to hear that she'd moved on from Randall.

Marissa shifted nervously. "Randall introduced us."

Kayla's eyes stretched. "What?"

Marissa wrung her hands together. "He's a friend of Randall. He was the one who introduced us."

Kayla couldn't believe what Marissa was saying. "He's Randall's friend?"

"Yes." She knew how Kayla would react when she told her about Jason.

"You'd better explain yourself, Marissa. Going out with your ex's best friend is foul."

Marissa tilted her head to one side. She was silent a moment. "I know it looks bad, but Jason is nice to me. We have a good time."

Kayla gave her a skeptical look. "You're not going out with him to get back at Randall?"

Marissa chuckled. "It started out with me talking to him about Randall, you know to get even with him, but we began going out, spending time together, and found out we have a lot in common. He's really a great guy. Good looking. Funny," she said dreamily. "And he treats me like a lady. Something Randall never did. I know that now. He's for real, you know."

"What about Randall? You were crazy about him."

"Not anymore," Marissa threw back at her. "I'm happy and enjoying myself."

Kayla noticed how Marissa beamed as she spoke about the new man in her life. She hadn't seen that expression on her face in a long time. It was good to see. "Take your own advice," Kayla said. "Be careful. Who knows what Randall will do when he finds out."

"Oh, and one more thing about Jason," Marissa said. She had Kayla's full attention. "He's white." Marissa tried not to laugh as she watched Kayla fall back on the sofa from surprise.

ʘϠ

Paul listened patiently as Liz scolded him about mistreating Kayla. He felt like a jerk. It was true that he'd allowed himself to get into an unforgivable situation, yet he had to find a way to clear things up with Kayla before he left for Fort Bragg. Nothing happened between him and Cheryl. It wasn't that he wasn't guilty because he was on the verge of consummating their evening when Kayla rang the doorbell. After the argument with Kayla, he threw a not-too-happy Cheryl out the door. He'd come to his senses, but it was too late, the damage had been done.

"I don't have an excuse," Paul said, exhaustion attacking him at every angle. He hadn't gotten much sleep the past couple of nights, trying to come to grips with the emotional ride his mind was on. As the effects of the alcohol wore off, he replayed the scene between him and Kayla. It was difficult for his mind to understand that he'd ruined everything.

"I know you don't have an excuse," Liz said, rolling her head as only a black woman could do. She sat at the dining room table and linked her hands over her stomach. Paul took the chair next to her. "How could you do that to her, Paul?"

Paul couldn't look Liz in the face. He hung his head. "I don't know what I was thinking," he replied.

"You weren't thinking."

"I was hurt after she turned me down. I went to the bar, got drunk, ran into Cheryl, and you know the rest. Have you heard from Kayla today?"

Liz glanced up at Paul. "Yes. She's dropping by later."

"I need to talk to her. Tell her how sorry I am. I didn't mean to hurt her. I would drop by her place, but I fear for my life."

"Good decision. You think my place is a safe haven?"

"Yes."

"I don't know how she will react to seeing you here."

He nodded. "I will never find another woman like Kayla or ever open up to a woman like her. I know you know what I'm talking about. I love Kayla. I messed up. I want to apologize to her. I don't want to leave with hard feelings between us."

"I do understand." A faraway look appeared in her eyes when she thought about Timothy. "But I think it may be too late for you to apologize."

Paul stood. He was trying to get used to Kayla not being in his life. It was a void he'd never be able to fill. "I have to try. It's the least I can do. "Whatever happens after," he shrugged, "I don't know."

"It's your funeral."

"Have you eaten?" Paul asked. "I promised Shupe I would look after you."

"Yes, we have eaten." She rubbed her abdomen again.

"Have you heard from Shupe?"

Liz dropped her eyes. "Not recently."

Paul reached out, clasping her hand in his. "No news is good news. We can take comfort in that." He offered a reassuring smile.

"Anything from your brother?"

"Nothing in the last week. The last time we spoke, he was doing okay. Just homesick."

"With everything that's going on, I can't believe you still want to join Special Forces."

Paul paused. "One time I knew for sure. Since I met Kayla, I don't know."

The chiming of the doorbell interrupted their conversation.

Paul gave Liz a questioning stare, to which she replied, "Like I said, it's your funeral."

Paul headed toward the door. It was probably Kayla. He collected his thoughts all the way to the door and took a deep breath to compose himself.

He opened the door to Kayla. She looked startled when her eyes landed on him. Paul breathed in slowly at the sight of her. His gaze took in her form-fitting, low cut shirt, which emphasized her full breasts. His gaze dropped to her flat, hard abdomen. He sucked in a deep breath and forced his gaze back to her face. "We need to talk."

She shot him a look filled with daggers. "I have nothing to say to you," she said, before turning and rushing down the sidewalk. She rushed toward her car, but Paul grabbed her by the arm, turning her around to face him.

"I just want to apologize for what happened."

"I don't want to hear it."

"I messed up, Kayla. I know it." He placed his hand to his chest. "I just want to say I'm sorry. I apologize, and I'm asking for your forgiveness."

Kayla was speechless. She couldn't believe he would ask for forgiveness, especially after the way he'd treated her. "You can't be serious." Kayla couldn't believe his nerve.

"Look, you and I are through. Keep your apology."

"I get it. Just listen to me. Let me explain what happened."

Kayla folded her arms across her chest in defiance. "What happened, Paul? You fell and landed in bed with her?"

Paul frowned. "No. After you turned me down," he said, in a soft voice, "I wound up at Cadence. Had a little bit too much to drink and well . . . " His voice trailed off.

"You slept with another woman." Kayla finished for him, as she envisioned him making love to another woman."

"You really believe that I proposed to you and took another woman to bed? I love you, Kayla. I would never do that to you."

"I found you with her. I know what I saw. How do I know nothing happened?"

"Because I said so."

"And I don't believe you."

"Look, I know I put myself in that predicament. I made a mistake. Haven't you ever made a mistake?"

Kayla dropped her eyes from his. She made mistakes. Lots of them. She thought her biggest mistake was turning down his proposal, but in the moment, it had felt like the right decision. She cleared her throat. "Yes, I have. What does that have to do with anything?"

"So have I. I just want to clear things between us."

"You know what, it doesn't matter because like you said you put yourself in that situation, which means you can't be trusted." Without giving him a chance to respond, she turned and headed toward her car.

The words came from her lips, but Kayla didn't know what to feel. She experienced so many mixed emotions. One part of her was elated to see Paul; another part was furious at the sight of him.

"Kayla," Paul replied, grabbing her hand, grateful for the opportunity to touch her.

"Paul, forget it."

"That's not why I stopped you." Kayla looked confused. "Are you going to see Liz? She needs you right now."

The color drained from Kayla's face from embarrassment. "Yes, that's where I was going." She hastily turned in the opposite direction.

Paul smiled softly, then turned and headed for his truck. With a quick wave of the hand, he drove off.

"Did you see Paul?" Liz asked, when Kayla came through the door.

"I saw him." Kayla dropped down in the chair opposite Liz. She looked up to see Liz, eyeing her closely. "What?"

"Did you talk to him?"

"It's more like he spoke and I listened." No matter how angry she was, she couldn't deny she had been happy to see him. He looked a little tired, but it did not take away from his handsome looks.

"Nothing to say to him, huh?" Liz removed the two glasses from the dining room table and strolled into the kitchen. Kayla trailed after her. Liz opened the dishwasher and began to load it with dishes. Kayla smacked her hand.

"Let me do that," she scolded. "Shouldn't you be resting or something?"

"I'm pregnant, not helpless."

"Dr. Maundry wants you to rest. If you don't follow his orders, I will have to call him." Kayla placed the remainder of the dishes in the machine and turned it on.

"You're ignoring my question about Paul. What did you two talk about?"

Kayla rolled her eyes, reached up in the cabinet, and

removed a box of cherry-flavored pop tarts. Besides cheesecake, it was one of her favorite snacks. She tore open the package and took a bite. "It was really nothing," she replied, as she leaned against the counter.

"Nothing?" Liz repeated in disbelief. "When he spoke to me, he had a lot to say."

"Then you know what he said."

"Kayla, don't you think you're being a little too hard on him?"

Kayla straightened. She had a look of surprise on her face. "He cheated on me. He's lucky he's still breathing."

Liz spread her hands apart. "I'm just saying you're not innocent in this whole thing."

"Are you saying I drove him into the arms of another woman?"

"I believe your actions did," Liz answered.

"If it was Timothy," Kayla said, her voice rising, "you would be ready to kill both of them, and you know it."

Liz sighed. "You're right. Paul told you what happened?"

"Yes, he told me. I turned him down. He went to the bar, got drunk, and picked up some hoochie." The more Kayla thought about it, the angrier she became.

"He told you nothing happened?"

"He told me that, too," Kayla quipped. "If you believe that, I have some swamp land in Louisiana to sell you."

"You really believe he slept with her?"

"I saw her wearing nothing but his shirt. Two plus two equals four."

Chapter Fifteen

"I really had a good time, Jason," Marissa said, as they stood in front of her barracks' steps.

Jason reached out and took her hand in his. "All we did was take a stroll around post. It's not the type of date I was expecting, but as long as I'm with you, it doesn't matter." He lifted her chin up.

"I know. I didn't really want to go out."

"You're not afraid of running into Randall, are you?"

"No," she said on a long breath. "It has nothing to do with Randall. I just wanted to spend time alone with you."

"I'm not going to argue with that, but we haven't been on a real date. People are beginning to think you don't exist."

Marissa took a seat on the steps. "What people?"

Jason dropped down, facing her. "My friends and family. Everyone wants to meet you. I figured we haven't been out because of Randall. For the life of me, I can't figure out what you ever saw in the guy."

Marissa shrugged. "When we first began dating, he was nice, attentive, caring, and loving, and then he did a 360 on me."

"I'm not trying to run him down. He seems like an okay dude, but you should be with someone you have more in common with." He reached out and removed a strand of blonde hair from her face.

Marissa smiled over at him. "Referring to yourself?"

He inclined his blonde head. "You know it. I was attracted to you the first time I saw you. I was jealous of him. I'm not going to lie; I wanted you for myself." To her surprise, she felt a tremor of desire racing through her. Her cheek colored from the touch of his hand.

"As long as we're being honest, I thought you were cute the day Randall bought you to my place." She tilted her face up toward him, grinning.

"But?"

"But nothing." Marissa blushed.

"I need to ask you something, Marissa." The tone of his voice was serious.

"Sure. What is it?"

"How many white guys have you been out with?"

Marissa leaned back in surprise at the question. Though she didn't know why, it was a question she wasn't used to answering. "Why?"

He laced his fingers together. "Just curious."

Her eyes flickered. She swallowed the lump in her throat. She knew some white guys looked down their noses at white women who had been with black guys. You would think in today's society that racism didn't exist, but it's very much alive.

"Does it matter?" she said, in a soft voice.

He lowered his head and shook it slowly from side-to-side. "I really like you, Marissa. I need to know that I stand a chance with you. I heard you only dated black guys, which is why I was surprised you gave me your number."

She nervously tucked a strand of blonde hair behind her

ear. "Well, counting the guy I dated in sixth grade, and you, that makes two."

He nodded and clapped his hands together. "Two, huh?"

"Is this going to be a problem?" she asked. "I'm not going to apologize for who I dated in the past."

"I never asked you to apologize for anything. I just need to know where I stand with you."

"I wouldn't be here if I wasn't interested in you. You don't need to worry about Randall," she assured him.

A moment of silence fell between them. She looked over to find Jason, admiring the June starry night. It was a picture perfect scene. Jason was the first to break the silence. "I believe you. Have you heard anything else about being deployed?"

"No. I hope they forget about 32nd CSH."

"I hear ya," Jason chimed in. "I don't want to see you go. I just found you."

"The only place I want to go is in a classroom at Penn State," Marissa said. "You ever thought about joining the armed forces?" Since he had been hanging out with Randall, she thought Jason was a soldier. She was surprised to find out he was a college student and in his second year of law school at American University.

Jason chuckled. "Are you kidding? I have never thought about it. Not to mention my father would kill me."

Marissa joined in his laughter. "My parents talked me into going. Money for college."

"I had to beg my parents to allow me to work at IHOP," he continued. Jason told her his family was from Houston. His father worked for the District Attorney's office and was pretty well-off. After graduating law school,

Jason hoped to become a prosecuting attorney, like his father. "It's only a couple of days a week, but it helps to break the monotony of studying all of the time."

"To become a successful attorney, you need to study."

Jason's large hand took Marissa's face and held it gently. His finger tenderly traced the outline of her cheekbone. "I have now found something better to study."

A shiver raced through her, and she knew that it wasn't going to be difficult to get over Randall. Jason was going places in his life. She wanted to be a part of his world. She wouldn't mind one day becoming the wife of an attorney. A Congressman? A Senator?

She watched as his lips slowly descended to meet hers. Jason forced her lips open with his thrusting tongue; their tongues began a special mating match, sweet and delicious. She didn't care who was looking and deepened the kiss.

The clearing of a throat interrupted the kiss. They looked up to see Sergeant Cage gawking at them.

"You want to take this to a room? And not your barrack room," he quickly added.

Marissa giggled like a schoolgirl. "Hi, Sergeant Cage." She stood. Jason followed her movement.

Jason glanced at his watch. "I…uh…better get going. I have some studying to do." He gave Marissa a quick kiss on the lips before strolling to his tan Sentra.

Cage watched Jason wave, then drive off. He refocused on Marissa. "He's kind of light for your taste, isn't he?"

"Ha. Ha," Marissa teased. "What are you doing here so late?"

"Well, if you must know, Specialist, I'm checking up on my soldiers."

"I'm doing fine."

"So I noticed. What happened with Randall?"

Her heart hammered at the mention of his name. But she had to move on. "We're through."

Cage flashed her a skeptical look. "You sure about that?"

"I have to be, Sergeant Cage. He's not good for me."

"That soldier is bad news. I'm glad to see you have finally come to your senses."

Marissa nodded in approval.

"Have you seen Private Springs?"

"No. I haven't seen her in the past couple of days."

Cage took a deep breath. "She hasn't been in formation or work the past couple of days, and she's still on extra duty."

⟡ ⟡

"I can't believe it went down like that," Paul was saying, as Victor and Gerald listened. They were at Victor's home, sitting in the living room. He'd just finished filling them in on the latest drama between him and Kayla.

"I can't believe you got caught," Gerald threw in. "I thought I taught you better than that. Never let the woman catch you."

"Give it a rest, Gerald," Victor scolded.

Gerald threw up his hands. "I'm just saying, if you're going to cheat, don't get caught."

"Don't you have something to do down at the club?" With a tip of his head, Victor motioned for his brother to leave him and Paul alone.

Gerald gave Victor a look of annoyance. "I have to check on the plans for your going away party," he mumbled, heading toward the door.

"Don't listen to Gerald," Victor said, as the door closed. "He has never been in a committed relationship and will never understand what you're going through."

"He may have the right idea. Never fall in love. No strings. Just get what you can get and get out." Paul strolled into the kitchen, opened the refrigerator door, and took out a can of Sprite. He popped the top and took a long swallow.

"Isn't that what got you in this mess?" Victor asked, bringing up the rear.

Paul turned toward Victor. "Yeah, but if I would have known things were going to go down like this, I would have gotten some."

Victor glanced at him and shook his head. "You don't mean that."

"No. I don't. I'm just mad at myself for ruining things."

They strolled back into the living room.

"I'm sure you apologized."

"It didn't help." Paul dropped down on the sofa. "With Kayla, it seems like I'm always apologizing for something."

Victor chuckled.

Paul glanced at him from the corner of his eyes. "What's so funny?"

"You. I remember when you and Dina broke up. You swore off love, said you were going to be a professional player. Kayla has had you going since you met her."

Paul shook his head in disbelief. "Tell me about it."

"I can't believe you proposed."

"This brother was desperate."

"I'm sorry I missed it." Victor shrugged. "Who knows, maybe things will work out later on, you never know."

Paul frowned. "No. It's over," he said quietly. "Kayla made it perfectly clear that she wants no part of me." He stood. "Let's head over to the club and check on Gerald and the plans for my party."

Victor patted Paul on the back.

"If we let him, Gerald will book only female strippers." The idea of a room full of half-naked women brought a smile to Paul's face, then his mind switched to Kayla. It was a half-naked woman that ended their relationship. "That's the last thing I need."

"You sure about that?" Victor asked, trailing Paul out the door.

α β

Kayla and Cage sat in the back row of the Majestic Theater in downtown Silver Spring. Kayla hadn't been to a movie in months. When Cage asked her if she wanted to go, she jumped at the chance and insisted on choosing the movie.

"The Rock is so fine," she whispered to Cage. They were seated in the last row of the large theater. He seemed to be enjoying the *Gridiron Gang*. She was glad he'd invited her out. Whether The Rock was wrestling in the ring or acting on the movie screen, he was easy on the eyes.

"I can't believe I let you talk me into seeing this movie so you can drool over The Rock."

"That wasn't the only reason I chose the movie. He's a great actor and it has a good plot."

"Yeah right," Cage said, turning his attention back to the screen.

When the movie was over, they headed back to Kayla's place. Cage was anxious to see the first game of the playoffs. The Washington Wizards were playing the Cleveland

Cavaliers. He led her to the car. He opened the car door for her, walked around, and settled in the driver's seat.

"Who's your team?" Kayla inquired. She wasn't a huge basketball fan, but managed to catch some games on television.

"I have to go with Cleveland. Lebron James is a beast. He's going to give Washington problems."

"I'm sticking with the home team, Washington."

"And you're going to lose," Cage bragged.

"We will see."

Cage glanced at her in surprise. "I didn't know you followed basketball. That's something else we have in common."

"I don't really follow it, but I manage to catch a Wizard's game from time to time. I like Gilbert Arenas."

Cage made a face. "He's all right."

"Men and sports."

"What can I say? Men like to compete."

"Yeah, you like to cheat," Kayla joked.

Cage threw his head back in laughter. "I said compete, not cheat. What are you saying—all men cheat because your man did it to you?" He was challenging her.

"That's exactly what I'm saying."

"You know that is not true. And you know women cheat, too."

Kayla didn't back down. "I never said women don't cheat, but I'm talking about men right now."

Cage glanced over at her. "All men are not dogs. There are some good men left, like me. Men who know how to treat a woman."

"Let's not spoil the evening talking about cheating. We're having a good time."

"You brought up the subject. I was putting it out there." He glanced over at her to register her response. When he didn't get an answer, he reached out, raising the back of her hand to his lips. "I can't help it if I can't get you out of my system." He parked the car in the parking lot of a 7-Eleven. "I'm going to pick up a few snacks for the game. "I'll be right back."

They made it to her place ten minutes before tip-off. Kayla headed into the kitchen and placed the bag of popcorn into the microwave. A few minutes later, she appeared in the living room with a bowl of popcorn, two sodas, and a bowl of nachos and cheese.

"Perfect timing," Cage said. "They're about to jump the ball." He rose to his feet to help with the refreshments. Kayla sat down on the sofa beside him.

"Way to start out," Cage yelled, when Lebron James hit a three-pointer from the right corner on his first possession.

"Whatever," Kayla quipped.

"You are just mad because Lebron will be doing that the rest of the game."

"Big talk," Kayla said in a stubborn tone.

"I guarantee Cleveland will get to the finals."

"It will be Washington, and when they do, you will be taking me to one of the games."

Cage leaned back. "I will be more than happy to take you, but I wouldn't count on it."

"Don't try and back out when they win."

"I won't. If they win, I will take you."

She pointed at him and dipped a nacho chip in the cheese. She jumped to her feet when Gilbert hit a three-point basket at the buzzer to end the first quarter.

"He's been doing that all year," Kayla boasted.

Cage dropped his head in amazement. "Yeah, he's a buzzer beater."

"Want a nacho?" She dipped another chip in the warm cheese. "Mm, this is good," she said, as some cheese fell to the side of her mouth. As she used her tongue to retrieve it, she looked up to find Cage staring at her.

"I could have gotten that for you," Cage replied.

"Oh, really?"

"Really?" he said, and refocused on the television.

"I think you are more focused on the game."

Her remark caused his head to snap back around to face her. She leaned over and gave him a kiss on the cheek.

"It's half-time," he said. "Don't play with me, Kayla."

Kayla reached out and gently stroked his cheek. "I'm not playing."

"Where is this coming from?"

"I never said that I didn't want to be with you."

"You want to talk about this with the second half about to start?"

"What if you had to make a choice between me and Lebron? Who would it be?" Kayla asked, as the third quarter began.

"You know you have my undivided attention."

Kayla stood, then sat in Cage's lap. With her finger, she traced the outline of his face, then proceeded to his chin and down to his Adam's apple. Her finger found its way to his chest, where she slid her hand into his shirt and began to unbutton his shirt. Leaning forward, she kissed his eyes, nose, and lips. She heard him take a quick breath. She thrust her tongue in his mouth, and she heard herself purr. She could feel Cage's hardness pressing against her feminine spot. Her breathing became heavy.

"What are we doing, Kayla?"

Not sure, Kayla responded, "What we have been feeling for a long time?"

He searched her face for sincerity. Finding the remote control, he turned off the TV and recaptured her lips. As the kiss deepened, one hand found its way to the small of her back. He began to move his hips in rhythm against hers. Kayla began to match him movement for movement. His hands slid beneath her knees, lifting her off him and onto the sofa. He positioned himself on top of her and kissed her deeply, his tongue continuing its exploration of the hot depths of Kayla's mouth.

She removed his shirt to feel the closeness of him. For a year, they had worked side-by-side and tonight their relationship would escalate to another level. Kayla opened her eyes to find Cage staring at her. She reached out, enclosing her arms around his neck.

Cage stood with Kayla's legs wrapped around his waist. He took her into the bedroom and laid her down in the middle of the bed.

"What about the game?" Kayla asked, a slight smirk on her face.

"I can catch the highlights later. Right now there's another game I'd like to play."

She unbuttoned his pants and slid them over his hips. He removed her shirt, shorts, and then her panties. After removing her bra, his large hand fondled one breast and then the other. His mouth replaced his hands as he suckled her breasts, then he recaptured her lips and his tongue found her breasts again. His tongue traveled to her flat abdomen and down to her navel. His head dropped and her legs parted. He kissed the inside of each thigh.

She could hardly wait as he leaned over the side of the bed and removed a condom from his wallet. She laid her head back on the pillow and closed her eyes, waiting for them to finally become one. Cage made his way back to her and positioned himself above her. A soft gasp escaped her lips. As he was about to enter her, she closed her eyes, but she didn't see Cage's face; she saw Paul's.

"Oh, Paul," she let out. She felt Cage's body freeze in motion. He jumped up, anger etched over his face.

"You called me Paul," he said.

Kayla was in a panic. Embarrassed. She placed both hands over her face. Cage looked for his clothes.

"No. I didn't," she babbled.

"This is the second time that you have burned me. There won't be a third. Why don't you just go back to him, and leave me the hell alone?"

"I made a mistake." Kayla propped herself up on one knee, still in bed. "I didn't mean…"

"No. I made the mistake of trusting you. Thinking you were over him. Now I know you will never be over him. You are in love with him." He dressed in record speed and raced out, slamming the door behind him.

Kayla slumped in bed. She banged her head against the headboard in agitation. She thought she could forget Paul by being with another man. Who was she fooling?

ʘ ⁊

Paul exited his car and hurried up the sidewalk to his apartment building. Caught up in his own thoughts, he didn't hear Cheryl calling his name until she grabbed him by the elbow.

"Didn't you hear me calling you?" she asked, looking up in his face.

"No, I didn't." He knew he shouldn't be mad at her, but he couldn't dismiss the fact that if she had not come on to him, his relationship with Kayla wouldn't be over. "What are you doing here?"

She did a flip-flop with her hand. She was looking like a little girl who wanted something, but was afraid of being told no.

She cleared her throat. "I…uh just wanted to say that I'm sorry about everything."

"Don't worry about it. What's done is done." Paul turned to head toward his apartment. Cheryl put her hand on his shoulder in a passionate gesture.

Paul took a deep sigh. He flashed Cheryl an irritated look. "Is that it?"

"I was just thinking, maybe I can come in. We could sit and talk or finish what we began."

Paul answered without hesitation, "Hell no!" He turned on his heels and continued up the sidewalk without a backward glance. "Woman must have fallen on her head," he muttered under his breath, entering his apartment building.

∞

Marissa didn't know how to react when she ran into Randall inside the training office. She managed to stay away from him as much as possible. She watched as he joked and flirted with another white girl. She appeared to be a few years younger than she was, maybe around eighteen or nineteen. Naïve. Fresh from home, like she had been three years ago. Whenever the girl giggled, Randall would look over in her direction to see if she was watching.

Marissa gulped and looked in the opposite direction. She was outraged, hurt, and in disbelief. She was determined not to let him get next to her. She held her head high, maintaining her composure. A female soldier sat next to her and struck up a conversation. Marissa was grateful for the company. For the moment, it kept her mind off Randall.

A few minutes later, she got the information she needed and headed back to Cage's office.

"You can't avoid me forever," Randall said, running to catch up with her.

She turned to face him. "I'm not trying to avoid you. I just don't have anything to say to you, and I don't want to be in your company."

"So you're going to pretend like you don't know me?" Randall snapped.

She looked at him through intense eyes. "I saw you, Randall. Everyone saw you flirting."

"Hey, I was just making conversation."

"Then why don't you go back and finish your conversation? Leave me alone." Her eyes misted, but she wasn't going to cry. She was more angry than hurt. Since she began seeing Jason, she clearly saw Randall for the dog that he really was. How could she have fallen for him?

"Because I'm talking to you right now," he insisted, his voice rising.

"I'm not listening, so step off." She threw up a hand and waved him off with attitude.

Randall reached out, grabbing her by the hand. "C'mon Marissa. Stop playing. Let's talk."

"You really think I'd talk to you after you were just all

up in another woman's face?" She withdrew her hand quickly. "Get real."

"You know how I am. I flirt. But it doesn't mean anything."

"Neither did I," she said and walked away.

"Marissa." Randall grabbed her hand again. "I get your point. I understand what you were trying to tell me. I didn't respect you. I took you for granted. Let's end this foolishness." He stepped closer to her. His face and eyes appeared sincere. She wasn't listening. "I miss you, Marissa."

She reached up and placed a hand to his cheek. Calmly, she said, "I don't miss you." She turned and began to walk away, but she was halted by an iron grip on her wrist.

"What did you say?" Randall tightened the grip, bending her wrist upward. The pain shot through her arm, causing her to stand on her tiptoes.

"Stop it, Randall," she squealed.

"What's going on, huh?" His face was clouded with anger. "Are you seeing someone else?" He didn't give her time to answer, bending her wrist harder.

"That's none of your business," she mouthed off, just as another jolt of pain flowed through her arm. "Let me go, Randall."

"You bitch, you better not be seeing someone else." He bent her wrist back further and this time the pain was twice as sharp.

"You're hurting me," she yelled, as she tried to remove his hand

Cage and a few other soldiers rushed out of their offices. Randall quickly let her go.

"What's going on out here?" Cage demanded to know.

Neither answered. His eyes shifted to Marissa, who was massaging her wrist. "Specialist Poe, are you all right?"

Marissa threw Randall a cold stare, then glanced over at Sergeant Cage. "I'm fine, Sergeant Cage."

Cage's gaze fell hard on Randall. He pasted on a fake smile. "Everything is fine, Sergeant."

"I didn't ask you, Specialist." Randall's smile slipped. Cage gave them one last look before heading back inside his office.

Marissa stepped forward, staring him in the face. "Don't you ever put your hands on me again," she said, through clenched teeth. "And for the record, I do have a new man." She left him standing in the middle of the hallway, his mouth wide open.

Chapter Sixteen

"I can't believe Randall put his hands on me," Marissa said to Kayla a few minutes later. "He's never done that before." They were walking out of the army shoppette, after picking up some snacks. "The man has lost his mind."

"You never know what you have until it's gone," Kayla added. The statement applied to her and Paul. After the fiasco with Cage, she'd come to the conclusion that Liz was right. She was in love with Paul and just as guilty for their breakup. It was too bad she'd had to drag Cage into the situation. Everything was a mess. "He knows he should have treated you right when you were together."

"Well, it's too late for that now." Marissa was proud she'd stood up to Randall. In the past, she would have folded like a deck of cards. "It's a good thing Sergeant Cage intervened when he did. Who knows what Randall would have done."

Kayla nervously looked away at the mention of Cage's name. Her action didn't escape Marissa, who frowned.

"What is it?" Marissa inquired.

"What's what?" She looked over to Marissa's come-clean look.

"Uh, huh. I know you. What happened? Did you and Sergeant Cage?" She leaned forward and whispered, "You know. Get it on."

"No. We didn't."

Marissa's shoulders sagged in relief.

"We didn't go all of the way," Kayla explained. "I really made a mess of things."

Marissa looked at her friend with concern. It wasn't the time to say *I told you so*. She was going through a lot emotionally since breaking up with Paul. "Well, what happened?"

Between small breaks, Kayla explained what happened between her and Cage.

"I was so embarrassed," she said. "I can't face him. I've been avoiding him all morning."

"I don't know what to say," Marissa gasped. "I'm speechless. I mean. Damn…that is a blow to a man's ego."

"Tell me about it. I'm not angry with him."

"One thing's for sure, you can't avoid him. He's your boss. You're going to have to talk to him sooner or later."

Kayla didn't like that option. She had been up all night, tossing, turning, and rehearsing what she'd say or how she'd react the next time she saw Cage. When she saw him arrive this morning, she hightailed it in the opposite direction. Sooner or later her luck will run out, and she'd have to face him.

"I'm surprise you haven't spoken to him today about Private Springs," Marissa said.

"I know she's AWOL. No one has seen or heard from her in days." A check of her locker revealed she'd only taken civilian clothing. Kayla figured the pressure of not knowing where her daughters were caused her to go AWOL. Though she was in a large amount of trouble, Kayla hoped Private

Springs would phone and explain everything. With the circumstances surrounding her family life, she thought the military might be lenient in punishment. "He hasn't spoken to me about Private Springs," Kayla added. "I have a feeling he won't be talking to me anytime soon."

ʘ ʘ

"I still can't believe it," Liz relayed to Timothy, sounding perky. She wanted to bring him up to date on all the latest news since their last conversation three weeks ago. She leaned back in the recliner, placing her feet up on the ottoman. She cradled the phone between her shoulder and ear; her fingers twisted the phone cord. Cocking a perfectly arched eyebrow, her voice dropped an octave. "I can't believe he did that to Kayla."

"I'm sorry, baby," Timothy said. "Someone was talking to me. I don't believe anything happened between Paul and that other woman."

In the background, Liz could hear other soldiers laughing and talking. "Kayla caught them together and the woman was wearing only a shirt. What do you think?" Liz massaged her temples, trying to head off the headache she was getting. Between Kayla's drama, the hormone changes her body was going through from the pregnancy, and the loneliness she felt with Timothy being in harm's way, she didn't know whether she was coming or going.

"You're kidding."

Liz continued twisting the cord in an attempt to calm her fragile nerves. She purposely left out telling Timothy about Dr. Maundry's orders to stay off her feet for a while.

"Who is she?" Timothy asked. "He never mentioned

another woman to me. All he ever did was talk about Kayla."

"I don't know, but Kayla said she was attractive."

"I'm sure she was."

"What are you saying?"

Timothy sighed. "I'm just saying Paul's a pretty handsome guy. It stands to reason the woman would be, too, that's all. I can understand you standing by Kayla, but baby, get real. She turned him down and hurt him. She made her decision, and my man moved on."

Liz retorted, "He was with the other woman a couple of hours later. He wasn't too hurt."

"Baby," Timothy explained. "Men deal with heartache differently than women. We pretend to be hard, emotionless, but deep down inside we want to be loved, too. Paul was hurt. He dealt with it the best way he knew how. Was he right? No. It's really a shame that it went down like that. I thought they were going to make it. I know Paul is crazy about her." Timothy paused. "With him getting orders for Fort Bragg, maybe things worked out for the best."

"I don't agree. I'm praying for the relationship to work out."

"From what you told me, only God can save the relationship. While you're at it, send one up for me. Now, how's baby Shupe? Everything okay?"

Liz's body tensed. She didn't want Timothy to worry about her and the baby. "Baby Shupe is just fine. Don't worry about us."

"How can I not worry?"

"Because you need to remain focused."

"That's hard to do over here knowing your condition."

"You have to try." Thoughts of him coming home to her and the baby removed all the doubts and fears she'd harbored about losing him. Those negative emotions had been replaced with solid love. Upon Timothy's return, her family would be together. "The baby and I need you. I will never forgive you if you allow anything to happen to you."

Liz could hear him smile over the phone.

"I hear ya," he said. "What could I do without you?"

"I pray I never have to find out." Liz returned the smile she could feel from thousands of miles away. "I love you."

"I love you, too, baby." Timothy cleared his throat. "Enough trivial talk." His voice dropped in a low, sexy tone. "What are you wearing?"

Liz threw her head back and laughed. That was one of the reasons she'd fallen in love with him. He could make her laugh. "A maternity dress. And what you're thinking is what knocked me up."

CR ED

Paul's cellular phone rang as he entered his apartment. He flipped it opened, maneuvering around some moving boxes. After placing an ad on the announcement board for someone to take over his lease, he'd received overwhelming responses for renters. He decided upon an army captain who'd transferred to the area a month ago from Korea. Captain Stork was a newlywed of two months. Paul figured he and Kayla would never live there as husband and wife, so why not rent to someone who would.

"Hello?" He headed into his bedroom and placed his black gym bag in the chair.

"What's up, little brother?" his brother, Devin, asked.

"Devin." Paul grinned. He was glad to hear his brother's voice. "How are you doing?"

"I'm okay under the circumstances."

"When I didn't hear from you, I was beginning to worry."

A deep chuckle came from the other end of the line. "I told you not to worry about me. I can take care of myself. How are things?"

"I was accepted into Special Ops. I leave for Bragg in two weeks."

A silence fell between them.

"Did you hear me, Devin?"

Devin took a deep breath. "Yeah, I heard you. Have you told Mom and Dad?"

"No. I was going to tell them once I'm at Bragg. Paul maneuvered the phone on his shoulder and headed into the living room. He plucked a piece of peppermint candy from the candy jar on the counter and put it into his mouth.

"That's not going to make it any easier to tell them. Call them and let them know what's going on."

"You're right. I'm ready to leave everything behind."

"Running from a woman?"

"What makes you think a woman is involved?"

"I know you. Who is she?"

Paul briefly told Devin about Kayla. He left out the intimate details.

"You really messed up," Devin scolded.

"Best woman I ever met."

"How are you going to fix this?"

Paul knew it was useless arguing with his brother. Ever since his wife, Jennifer, gave him a second chance for cheating on her before they were married, he believed all women were forgiving.

"I tried," he said. "Kayla isn't trying to hear it. She's a very strong, independent woman. It's over between us."

"I didn't think you were the type to give up so easily."

"I'm just being realistic. If the shoe was on the other foot, I don't know if I could be so forgiving."

"I thought you said nothing happened."

"That's true. I told her that, but she didn't believe me."

"If she's worth as much as you say, then try again. Don't give up. I wouldn't be happily married if I had given up. This brother did a lot of begging. You may have to do the same thing. Fight for what you want."

"Not all women are as forgiving as your wife. Plus, matters of the heart can be difficult sometimes."

"You're a Lake," Devin reminded him. "Nothing is too difficult involving love. You need to get back in there and give it another try. Call her up. See what happens."

"She will hang up in my face," Paul said.

After an hour of talking about his messed up situation with Devin, Paul hung up and phoned his parents. They took the news better than he thought they would. Afterward, he was restless. He turned on the TV. He channel surfed for several seconds, then shut it off. He then placed a CD in the player and the smooth sounds of Carl Thomas' "Lady Lay Your Body" filled the room.

While listening to the music, he attempted to finish packing. As a bachelor, he didn't have many household goods. He needed to complete the kitchen and the bathroom.

Several hours later, his nerves were still on edge. Times like this, Paul missed Kayla the most. Devin's advice still rang in his ears. He headed into the bedroom, picked up the phone, and dialed her number. On the third ring, he lost his nerve and hung up.

ଔ ଓ

The phone rang and Kayla grabbed it. She was met by a dial tone. Checking the Caller ID, she was surprised to see Paul's name and number. Without thinking, she pressed star sixty-nine. He answered on the fifth ring.

"Hello?" he answered.

"Paul, you phoned?"

Paul felt his middle tighten at the sound of her voice. He wasn't prepared to speak to her. "I was just calling to see how you were."

"I'm okay." She missed him so much. She was so giddy. She had to compose herself. "What about yourself?" She plopped down on the edge of the sofa.

"I'm finishing up some packing."

"I guess this is it." She didn't try to hide her disappointment. "In a couple of weeks you're leaving."

"Looks like it."

"I'm glad you're getting what you want."

Silence fell between them.

"Not really," Paul said softly. "Again, I just wanted to say how sorry I am. I didn't mean to hurt you, Kayla."

"Then why did you hang up?"

"I figured I was the last person you wanted to talk to."

"If I felt that way, I wouldn't have called you back."

"I can't say I blame you. I was stupid. I allowed my ego to get the best of me. I hurt the person I love. I'm asking you again, Kayla, to forgive me."

Kayla couldn't miss the sadness in his voice. It touched her deep down inside. "I forgive you, Paul. I share part of the blame. If I would have accepted your proposal..." Her voice trailed off.

"No, baby. You were right. I should have given you more time." Paul was on cloud nine just talking to Kayla. He lay down across the bed, wishing she was lying next to him. He missed the times when they would just cuddle in each other's arms and talk.

"Maybe we can talk about it." Paul made the first move, reaching out to her. She didn't want to ruin the opportunity. "Do you have any plans for tomorrow night?"

Paul pepped up. "My cousins are throwing me a going away party at Cadence. It's at 8 p.m. Can you make it?"

"It's a date."

"I'll see you then."

"Yes, you will," Kayla said, in a sultry low tone. After she hung up with Paul, she quickly dialed Victor's number. She had some planning to do.

℘ ℘

"You want me to move to supply?" Kayla swirled around to face Cage. He stood in the middle of her office, returning her empty gaze.

"I think it's best for both of us." Cage's voice was sharp and unfeeling. "We can no longer work together, and you know it."

Kayla understood. She just wished it didn't have to come to this. She enjoyed working in Training. She didn't want to transfer to another section. "I never meant—"

Cage raised a hand to cut her off in mid-sentence. "Sergeant Perry," he placed an emphasis on her last name, "save your apology. I don't want or need it. From now on, our relationship will only be professional. Got that?" He turned and walked out the door without giving her a chance to reply.

251

Kayla quivered from the coldness that pushed throughout her body. She felt bad for what had occurred between them, but she wasn't going to allow it to get her down. Especially now that it looked as if she and Paul had a chance to patch things up between them. That was all that mattered.

A few minutes later, she walked next door to the café. She strolled to the counter and poured herself a cup of coffee. She was still trembling from the confrontation with Cage. She added cream and Sweet N Low. She ordered a glazed donut. She headed to the cashier and paid for the items. On her way out the door, she took a napkin from the stack, blew soft puffs of air in the hot liquid, and carefully took a sip followed by a bite of the donut. She pushed opened the door and ran into First Sergeant Chambers.

"Sergeant Perry," he said, "I need to see you in my office." He glanced at his watch. "Let's say in about ten minutes."

"I'll be there, First Sergeant." She took another sip of coffee, then hurried along the sidewalk, wondering what he wanted to talk to her about. It was the first week of summer, too warm for hot drinks, but she needed the concoction to calm her frazzled nerves.

She made it back to the company just in time to see Randall drive up in his cherry red, renovated Camaro. The window was down and loud Rap music was blasting in the air. He brought the vehicle to an abrupt stop in front of her. Keeping in mind her dislike for him, she cast him a look that could kill him on the spot. She made her way up the barracks' steps.

Randall exited the vehicle and trailed her. "I wasn't going to hit you, Sergeant Perry," he said to her retreating figure.

"Just watch yourself," she said over her right shoulder.

"I need to talk to you, Sergeant Perry."

Kayla frowned before turning to face him. She offered a weak smile. "About what?" she asked, irritated. She didn't want to talk to Randall at all. But they had one thing in common, Marissa. "Or should I say who?"

"Marissa."

"What about her?"

"Can you talk to her for me?"

"What about?"

He threw her a give-me-a-break look. "About us."

Kayla shook her head. "You have to speak to Marissa for yourself."

"I've tried talking to her. She's not listening to me. She told me she has another man."

"I can't blame her."

"Sergeant Perry, I know how you feel about me. You never thought I was good enough for her. I love her. I want her back. Tell me what to do."

"Regardless of what I think, I'm not the one you have to convince."

"We had a relationship, a love that you wouldn't understand. I miss her, and I want her back."

Kayla remembered once hearing the same confession from Marissa. She didn't understand what Marissa was trying to tell her about love and heartache until she'd experienced it firsthand with Paul.

"You're wrong, Specialist Randall. I do understand. But you have to talk to Marissa for yourself. I'm on my way to see First Sergeant. You know he doesn't like to be kept waiting."

Kayla walked to Liz's empty desk and placed her cup of coffee there. Liz was still out of the office on bed rest.

Kayla knocked once and opened the door to First Sergeant Chambers's invitation to enter his office. She threw her shoulders back, stood straight, and assumed the position of parade rest before him.

"Stand at ease," he commanded.

Kayla clasped her hands loosely behind her back.

"I'll get straight to the point." First Sergeant opened the top desk drawer and removed a stack of papers. "Some orders came for you late yesterday evening."

She felt her heart drop in her stomach. What type of orders? Deployment orders to Iraq? College? "Orders, First Sergeant?" she managed to say.

"Congratulations." He handed her the copies of the orders. "Looks like I'll be saluting you one day soon."

Kayla let out the breath she was holding. She was pleased it was the news that she wanted to hear. She would be sitting in a classroom at the University of Maryland instead of on a battlefield come fall.

She accepted the orders, glancing down at them to make sure they were real. A huge smile spread across her face. "Thank you, First Sergeant."

"I'm very happy for you, Sergeant Perry. I know you will make a fine officer."

"I promise I will make you and the army proud." She pressed the orders to her chest in jubilation.

First Sergeant returned her smile. "You better." His expression became serious. "Sergeant Cage tells me he wants to move you to the Supply section. Is something going on I should know about?"

Kayla shrugged. "No, First Sergeant."

First Sergeant glanced at her a moment, as if trying to read her facial expression. He must have been satisfied because he said, "You both worked very well together."

She lowered her gaze. "Yes, we did."

"It looks like you will be clearing at the end of the month. So it doesn't make sense for you to move from the Training section. I will speak with Sergeant Cage. Will you be taking leave before you begin clearing?"

Kayla's face beamed. Going on vacation would fall in line with her plans. She had thirty days to use. She knew how she wanted to spend them and with whom.

ଓ ଇ

"I wish you could be there," Kayla said to Liz, who lay in her bed. "It was you who helped me see the light. Paul and I have a lot to talk about. He just doesn't know how much."

"Being in this bed," Liz said, "I'm missing out on all of the fun."

"I have worked out everything with Victor. He was more than happy to be involved."

Liz giggled with excitement. "I would love to be there to see the look on Paul's face."

Kayla sat down on the foot of the bed and Liz sat up straight. Kayla's mouth curved up in a grin. "This is what I have planned so far."

Chapter Seventeen

Victor flicked on the light. "There's a room full of people at your party," he said, as he walked into the dark office to find Paul stretched out on the sofa, his long legs crossed at the ankle. "The guest of honor is missing."

"The only guest I want to see isn't here."

"If she said she will be here, she will be here."

"Maybe she changed her mind," he said gloomily. "I should have stopped by her place. Called her or something. I didn't want to appear too anxious."

"You did the right thing. Just let the evening unfold," Victor replied. "I guarantee it will be an evening you won't forget." He turned away from Paul to smother the grin on his face. Kayla had informed him of her plan for Paul this evening. He couldn't be happier for his cousin and was more than happy to pitch in.

Paul stood, put on a fake smile, and followed Victor out of the office and into the club. "Let's go get this night over with."

ʘ ʘ

"Do you see him anywhere?" Kayla whispered to Marissa. She craned her neck, looking around the packed club.

"Relax. Relax. The party is probably in another room."

"I didn't think about that." Kayla sucked in a breath and slid a nervous hand over the eggshell white dress she was wearing. Her hair hung loose and full, surrounding her perfectly made up face. Let's go check and see."

The women sauntered toward one of the back rooms. All heads, male and female, followed their movement. As they headed toward one of the door entrances, a good-looking host, in his early twenties, stopped them in their tracks.

"Good evening, ladies. May I help you find something?"

Kayla quickly turned in his direction. "I'm looking for Paul Lake's going away party."

"It's in the Rose Room." He pointed to the end of the hall. "Two doors down. You better hurry. It's filling up fast." He then gave Marissa a slow once over. "If you need anything, anything at all, let me know."

"Thanks, but no, thanks. My man is meeting me here," Marissa said.

"If he doesn't show up…"

"I won't call you," Marissa echoed. She refocused on Kayla and grabbed her by the hand. "C'mon, we have serious business to take care of." Kayla's hand trembled. "Calm down." Marissa led her to the banquet room.

"I'm shaking like a leaf," Kayla whispered.

Marissa patted her on the hand. "This is the beginning of the rest of your life. You got into school. Now, go and get your man."

The women stepped through the doors. The first person they spotted was Victor crossing the dimly lit room. "There is Victor," Kayla said. "I don't see Paul."

"Stay out of sight," Marissa instructed. "I will go and let

Victor know you're here." She disappeared through the thick crowd.

A few minutes later, Victor stood in front of the crowd. "I want to thank everyone for coming out. As always, it's difficult to say goodbye to loved ones. Tonight, we're doing just that. We're saying goodbye to my cousin, Sergeant Paul Lake." He glanced over in Paul's direction, seated at the front table. "As some of you know, he's leaving for Fort Bragg. But before he leaves, there is something we have to give him. Something very special that I know he's going to like very much."

Almost on cue, Kayla appeared from the back of the room.

In a lightning fast motion, Paul jumped from his seat. "Kayla."

Kayla stopped in front of him. A warm sensation flowed through her veins at the sight of him standing in front of her. Paul outstretched his arms, and Kayla walked into them. He held her tightly, as if she might disappear.

Her heart raced, she could barely breathe, but she kept her composure. She was in his arms again. All she wanted to do was show and tell him how much she loved him. Tonight was the perfect time to do it and in front of everybody.

She stepped out of his embrace and took the microphone from Victor. She stood in front of the crowd.

"Kayla?" Paul said, a look of confusion on his face. He glanced over at Victor, Gerald, and Marissa. All three looked like they'd swallowed a canary. "What is she up to?"

"You will see," Marissa replied.

"First, Paul, I want to tell you that I was foolish not to trust you. It jeopardized our relationship." Whistles, loud whoops, and applause followed her admission.

Paul could hardly believe his ears or his eyes. Standing in front of him was Kayla, pouring out her heart to him before the world.

"I love you, Paul, from the bottom of my heart. I never want to live without you." Her eyes pleaded with him as she strolled toward him.

Paul stood rooted to the floor. His knees nearly buckled as he watched the woman he loved drop to one knee in front of him. They'd made amends last night, but he'd never expected this.

"Oh, my God," someone in the crowd said.

"Go on, girl," was followed by another round of applause.

Kayla knew that what she was doing was out of the ordinary for women, but she didn't care. "Marry me, Paul," she said. "Right here. Right now."

Paul could only nod in disbelief.

"Is that a yes or no?" Gerald screamed.

"It's a yes," Paul said, after finding his voice. "Right here. Right now. I will marry you." He helped Kayla to her feet. Taking her in his arms, he twirled her around. Putting her back on her feet, he brought her mouth to his, kissing her deeply.

Victor walked toward them, applauding wildly. "There's going to be a wedding," he announced to the crowd. "You're all invited." He motioned for Reverend Martindale to take his position.

ଓ ଛ

Liz leaned her head back against the headboard. She wondered how the evening was going for Kayla and Paul.

She hated not being there, but hoped everything went as planned. If so, Kayla and Paul would be husband and wife by now. Mr. And Mrs. Paul Lake, she grinned to herself, then grimaced. The pain wouldn't subside. "Oh, God, not again."

She picked up the cellular phone she kept in bed with her in case of emergencies.

She knew Kayla and Paul wouldn't be available. She quickly dialed the number to the one person she never thought she would: Marissa.

The call was finally answered. Loud music, voices talking, and laughing could be heard in the background. Marissa's voice came across the line.

"Hello?"

"Marissa," Liz said, swinging her legs over the side of her bed. "It's Liz. Can you come quick?"

"Liz," Marissa squealed. "What's wrong?"

Liz sat on the edge of the bed. Looking down, she noticed blood on her gown and sheets. "I'm bleeding."

"Hold on, Liz. I'm calling 911. I'm on the way."

⚛ ❧

Marissa made it to Liz's place ten minutes shorter than the usual thirty-minute drive. She was surprised she didn't receive a speeding ticket. Jason appeared to be scared out of his skin. He threw her glances, but he didn't open his mouth. They arrived in time to find Liz being loaded into the back of an ambulance.

Frantic, Marissa threw the car in park and sprinted to the ambulance. "Liz," she yelled out, but didn't get a reply. She focused her attention on the young, white attendant for answers. "How is she?"

"She appears to be in labor. We won't know until we get her to the hospital and evaluate her."

"Marissa. Marissa. Thanks for coming," Liz cried out, reaching for her.

"I'll follow the ambulance and meet you at the hospital," she replied in a soothing voice.

Liz was frantic. "My baby. Don't let anything happen to my baby." A tear slid down her face.

"Liz, everything is going to be fine," Marissa assured her.

"We have to get going." The EMT hopped in the back of the ambulance and closed the doors behind her.

A few minutes later, Marissa rushed through the doors of the Shady Grove Adventist Hospital emergency room. She stood at the registration desk. She couldn't believe how over a matter of hours, her evening had gone from happiness to anxiety.

Several hours ago, she was at Kayla and Paul's wedding. It was a lovely ceremony. They were now on a weeklong honeymoon. Now she paced, awaiting news about Liz and her baby. Her pulse beat uncontrollably as she struggled to keep it together.

Around two in the morning, Liz gave birth to a premature four-pound baby boy by cesarean section. Coming into the world so soon, the baby was rushed to the Neonatal Intensive Care Unit. He was fighting for his life, and Liz was resting.

Dr. Maundry found Marissa and Jason sleeping in the waiting room. He shook Marissa awake. She jumped to her feet.

"How are Liz and the baby?"

"Both are resting comfortably. The first twenty-four

hours are crucial. We will know more in the morning.”

“Can I see her?”

“Not tonight. Come back tomorrow morning. I know Liz will be glad to see you.”

Marissa and Jason left the hospital hand in hand. “I’m glad she called me. I just wish I could have done more.”

“What more could you do? Mom and baby are doing fine.”

Marissa shrugged. “I don’t know.”

Jason wrapped an arm around her waist. “Being with you has never been a dull moment.”

“Stick around.” She leaned over and kissed him softly on the lips. “There’s more to come.”

Jason’s smile widened across his face. “I can’t wait.”

☙ ❧

Sunlight streamed through the curtains of the room. Kayla stretched, feeling tired and satisfied. Yesterday had been a busy day. Planning a wedding at the spur of the moment was more than tiresome, but it had been rewarding.

A reception followed the wedding in another room set aside for them. Victor and Gerald surprised Kayla and Paul with a honeymoon trip to the Poconos and the two exchanged their vows.

Kayla smiled, thinking about the look of surprise on Paul’s face when she proposed. She was now Mrs. Paul Perry-Lake. She glanced over at her husband, sleeping peacefully. A heat wave washed over her as she thought about last night. The sexual positions they’d performed even made her blush. She enjoyed all of them. Thinking about her honeymoon night caused a stirring in her erotic place. She edged closer to Paul. He didn't move. She grinned again. She'd really put something on him. Deciding to let him sleep, she pushed the sheets aside and headed into the bathroom for a shower. Already naked, she opened the shower doors and stepped inside. She turned on the showerhead and allowed the warm water to spray over her body.

"Mm, that feels good," she said aloud.

"I hope you were talking about me." The shower door opened and Paul stepped inside, deliciously nude.

"I thought you were 'sleep."

"You did put me out." He smiled mischievously. "I'm wide awake now. Ready for round two, Mrs. Paul Lake."

She loved the sound of her new name and couldn't help but recognize the gleam of passion in his beautiful brown eyes. It was impossible to ignore the gratifying arousal standing out between his legs.

"I love you," she whispered to him, as she backed up against the tile wall, pulling Paul with her.

"I love you, too," he murmured, pressing his hard, wet body up against her. "I can't believe you're my wife." He moaned huskily with anticipation. "I'm your husband." Paul's hands cupped her nice round, firm bottom, lifted her, and parted her legs in the process. He lifted her higher so that her breasts were even with his mouth."

"That feels so good." She moaned at the excruciating pleasure of his mouth suckling her. "Were you surprised by the proposal?"

With calmness, his expert fingers began working magic over her body. The shower continued to spray hot water on both of them. "I would have been just happy to see you. I never dreamed you would become my wife. But last night you made me the happiest man in the world."

He closed his eyes as he moaned and lifted her once again, wrapping her legs around his waist. Grabbing his own erection, he carefully guided himself inside of her.

"Just come back to me, Paul," she stammered out.

"I will, baby," he whispered on a gasp. She immediately began to feel her womanhood convulse. "I will. I promise."

Paul could feel her climax. He drove deeper inside her.

Kayla could feel him grow larger inside her feminine spot. She felt him release inside her, then tremble.

Placing her feet on the floor, Paul grabbed her face within both of his hands. "This is a new beginning for both of us," he said. "Me in Special Ops. You in nursing school. We will be a good team."

"Forever, Paul," she said softly.

"Forever, Kayla." Paul leaned down, pressing his lips to hers. "I will love you forever."

ℝℤ

The next morning, Marissa and Jason stopped by Liz's apartment to pick up clothing and toiletries before heading to the hospital. As they were getting into Jason's car, a bewildered Randall rushed toward them.

"What's going on?" Randall said, closing the gap between them in record time. "You and Jason good buddies all of a sudden?"

Jason protectively moved between Marissa and Randall. He put an arm around her waist.

"You need to be talking to me," he snapped. "Not Marissa."

"Who are you supposed to be?" Randall yelled.

"I'm her man," Jason screamed back.

Randall's eyes bucked at the news. His face twisted in anger. Jason stood an inch taller than Randall. Both men sized each other up like gladiators ready to do battle, each daring the other to make one false move.

"You were supposed to be my boy, my friend, and this is how you repay me? Sleeping with my lady," Randall asked. He hit himself in the chest expressively with extra emphasis. "That's foul, man." He choked on his own words. He panted at Marissa. "And you, you lowdown—"

"That's enough," Jason threw in.

Randall's voice climbed. "I'm not talking to you, but I'm getting ready to kick your ass." He lunged at Jason.

Marissa stepped between them. The situation was getting out of hand. "Knock it off, guys," she said.

"Bring it on, Randall," Jason spat out.

In the blink of an eye, Randall reached around Marissa, striking Jason in the face. The punch landed on his left eye, staggering him backward. Before Jason could retaliate, Marissa began striking Randall in the chest. Her face turned beet red. "Leave him alone, Randall." She shoved him so hard, he almost lost his balance. "Can't you get it in your head, we are through?" She was screaming at him. "Go home, Randall."

"You were creeping around with Opie, and now you're treating me like I'm the bad guy."

"Randall, you are not a bad guy," Marissa said, sighing. "You are just not the right guy for me."

"And you think Opie here is." He smirked. "You can't be serious. He's not the man for you. I love you, Marissa."

She stood motionless for a moment. A few months ago, she would have given anything to hear those three little words. She thought she loved Randall. Since meeting Jason, she came to realize that the kind of love she felt for Randall wasn't love at all. She deserved better. At the moment, she had that with Jason.

She looked Randall square in the eyes. "I don't love you."

Randall leaned back. He stepped toward Marissa. Marissa could see on his face he was surprised by her revelation.

"You don't mean that, Marissa." His voice softened. "Not after all we have been through. How much we meant to each other. Opie will never love you like I do or care for you like I do."

"You're right," Marissa replied. "Jason loves and treats me like a woman, a person. Something I never had with you. All you did was use me. Disrespect me."

"That's not true," Randall said.

"Yes, it is. It wasn't your fault," Marissa said calmly. "I allowed you to treat me like that, but not anymore." Jason stood next to her. "Jason and I are together. Get used to it."

She watched Randall struggle to keep his composure. "You will be back," he replied sharply.

"No, I won't," Marissa reassured him.

"Yes, you will, because you're a freak, and Opie won't be able to please you the way I did."

Jason tried to leap at Randall, but Marissa held him back. "Don't even bother. That's what he wants. We are not going to give him the satisfaction. Goodbye, Randall."

"When you get tired of Opie," he said, chuckling nastily, "you come on home to Daddy." He glowered at them, turned, and stomped off.

ʘ ‰

"Liz, he's gorgeous," Marissa said, entering Liz's room. She'd stopped at the hospital gift shop and purchased several *It's A Boy* blue balloons and a plant. "He has Timothy's nose and forehead."

Liz gingerly sat up straight in the bed. She was glowing. Motherhood agreed with her. "He is beautiful," she said. "Just like his daddy. I can't wait to take him home."

"Did the doctor say how long he will be in the NICU?"

"They don't know for sure. It all depends on how well he does. If..." Liz started to say.

"When?" Marissa smiled and corrected.

Liz nodded in agreement. She was all smiles. "When he gains more weight and his vital signs remain stable, I can take him home."

"You will be taking him home before you know it." Marissa placed the plant on the table next to the bed. She tied the balloon strings to the bedrail.

"Thank you," Liz replied.

Marissa dragged the chair closer to the bed and placed the bag in it. "I hope I brought everything you asked for."

Liz rummaged through the overnight bag Marissa brought earlier. "Everything is here. Thanks, again."

A moment of awkward silence fell between the two women.

Marissa was the first to break the silence. "Is Timothy coming home?"

"I doubt it. I sent a message through the Red Cross, letting him know he's a father. Of course, I will send him pictures."

"He's going to love the pictures."

Silence fell between the two women again.

"So, tell me," Liz began, "how was the wedding?"

Marissa's face broke into a wide grin. "Liz, it was beautiful." She filled Liz in on how smoothly the ladies' plans had been executed. "Victor videotaped it. He promised to give us a copy."

"I wish I could have been there. I knew they would make a good couple. They were made for each other. It will be rough for a while with her in school and Paul in OPS, but the love they have for each other is strong. Unbreakable."

"Like you and Timothy," Marissa added.

"I'd like to think so. We have had our ups and downs like most couples. But our love has pulled us through," Liz said. She paused for a moment and looked at Marissa, who sat quietly and attentively beside her. "We have had our moments, too."

Marissa pepped up.

"I'm sorry, Marissa," Liz said. "I was so caught up in my own personal grief and hatred that I took it out on you. You didn't deserve that."

"It's okay," Marissa said.

"You're being polite. I said some pretty nasty things to you. I want to thank you for overlooking my ignorance. It says a lot about you."

"I just want us to put the past behind us. Move ahead."

"Good. I'm hoping we can be friends."

The grin on Marissa's face widened. "Really?"

"What the hell, you're always around," Liz teased. "We may as well get along. Call a truce?"

"May as well," Marissa agreed.

"So, uh, who's the white boy you're hanging out with?"

Jason had dropped Marissa off at the hospital and was returning later to pick her up.

"That's my new man, Jason."

Liz leaned her head to one side. She placed a hand to her chest, pretending a heart attack. "You, with a white guy. It's going to snow in June."

☙ ❧

"Why didn't you call me?" Kayla asked the following week. She'd returned from her honeymoon to find a voicemail message from Marissa, informing her that Liz delivered Baby Shupe. Both mother and son were doing well.

"You were on your honeymoon. The last thing you needed to do was worry or think about me." Liz slowly walked over to her spacious closet. She replaced the house slippers on her feet. "Besides, Marissa was here."

Kayla folded her arms to her chest. "I heard you guys called a truce."

"I don't know how long it will last, but I'm willing to give it a try."

"It's a huge step in putting your past behind you."

Liz waved a hand in mid-air. "I know. Have you met Jason?" she asked, changing the subject.

"I have. He seems like a nice guy. He treats her good. That's the most important thing, and she's happy."

"Very true. What time is Paul leaving in the morning?"

Kayla dipped her head. "He's driving out around eight o'clock."

Liz couldn't miss the somber expression on Kayla's face. She walked over and gently placed a hand on her back in comfort. "Still worried, huh?"

Kayla shook her head to one side. "Yes. What if something…" Her voice trailed off.

"I know." Liz could relate to the uncertainty of a loved one being in harm's way.

"How do you do it, Liz? How do you keep it together? Dealing with the stress of not knowing what or if something is going to happen. It's like waiting for a shoe to drop. It's supposed to be easy for me being a soldier, but it isn't. I'm scared out of my mind."

"It's not easy, Kayla. You just have to take it one day at a time. Keep yourself busy. You will have nursing school to keep your mind occupied. Before you know it, Tim, Paul, and Devin will be back. You will see," She tried to cheer Kayla up as best she could.

Kayla gave her a weak smile. She nodded. "You're right. Thanks for listening."

"That's what I'm here for. We have to give each other support. We're both going through the same thing right now. Anytime you need to talk, I'm here." Liz reached out, giving Kayla a tight hug. A knock on the door interrupted them. "Come in," Liz answered.

Paul stuck his head around the bedroom door. "You ladies ready to go to the hospital?"

"Yes, we are," Liz said, as she handed Kayla several stuffed teddy bears to place in her son's crib. Timothy Antoine Shupe II was doing better. The doctors moved him into an open crib. He should be coming home within another month or so.

Paul moved further into the room. He looked at his wife's troubled face. "Honey, are you all right?" He tilted her chin up to look directly into her eyes. She tried to smile. The last couple of days she'd been a little distant. He knew it was because it was almost time for him to leave for Fort Bragg.

"I'm fine," Kayla said.

He planted a quick kiss on her lips. "Okay. Let me take those." He removed the stuffed animals from her hand. "I will be out in the car. I can't wait to see what the little rug rat looks like," he joked.

"Who are you calling a rug rat?" Liz chimed in animation. "I can't wait until you and Kayla have your little…" She couldn't come up with a good comeback. "…I can't think of anything right now."

They all burst out laughing.

"Good comeback, Liz," Kayla closed the door behind them.

ର ଡ

"I don't know how I'm going to make it," Kayla said to herself in a low, deep growl of anguish the next morning, as she watched the brake light of the truck make a left at the light and disappear. Marissa and Liz were there for moral support, but it didn't make his departure easier.

Paul promised to phone, e-mail, and write as much as possible. But Kayla knew with the type of training he was going into, communication from her new husband would be nonexistent for a while.

Kayla's thoughts shifted to Paul, their whirlwind romance, marriage, and honeymoon. The past couple of months they had been together and the love they had for each other. She hoped and prayed it would be enough to carry them through all that lay ahead.

"Kayla?" Liz inquired. "Are you all right?"

She looked back at Liz and Marissa standing on the sidewalk. "I'm fine."

Kayla turned and headed back toward them. Liz and Marissa placed their arms around her in comfort. They said a prayer for their loved ones to return home safely.

Several days later, Kayla flew to Alabama to spend two weeks with her parents. She divided the time between her mother and father's home. Her parents were not pleased that she'd gotten married without them meeting the groom. Paul managed to call. Her father took the opportunity to interrogate his new son-in-law.

Before she knew it, her leave was over, and she headed back to 32nd CSH. Now that Paul was gone, she looked forward to out-processing and attending college in a month. Being in nursing school would give her the opportunity to keep her mind off Paul. She knew it was going to be easier said than done. She had no other choice.

She didn't even want to think about the lonely nights without Paul, the warmth and feel of his body on hers as he lay on top of her: The sounds of their heavy breathing, moans, and groans of passion often haunted her in the middle of the night. The thoughts caused a moist pool at her core. She was lonely. It was unbearable. Tonight would be another cold shower and another round with her favorite toys.

Eighteen Months Later

ayla listened to the seven-to-three shift nurse at the Walter Reed Army Center. She was scheduled to graduate in May as a second lieutenant. After graduating, her next assignment would be at Womack Army Community Hospital at Fort Bragg. She would be stationed with her husband.

So much had happened in the last year and a half. Timothy returned from Iraq a month ago. Marissa was going into her junior year at Penn State. She and Jason were engaged. Sergeant Cage, Specialist Randall, and several other soldiers from the 32nd were deployed to Kuwait. Private Springs never returned. She was dishonorably discharged from the army. Devin suffered a minor injury to his arm. His unit was being deployed to Iraq for a second tour in a year.

Kayla hadn't seen Paul in six months. Since then, he had been deployed on mission after mission. Because of the secrecy surrounding the missions, he wasn't allowed to tell her where he was going, what he was doing, or when he'd return.

"We're expecting four soldiers this evening from Germany," Captain Borrows relayed. "Three are litter patients and one is ambulatory."

Kayla removed the copy of the flight manifest from Captain Borrows's hand. "Who are they?" Her eyes scanned the list of names.

"Lieutenant Lake's name isn't on the list," Captain Borrows assured her.

She breathed a sigh of relief. "Thank God," Kayla managed to say.

Whenever a flight from Germany was due in, Kayla would check the roster to make sure Paul's name wasn't listed among the injured.

"You and I both know that there are often add-ons," Kayla added.

"You're reading too much into it. His name isn't on the list, that's enough. Leave it at that." Captain Borrows rolled her chair into position behind the computer. "So let's get to work."

☙ ❧

Paul sat the duffel bag outside the door with a thump. He pulled the keys from his uniform pocket, activated the lock, and entered the apartment. He was home. All he needed now was to see his wife. He glanced at his watch. She was due home in a couple of hours.

The team landed back on U.S. soil several days ago. He was debriefed, and they were allowed to go on leave. Though he was tired and needed much rest, since he'd only seen his wife once within the last six months all he wanted to do was immerse himself completely in Kayla.

Paul made his way to the shower. In fifteen minutes, he was dressed in black army shorts and a T-shirt. In bare feet, he made his way to the refrigerator. He knew she hadn't prepared anything. He opened the freezer and found a pair of pork chops. Before long, the kitchen was filled with a mouth-watering aroma. While the chops marinated, he tossed a salad and baked some potatoes. He popped some rolls into the oven. For dessert, he discovered a strawberry cheesecake in the freezer. Her favorite.

He set the table for two, adding candles, dimming the lights, and lowering Luther Vandross' music to set an intimate mood. This time it would be Kayla who was going to be surprised, he thought to himself.

Å ℯ

"I'll see you tomorrow." Kayla waved to Captain Borrows, sliding behind the wheel of her car. Twenty minutes later, she turned onto Brackett Street. Her apartment was on the bottom level. She could see a dim light in the living room window. Her brain kicked into high gear, registering the fact that Paul must be at home. Her heart began to gallop into full speed. She was out the car door and rushing to the apartment in record speed.

"Paul?" she called, closing the door and tossing her purse on the sofa cushion. She spotted his duffel bag in the middle of the floor. He was really there.

"In the dining room," he answered.

A soft gasp escaped her when he stepped from the dining room. He wasn't an apparition. He was real. Her heart danced with excitement.

"Hi, baby." He moved toward her to prove he was actually there.

Kayla suddenly ran toward him. Paul opened his arms and she flew into them. He caught her and twirled her around in mid-air. When he set her down and gazed into her eyes, she saw love and passion in them.

"I've missed you so much." His voice was laced with emotion, making her insides tingle. His mouth swooped down to capture hers. The kiss began softly, with tenderness, and deepened with demanding mastery as their tongues took on the special kind of intimacy that only they shared. Kayla responded to his kiss with the same passion that blew her mind every time she was in his arms.

She angled his head to one side, thrusting her tongue deeper inside his mouth. His lips tasted so good. "I can't believe you're here," she spoke into his neck. Then she kissed the tip of his nose, his eyes, and recaptured his lips again. "Tell me I'm not dreaming; it's really you." She leaned her head into his chest, touching him again to make sure he was real. She could smell his soap and the male essence of him.

"It's really me. I'm here," he groaned.

Her arms circled around his waist, pulling him closer to her. She pulled up his shirt, touching his smooth, brown, warm skin. She rubbed her hand up and down his back in a caressing motion. Then her hands dropped down, cupping his nice firm bottom. She stood in his embrace, feeling the true love that surrounded them.

"How long will you be here?" she asked frantically.

He leaned into her, tilting her face up to look at him. "You have me for two weeks."

She stared lovingly at him. "Two whole weeks." Happiness filled her as she talked. She tightened her grip around his waist.

"What are you going to do with me?" The meaning of his gaze was very obvious.

"I can think of a lot of things."

"I bet you can." Paul's smile widened in approval, sending her pulse racing.

"I'm not hungry for food right now." She grabbed his hand, leading him toward the bedroom. "But we are going to work up an appetite."

About the Author

$\mathscr{S}$ammie Ward has written over forty short stories for Black Romance, Black Confessions, Black Secrets, Bronze Thrills, Jive, True Black Experience, and True Confessions Magazine. She's also the author of *In The Name of Love*, *Love To Behold*, *7 Days*, and *It's In The Rhythm*. She was recognized as a Literary Diva in Heather Covington's *Literary Diva: The 100+ African-American Women in Literature*. She's also the CEO/Founder of the Online/POD publishing company, Lady Leo Publishing. You can visit the website at: www.ladyleopublishing.org. She loves to hear from fans. Drop her an email at: ladyleopublishing@comcast.net or by snail mail at P.O. Box 14283, Silver Spring, MD 20911.

LADY LEO PUBLISHING

Bringing You The Best In Confessions, Short Stories &Novellas

Lady Leo Publishing
P.O. Box 14283
Silver Spring, MD 20911
Email: info@ladyleopublishing.org
Website: www.ladyleopublishing.org